Are You Reading the Best?

You will find a wealth of fascinating stories in WEIRD TALES, *the unique magazine*. The brilliant success of this magazine has been founded on its unrivaled, superb stories of the strange, the grotesque and the terrible—gripping stories that stimulate the imagination and send shivers of apprehension up the spine —tales that take the reader from the humdrum world about us into a deathless realm of fancy—marvelous tales so thrillingly told that they seem very real.

WEIRD TALES prints the best weird fiction in the world today. If Poe were alive he would undoubtedly be a contributor. In addition to creepy mystery stories, ghost-tales, stories of devil-worship, witchcraft, vampires and strange monsters, this magazine also prints the cream of the weird-scientific fiction that is written today—tales of the spaces between worlds, surgical stories, and stories that scan the future with the eye of prophecy.

Read

The Unique Magazine

On Sale At All News Stands

Fascinating Tales of the East

ORIENTAL STORIES

VOLUME I   **NUMBER 1**

Published bi-monthly by the Popular Fiction Publishing Company, 2457 E. Washington Street, Indianapolis, Ind. Application made for entry at the postoffice at Indianapolis, Ind., as second class matter. Single copies, 25 cents. Subscription, $1.50 a year in the United States, $1.75 a year in Canada, $2.00 in other countries. The publishers are not responsible for the loss of unsolicited manuscripts, although every care will be taken of such material while in their possession. The contents of this magazine are fully protected by copyright and must not be reproduced either wholly or in part without permission from the publishers. All manuscripts and communications should be addressed to the publisher's Chicago office at 840 North Michigan Avenue, Chicago, Ill.

FARNSWORTH WRIGHT, Editor.

Contents for October-November

THE YELLOW RIVER
By HUNG LONG TOM

Some say the Yellow River
Rises and flows
Across the breast of China,
That the color of the water
Is caused by loess
And mud deposits
Drifting on the river shallows.

But I say
The Yellow River
Is the rising tide
Of yellow men
That sweeps throughout
All China,
Mongolia, Manchuria, Kansu,
Splashing and foaming
On the shores of other countries.

It is a Yellow River.
The yellow is a reflection
Of the sun
That shines upon the people,
Though sometimes
It is due to the gold
That lies within the man.

Singapore Nights

By FRANK OWEN

*The East never sleeps, never rests. Its maze of confusion
and mystery flows onward endlessly*

1

DICK VARNEY stood on the docks in Singapore gazing idly at his surroundings. This was a new life, a new world, and it was just as well. He had been bored with New York anyway, aside from the fact that it was a dangerous place for him to remain. He had come to the East as a member of the crew of a large freighter. The fact that he was a rather worthless member hadn't really mattered. The main thing was that no one suspected he was the famous Richard Varney.

Along the waterfront Chinese junks piled up everywhere like so much kindling wood. Hordes of sleek-eyed Orientals pattered about jabbering, laughing, chanting incessantly. Near at hand scores of steamers lay at anchor. Almost every nation was represented in the kaleidoscope of flags. They helped to make the color of the morning even more vivid.

At last Dick turned his steps inland. He walked through spacious avenues on which fronted magnificent government buildings and enormous hotels which might have been in New York or London, so resplendent were they with gayly dressed ladies and well-groomed men. He shunned the big hotels. His clothes were not in fit condition for him to stop at them. Oddly enough it did not enter his head to buy better ones. He was dressed like a common sailor, in clothes of cheap blue shoddy material, and yet he had grown accustomed to them. He dreaded the thought of being forced to wear full-dressed shirts and stiff white collars again.

He crossed the Singapore River, pausing for a moment to appreciate the beauty of the gay-hued sampans which almost completely filled the stream from bank to bank. It was extremely interesting. He was a born artist. Every new scene attracted him. He smiled at the rikshas containing well-dressed perfumed ladies and drawn by poor coolies who had advanced no farther in life than to be beasts of burden. Lean, raw-boned fellows, the very expression of their emaciated faces showed plainly the years of toil and privation through which they had passed. Wealth and poverty are responsible for some grimly provocative pictures.

Dick Varney entered the business section where stood the enormous banks and office buildings, so modern that they would not have seemed misplaced in the heart of any large city. The glamor is fading from the East. Modernism is creeping in.

He was amazed at the motley throngs which he met everywhere, Europeans, Hindoos, Japanese, Malays, Filipinos, Dyaks and Javanese. Every quarter of the globe was represented and the costumes were as varied and absurd as any in Barnum's circus.

In spite of himself he chuckled. "I'd hate to keep a clothing store here," he mused.

At last he journeyed into the low-built poorer section of the city, and there, almost hidden among the blue, yellow and pink dwellings of the Chinese, he found an odd little ramshackle building which was used as a combination bar and lodging-house and kept by a wizened little old fellow who spoke as many languages as a month has days and was known by the extremely uninteresting name of Mr. Isaacs.

He looked shrewdly at Dick Varney when he applied to him for a room. He rubbed his hands together. He was trying to decide whether he could be trusted for a night's lodging. In the appraisal Dick evidently lost out, for in a high-pitched, quavering voice he said, "Have you any money?"

Dick's anger flared up at once. "Have you any rooms?" he cried.

The old man shook his head dolefully. "I think not," he said.

"Well, you'd better think again. I'm going to stop here if I have to pitch you out bodily into the alley. I've got enough money to buy this filthy hovel but I'm not going to buy it. All I want is a room."

Mr. Isaacs adopted a conciliatory attitude at once.

"Be calm," he said, "be calm. Never give vent to anger. Anger is foolish. It might bring on a stroke. I have some of the best rooms in Singapore. They are old but they are clean. They are small but they are good."

As he spoke he led Dick up a rickety staircase to a little dingy room that was so filthy it might have been the forecastle of an abandoned schooner.

"This is a splendid room," he said. "Nice and quiet, nobody to bother you, and only a pound a night."

"You're lucky if you even get a couple of ounces," said Dick. "I appreciate your sense of humor, but don't carry it to an extreme. I'm used to the Orient. Don't mistake me for a fool. If you do not ask something within reason you won't get a thing."

Mr. Isaacs hesitated. "How about two pounds per week?" he asked at last.

"That's more than the whole building is worth," was the reply, "but I'll pay it to you."

He did not add that Mr. Isaacs was interesting to him, that therefore he did not wish to stop anywhere else. If he had, Mr. Isaacs would probably have attempted

"As Dick spoke, Mr. Isaacs whipped out a revolver."

to charge extra for his own personality. Mr. Isaacs was the type of individual whom one often meets and yet who never seems in the proper place. One could never imagine him as a child. He looked as though he had been born old. Even in Singapore he was a man of mystery. No one knew from whence he had come. He apparently had no relatives. He received no mail. It was rumored that he was enormously wealthy but then such rumors spring up about all old men who are eccentric.

THAT night Dick suffered from insomnia. He retired early and yet he could not sleep. The little room was like an oven. It was stifling, suffocating. He rose and threw open the hall door, which permitted a dozen weird odors to creep in. Nevertheless the breeze that occasionally blew through was cool, or so it seemed compared to the stagnant torpid heat when the door was closed. From the Chinese houses across a narrow court came the echo of laughter or the occasional guttural speech of some Celestial merrymaker. Over all floated the wild, unearthly din of Chinese music, the sing-song notes of the same unrhythmic tune crashed out over and over again.

Dick tossed upon his bed. He would have gotten up if there had been any conceivable place to go. Singapore was a city of horrors, grand by day, sinister by night.

He closed his eyes, striving to shut out his thoughts. For a few moments he lay still. If only he could doze even for a few moments! Then suddenly he was wide awake, every muscle taut, but he did not move. Some one was moving cautiously across the floor of his room. He could hear the stealthy patter of bare feet. He hesitated only long enough to locate where the intruder walked; then

with an oath he sprang from the bed and crashed to the floor on top of the wizened, wrinkled figure of Mr. Isaacs.

"Let me go," he whined, "let me up! You're killing me. Oh, my poor old bones! They will all be broken."

Dick stumbled to his feet, dragging Mr. Isaacs after him. He shook him until his teeth rattled.

"What are you doing in my room?" he demanded.

"I meant no offense," quavered Mr. Isaacs. "I only came in to see if you were sleeping soundly."

"And were disappointed to find I wasn't."

"Certainly."

"Well, don't worry about my welfare any longer. Better watch yourself. If I catch you skulking around my room again I'll fix you so you won't sleep for a week. Furthermore, you won't find any money here. I took the precaution to deposit it today with a local bank. Of course I would not have done so had I known I was to have such a solicitous host."

2

THE incident would have driven a less hardy wanderer from the unsavory lodging-house, but not so Dick. He viewed it as a prelude to adventure. What form the adventure would take he could not tell. One could not, however, dwell long at such a house without some sort of excitement. Until it broke, he would remain.

Every day found Singapore a constantly changing mass of color. Almost from dawn till sunset he tramped around the city, even journeying into the most wild and dismal of the filthy alleys.

Sometimes in the evenings he went into the bar in the house of Mr. Isaacs, and a more forbidding room could not be imagined. It was lit by a single oil lamp which hung from a huge black hook in the center of the room. Instead of illuminating the chamber it only served to make the gloom of the farthest corners more pronounced, and yet it seemed fitting for the room to be almost in darkness, for it was a place of shadows. The men who lolled there, bleary-eyed, unshaven and half drugged with liquor, seemed only to be shadows also. They sat and consumed glass after glass of the strong golden-yellow wine for which the establishment of Mr. Isaacs was famous. A few drinks were sufficient to sink them into a torpor, after which they just sat and mechanically drank and drank like inanimate things, scarcely conscious of their actions. Mr. Isaacs continually filled up the glasses as fast as they were emptied, never waiting for a second order, and always when one of the revellers roused himself sufficiently to make a settlement, Mr. Isaacs charged for twice as many drinks as had been consumed.

In one corner of the room was a dilapidated piano, so decrepit-looking it had probably found its way there because it was unfit for any place else. Every key was out of tune. Whenever any one tried to play it the symphony of discord was maddening. A young fellow named Bourse McGill was banging away at it most of the time. He had a rather doleful, gloomy voice, not without a certain charm, and hour after hour he would sing *My Mother Was a Lady*.

Sandy Lawrence, who represented an American trading company, would stand it as long as he could, then he'd shriek, "If your mother was such a fine lady, why the hell did you leave her?"

In spite of himself Dick Varney became interested in studying the weird stream of patrons which continually surged in and out. A perpetual habitué was a one-eyed man named Lew. He sat alone at a table, never saying a word, scarcely even moving, and yet his single eye kept constantly searching for something—perhaps for the other eye. Then there was the Welshman. He never told his name. He went about Singapore anonymously, an enigma which nobody took the trouble to solve. He was neither pleasing-looking nor ugly. He was neutral, the type that submerges itself into the throng unnoticed. He lacked individuality. He never said a thing worth listening to, and yet he talked a lot. Nobody heard him. His voice was low and monotonous. It failed to carry. About his drab person there was only one thing that distinguished him from the common herd: a huge wart on the side of his nose, a wart as big as a bean. It bobbed up and down as he walked. It seemed momentarily in danger of falling off.

"When it does," mused Dick, "the Welshman will lose his last flicker of individuality. He'll go out like a candle. Nobody'll ever look at him again. It is rather pathetic because he seems to yearn for notoriety, to be constantly in the spotlight. Where did he come from? Where did any of this crowd come from? Where are they going? Here they are, sitting and drinking. They have paused at a bar in Singapore, the Highway of the World. Where does the Highway lead? What will be the end?"

He motioned to Mr. Isaacs. "A glass of wine," he said curtly.

Mr. Isaacs conferred upon him a look of such undisguised hatred that Dick would probably have commented upon it if he had noticed. Nevertheless he brought the wine, a quart bottle and a glass. Dick poured a generous drink and then another. It tasted rather good. It caused the spell of ennui to lift somewhat.

His blood coursed through his veins with new energy.

THE bar-room was almost in darkness. The faces of the men loomed up grotesquely. Many of the gaunt, haggard faces seemed whiter than ever. The men who were sunburned and unshaven looked as black as negroes. Lew's single eye kept up its ceaseless quest. Bourse McGill, bent low over the piano, sang *My Mother Was a Lady* in a drawling monotone. The squeaks and discords of the piano blended eerily with the clanging din of Chinese music from the house next door. Dick gazed at his glass of golden wine. In the fantastic light it seemed to glow with a splendid insistence. The wine he had already drunk had gone to his head. It was a mad moment. Singapore was mad, life was mad, everything was out of key, all sounds echoed in falsetto notes.

Mr. Isaacs crept over and seated himself at the table opposite him. He laughed gratingly.

"Did I disturb you?" he asked.

"You always do," replied Dick. He did not bother admitting that he was really glad of his companionship. He longed to fathom the mystery of Mr. Isaacs. With such an education what was he doing in the very dregs of Singapore?

"I am unwelcome," said Mr. Isaacs, "because you think I am a Jew."

"You are wrong," snapped Dick. "You are unwelcome because you do not appeal to me. I may be a bit crude in my speech but I do not believe in wasting words."

"You hold me in contempt because I am a Jew."

"Rot!"

"It is true. You loathe me because you fear me. It is so the world over. A Jew is a composite type made up of all the races of the world. He has no country because he is of all countries. When

necessity forces him to it he can live as cheaply as a Chinaman, or he can save as clutchingly as a Scotchman. On the other hand, there is no one in the world who can entertain so lavishly, who understands drollery and humor so well. He is a better trader than an Arab. He knows ivory better than an Abyssinian, and pearls better than a Ceylonese diver. He is a connoisseur of diamonds and other precious stones. He will deprive himself of every pleasure to obtain an education. He is often crafty and untrustworthy in his business dealings because he knows that the survival of the fittest is governed solely by the caliber of individual wits. He has been harassed and oppressed for centuries. He is disillusioned. His faith in everything, except himself, is ruined. He is disliked because he is feared. He adapts himself to any environment and every condition. He is a universalist. He flourishes in any climate. He has most of the vices of earth and all of the virtues. His home life is ideal. He is a good husband and a loving father. His children look up to him. He is progressive and therefore misunderstood." Mr. Isaacs spoke with great vehemence. His earnestness made him truly eloquent despite the shrill, guttural tone of his voice. "And yet you hate me because I am a Jew."

Dick was amazed at the torrent of words. He was impressed. Not for a moment had he imagined that Mr. Isaacs was capable of rising to such rhetorical heights.

"For the last time," he said in a voice far more amiable than it had been before, "let me assure you that you are absolutely wrong."

As Dick spoke Mr. Isaacs whipped out a revolver with an alacrity that would have done credit to a boy of twenty. He levelled it at Dick in a horribly deliberate manner.

"You lie!" he cried in a voice which rose almost to a shriek, almost beyond control. "And as sure as you're a dirty rat I'm going to make you admit it."

Bourse McGill stopped playing. For a moment he forgot that his mother was a lady. He swung lazily around on his stool. The incident promised to be interesting. He rolled a cigarette nonchalantly as though he were in a theater waiting for a show to begin. Lew's one eye stopped its roving, its mate forgotten. It focussed itself upon the scene. Every man in the place stopped talking. It was a breathless moment, although not an uncommon one in the sordid bar-room. There was not a single friendly face. Most of them were mask-like. The emotions lying underneath were unreadable. Dick realized that he was in a precarious position and yet he disliked the thought of groveling at the feet of Mr. Isaacs.

Mr. Isaacs kept the revolver leveled at him. His hand did not shake. It did not quiver.

"You detest me because I am a Jew."

It was the one sentence Dick needed. It was the spark that touched off the fuse of his anger. With an oath he sprang up, and seizing the chair on which he had been sitting he hurled it at the oil lamp less than a dozen feet away. The next moment there was a muffled roar and a sheet of flame shot from the lamp. In the confusion Dick sprang for the door. Lew barred his way. There was no time to lose. Dick's clenched fist shot out and successfully closed the weird remaining eye. Then he fought his way to the door. He walked over several prostrate bodies. Bourse McGill clutched at him but failed to get a hold. Mr. Isaacs was on his knees moaning and wailing like an idiot.

"Oh, my poor house," he shrieked, "my poor house! It is afire and it is not insured. Oh, my poor house!"

As Dick dashed past him he yelled, "I despise you not because you are a Jew but because you are a yellow thief!"

A great body loomed up before him. Dick seized a chair and crashed it down over the head of the black, shadowy form. Now he was in the street. He ran as if all the fiends of legend were after him but he was pursued only by a half-dozen or so of the less drunken patrons of Mr. Isaacs. These, however, increased as they pursued him, for almost every idler, and there seemed to be hundreds of them, joined in the hunt. A man-hunt is always far more interesting than any other kind. In the distance, far behind him, the sky glowed red as the fire gained headway in the box-like structure of the hotel. He quickened his pace. He dashed down a crooked winding alley to shake off the throng behind him. They kept up a continuous yelling that made pandemonium out of the peace of the night, an endless babble of shrieks and curses.

A sailor stepped into the center of the alley. Dick didn't know whether he was going to attempt to stop him or not, and he could not afford to take any chances; so he struck him on the chin and with a groan the sailor toppled over, not stunned but surprized at the suddenness of it. Dick continued on toward the waterfront. It seemed endless miles away. He crossed the bridge over the Singapore River. He was far in advance of the mob. It had grown enormously. There must have been hundreds, so many of them they got in one another's way. Once a huge Javanese fell and immediately a half-dozen piled up on top of him. It was a confusing chase because there was no leader. Scarcely anybody knew what the excitement was all about. Of the original bunch that had started from the bar-room only three remained and they made no effort to explain anything.

At last, almost exhausted, Dick reached the waterfront. Not for a moment did he pause. He rushed up a narrow strip of board that led to a Chinese junk. His breath was almost gone. His heart crashed against his ribs frightfully. At the dark doorway that led into the mystic interior of the ship he paused. The gloom of it was forbidding. It was creepy. Yet the howling mob, which was now dangerously near, was a far more definite menace. As he hesitated, something struck him a terrific blow on the shoulder and sent him headlong into the eery blackness.

3

FOR a few moments he lay in the darkness afraid to move. He was unhurt, for he had fallen scarcely a half-dozen feet. The interior of the junk was totally black. He did not know whether he was in a cabin or not. He knew nothing about the construction of a Chinese junk. He didn't suppose it amounted to much, or else it would have had a more flowery name. As his eyes grew accustomed to the gloom, he tried to see about him, but he could not. For all the good his eyes were to him in that velvet blackness he might have been blind. He had no idea who had struck him. It could not have been one of his pursuers, for they were far behind. He made no effort to rise. He was afraid that the least rustle of his body might make known his position to the hidden foe, who he was sure lurked in the velvet shadows. Once as he felt cautiously about him his hand encountered a cold damp hand, so bony and with such sharp nails it might have been the claw of some monstrous bird. He shrank back. Yet the hand pursued him. He heard no sound. The hand seemed bodiless, to be groping eerily around in the darkness, an unexplainable menace. He crouched back from it. It was foolish,

but nevertheless he was in a condition bordering on panic. Now he was against the wall, but still the hand came on. With an effort he pulled himself together. He could retreat no farther. He put out his hands frantically and in the gloom he found and held a scrawny throat. He squeezed it as though his fingers were a vise. The thing struggled. It uttered a shriek. Dick's grip relaxed. The menace was human. Fear slipped from him. The Chinaman feared him as much as he had feared the groping claws.

Instantly a door opened and an old Chinaman carrying a lantern appeared, a golden-yellow lantern that looked as big as the moon. His face was yellower than the wine of Mr. Isaacs. He was dressed in a long coat of yellow and on his head was a fantastic contrivance which looked as though it might be a shade for the lantern. It could not by any stretch of the imagination have been called a hat. He came forward slowly, as though the years bore down heavily upon his shoulders, and yet there was a majestic air about him which was exceedingly impressive.

Before Dick Varney he stopped. "I am Wing Lo," he said in perfect English. "I have sailed the Yellow Sea for over sixty years. And only now in my advanced age am I molested."

Dick looked at the old fellow in amazement, then at the yellow-brown coolie who was dimly discernible not far off in the shadows, rubbing his scrawny throat with his claw-like fingers.

"It is not I who am the oppressor," he replied. "Until this moment I did not know of your existence. How then could I oppress you? I was held up at the point of a gun in a questionable resort far on the other side of the river. In the ensuing fight I was forced to smash the lamp so that I could escape. Almost half of

Singapore rushed pell-mell after me. My life wasn't worth a pumpkin-seed until I beheld the plank that led to this junk. I had no alternative. Either I must surrender myself to the mob or trust to the good nature of the occupants of this vessel."

"I am the owner," said Wing Lo, "and I am sorry that my faithful servant mistook you for a robber. I am a trader, and rumor has spread throughout the city that my ship is laden with rich silks."

As Wing Lo spoke Dick Varney glanced up quickly. The sight that met his eyes made his heart stop beating; for framed in the doorway was the most beautiful girl he had ever beheld. She was dressed in black, which made the ivory whiteness of her face more pronounced. Her eyes were dark and her lips were as red as roses. Dick Varney had never cared much about women until that moment. They had been insignificant things in his cosmos. Now his cosmos had suffered an earthquake. All his ideas had changed. Perhaps it was the exotic circumstances under which he beheld her that made his pulse go galloping at a frightful speed. Only the light from the moon-lantern illuminated the room. It cast a strange radiance over everything. The girl stepped forward and held out her hand.

"I have been studying your face," she said slowly, "and I believe I can trust you. I heard you say you were an American. I am an American, too. It is rather good to meet one of my countrymen on this old ship in Singapore."

Dick grasped her hand mechanically. What was that verse in the old Chinese poem by Lai Tai Po? "She was of a loveliness to overthrow kingdoms." The old poet must have been thinking of just such a girl when he wrote that immortal line. Whether he muttered anything by way of greeting, Dick never knew. He was dazzled by the beauty of her. Her loveliness was as intoxicating as old wine.

"I am in great trouble," she whispered softly and her voice seemed to tremble. "Will you help me?"

"Nothing would make me happier," he said huskily. "From this moment forth I am your slave. Bondage with you would be better than kingship with any other woman."

"Are you married?" she asked abruptly.

"No," he replied quickly. "I guess all my life I've been waiting for you."

She smiled wanly. "That is good," said she. She seemed unable to go on. Sudden agitation seized her and she sank upon a rude bench.

"Life is a maze," she faltered. "Why must we all struggle through it blindfolded? Why is there so little happiness in the world?"

"You are in trouble," said he. "Let me help you."

"Yes," she admitted. "I am. I'm not afraid, but it rather gets on my nerves. In all of Singapore Wing Lo is the only one I can trust. That is why I am hiding on his boat."

"Confide in me," suggested Dick. "Maybe I can help you."

She rose to her feet and faced him. "You can," she said emphatically. "In spite of everything I will not fail. My name is Dolores Cravat. No Cravat has ever been able to accept defeat. I want you to marry me tomorrow morning as early as it can be arranged. But I must warn you beforehand, marriage to me will not bring you happiness. It will plunge you into extreme danger. It will be a marriage of convenience only. When the ceremony is over you must leave me. I shall pay you well for any inconvenience the affair may cause you."

Dick was speechless. Marry her?

Nothing in the world would please him better. But the rest of her words were far from reassuring. They were almost an insult. But she was very lovely, adorable. She was far too gorgeous for him really to be angry. Nevertheless he said decisively, "Of course I'll marry you. Did I not say I was your slave? The suggestion of payment, however, is disagreeable to me. Anything I do will be done because I am mad about you. You can send me away if you like, but let there be no mention of money between us." He smiled wickedly. "Let us set it down merely as American courtesy," he added.

Dick Varney had always been impetuous. He had been in more tight corners than an African explorer. But always he had succeeded in wriggling out. By nature he was daring, impulsive, reckless. He was used to making snap judgments. Hence there was now no half-measure in his devotion. He was intoxicated by the beauty of the girl and in a few hours they would be married. It was like a dream of loveliness. Unbelievable.

SOMETIME later he sat on the side of the ship and gazed at the low-hanging moon. Before him lay Singapore, city of mystery and romance, of strange whisperings and quaint shadows. But nothing in Singapore was stranger than the chaos into which his life had been plunged. Put it down that he was mad. The moon glowed in yellow splendor over the blue-purple shadows of the city. Life was very wonderful indeed. And then she came to him. The perfume of her hair was sweeter than the breath of flowers. It was the deepest hush of the night, the blackest hour before sunrise.

"Come," she whispered, "a tiny boat is waiting for us."

He followed as she led the way to a rough rope-ladder. The night was intensely black. No light was visible anywhere on the junk. He groped his way down the ladder and she followed. Soon the sound of oars broke the silence as the little boat floated off down the black river. Here and there along the banks specks of light peeped out like stars. The East never sleeps, never rests. Its maze of confusion and mystery flows onward endlessly.

Dick sat in the stern of the boat. Dolores was beside him. It was enchantment. This glorious girl, a girl whom he scarcely knew, was to be his wife before another sun had set. He was plunging headlong into romance and adventure. His whole life had been a jumble. Softly his arm crept about her shoulders. It was a mad moment, a night of witchery. Who could act sanely on such a night? He drew her to him and pressed his lips to hers. She sighed softly. "Don't," she whispered; "please don't."

At once he released her, but it did not matter. He had kissed her lips. He had expected anger. Instead she had pushed him gently away. Was it only imagination or had she really yielded to him for a single moment?

The oars swished softly in the water. A gentle breeze sprang up and caressed their cheeks. The moon had set, leaving the sky a deeper blue than ever. Like lamps the stars gleamed forth, making the waters weirdly black. At last the little boat stopped. As it did so the dawn thundered up in the east. It burst in a flame of orange-rose and gold. The blue-purple mists of night fled in terror before its glory. The country loomed up sleepily. Birds began to twitter in the tree tops. The distant lantern lights flickered out. The stars dimmed.

Dick helped Dolores to alight from the

boat. Now they were in an enchanted garden, a garden filled with willow trees and cherry blossoms. There was a great ghinko tree like an ogre standing guard over a Moon-Bridge that arched above a tiny winding stream. A tiny red-roofed house peeped out from among the trees.

"It is the garden of Doctor Placid," she said softly. "He it will be who will unite us in marriage."

In back of them walked old Wing Lo like a gentle shadow.

"Wing is my friend," said she, "the most faithful friend that dwells in all the world. He will be a witness to the ceremony."

An hour later they were back in the tiny boat again, floating upon the river. Dick's senses quickened. This lovely girl beside him, who was like a flower, this gorgeous, wondrous stranger was his wife.

4

BEFORE parting forever they decided that they would have a little wedding breakfast somewhere in an out-of-the-way alley in the labyrinths of Singapore. He longed to ask her why she had married him. He wished her to confess to him the sinister mystery that hung over her, but somehow he could not bring himself to question her. If she wished to speak, she would; otherwise the matter would remain an enigma to the end.

For their rendezvous they chose a tea-house kept by a bland-faced Oriental that Wing Lo had recommended. It was a rather dim-lit restaurant, though by no means small. In the wraith-like lantern-light it seemed very vast. A few Orientals lolled over their tea and gazed sleepily into the shadows. Outside it was broad daylight, but within the tea-house it was very dark, for the windows were covered by heavy draperies.

For a wedding breakfast it was an ex-tremely sketchy thing, merely rice-cakes and tea. Dick had no appetite whatsoever. He was very gloomy. It was hard to lose the most beautiful wife in the world within a few hours of one's marriage.

"I shall never forget what you have done for me," she said softly.

He smiled wryly. "Spoken like a constant and true wife," he drawled, "and yet you are sending me away."

"I must," she said. She hesitated for a moment; then she went on quickly. "You must think me mad, and therefore I will give you some slight explanation of my actions. My father was a rich tea-merchant, but eccentric. He had few friends, only one that he recognized. This one was Mortimer Davga. I was never able to understand why Davga of all men had been singled out by my father as a confidant. I could not trust him. He was like a sleek cat purring about one, a man of studied culture and refinement, fastidious in his eating and dress. His tastes were of the finest, both in women and jewels. A year ago my father died, leaving me as his sole heir. He made Davga executor of the estate with full unrevokable power to act over my affairs until such time as I should be married. Mortimer Davga proved himself a very thoughtful companion during the funeral. He attended to everything, but immediately thereafter his conduct changed. He came to live at the huge house which was my home. I had no brothers or sisters. My mother died when I was born. I do not know of a single living relative except an uncle in England whom I have never met.

"Existence at that house after the coming of Davga was not a pleasant thing. He moved soundlessly about as though he were a ghost or a spy. Continually I would look up from my book to find him standing over me. Several times I thought I caught a malevolent look in his eyes that made me very uncomfortable. He was ugly to an extreme, thin and wizened. He might have been taken for a Jew but he was not. He was, I think, of French extraction, although of his origin I knew little.

"It was distinctly unpleasant to have that soundless prowler living constantly under one's roof. I grew to abhor him, despite the fact that he was very solicitous of my comfort. Things were in a sorry plight. I was very unhappy. Then they grew worse. Davga tried to force his attentions upon me. He was several times my age, but that made no difference to him. His eyes shone like those of a snake whenever he approached me. He sent me flowers, candies and jewels. He wooed me in a hundred subtle ways, but his interest made him only the more repulsive to me. One night, unexpectedly, he took me into his arms and kissed me. It was the final straw. I grew more frightened than ever. There was something menacing about him. I knew that he wished to marry me, not because he cared for me in the slightest, but because he wished to get control of my money forever. I wondered what my chance of continued life would have been if I had yielded to him.

"That night I fled from the house. I sought refuge with old Wing Lo, who had been my faithful servant for years. Davga had discharged all the servants on my father's death. In the entire house there was not one left that I knew. There was only one thing to do, I decided after thinking the matter over calmly. I must marry to get control of my money. But whom to marry was a problem. I had to marry some one I could trust. I wanted it to be an American or an Englishman. Then you came along and I knew you possessed both requisites. To judge from your appearance, if you do not mind frankness, I imagined that you were poor. A bit more money honorably earned might appeal to you. It was thus that I reasoned. Now your work is ended. You are free. When control of the estate passes to me, I will divorce you. You need not give me another thought."

He leaned across the table and seized her hand. "Free?" he repeated. "Free? I shall never be free again. I have gazed into your eyes. I have kissed your lips. Though I live for ages I shall never be free again. But I will go away; I will leave you if you wish. However, do not decide too quickly. You are in danger. At least let me remain until you are safe."

Even as he spoke a shot rang out. It smashed to atoms the tea-cup which he held in his hand. The next moment the lights went out, plunging the room into darkness. The sudden crash surprized Dick despite the fact that his experiences in life led him to expect anything. He sprang back, upsetting a table as he did so. In the room he could hear sounds of scuffling. He called to Dolores but she did not answer. He groped frantically about in the darkness, but to no avail. Then the lights flared on again. The tea-room was deserted. No trace of Dolores could be found. He searched the building from ground to roof but could find no one. It was absolutely deserted. Even the few loiterers had departed. He was quite alone.

At last he rushed from the building. He felt as though his head would burst. What had happened to that lovely girl, the girl who was his wife? The seething lanes of Singapore were crowded with laughing, jabbering, shrieking humanity. Everybody was talking at once. Dogs barked discordantly to add to the confusion. A Chinaman driving a pig before him jostled against Dick but his expression was so smiling and friendly he could not take offense. He walked along, his head in a whirl. How was he to find her in this mystic maze which was Singapore?

Then he met Wing Lo, the gentle, faithful servant.

"Would it not be well," Wing Lo whispered softly, "to search for the beloved mistress in the great house, her former home, from which she fled? It is a grim, bleak house wherein a thousand tragedies might lie buried."

It was an excellent suggestion and Dick acted upon it. To have rushed blindly through the tempestuous city without any design at all would have been useless.

He longed to rush off at once on his quest, but he refrained. Before going he decided he must buy suitable clothes. The delay was irksome but it was necessary. Toward evening Wing Lo led him to the great house which stood in the center of a vast garden like a great gray elephant. At the gate Wing Lo left him.

"For me to go farther," he explained, "would only plunge you into grave danger. By the household of Mortimer Davga I am not liked. I do not think they would hesitate at any means to exterminate me. But I shall be in the neighborhood and if I divine that you are in need, I may come to you."

So they parted and Dick Varney walked up the crooked flower-bordered path that led to the house.

THE garden was a rug of lovely flowers and stately trees that stood out in silhouette against the sky. It seemed impossible that danger could lurk in such a charming garden. And then a snake came hissing out from the bushes. Dick had barely time to spring aside to

O. S.—2

avoid it. It broke the spell. After that even the gorgeous flowers seemed deadly. Sudden death might lurk in those lovely blossoms.

He hurried on until before him loomed the monstrous gray house, vast, bulky, shapeless. It must have been designed by an architect in the last stages of insanity or by one of utterly morbid tendencies. It was all of gray without even the slightest trace of color to form a contrast. It might have been some monstrous prehistoric animal resting for a moment in the garden.

As Dick walked up the steps that led to the house the door was flung open and a rather repulsive Chinaman stood before him. He was elegantly dressed but his face was mottled yellow. His nose was shapeless, his lips thick. His eyes were tiny and crafty. They were shifty eyes that seemed to take in everything at a single glance. He would have made, to judge by his appearance, an excellent henchman for Genghis Khan, whose cruelty surpassed any other person in Chinese history.

He bowed low as Dick Varney entered. "I wish to see Mr. Mortimer Davga," he announced simply.

"I will lead the way," replied the Chinaman, "and acquaint the master with the fact of your presence."

Dick followed him through velvet-carpeted halls, halls heavy with delicate vases, lacquer screens, rich tapestries and fantastic lanterns. Finally they emerged into a great room that might have been a gorgeous corner of a vast museum. The walls were lined with cabinets of curios, precious jades and art objects that would have enthralled a collector. In the center of the room was a massive table littered with heaps of books and documents, maps and diagrams. Mortimer Davga sat behind the table busy writing. This was the sanctum in which most of his schemes and problems were worked out. He was faultlessly attired though rather somberly in a suit of black. Even his tie was black, as though he were still in mourning for the noble friend he had lost, the friend who had trusted him beyond all others by making him executor of his will.

As Dick Varney gazed upon him he could scarcely credit his eyes; for Mortimer Davga was none other than Mr. Isaacs who had kept the vile lodging-house in the poorer section of Singapore, the keeper of the house which Dick's deliberate smashing of the lamp had ultimately laid in ruins. There was no chance that the likeness was only a resemblance. Dick had an excellent faculty for remembering faces, and that sly, sinister, ancient face could belong to none other than Mr. Isaacs.

Dick realized that his position was more than precarious. The man at the door had resembled a scoundrel. Such a man might stop at nothing. And Mr. Isaacs, or to give him his real name, Mortimer Davga, looked capable of formulating any despicable plan. It made his fears for Dolores all the more acute. He longed to flee from the house, and yet he vowed that he would not. Not for a moment did he doubt that Davga had spirited her away from the tea-house. Perhaps the tea-house itself was owned by Davga. The fact that Wing Lo had recommended it meant nothing. Wing Lo was a gentle character. He had merely recommended a tea-house in which he had been wont to linger in the heat of the afternoons. The restaurant was dream-like, the tea superb, and Wing Lo had found contentment. No further credentials were necessary. At last Mortimer Davga looked up from his writing. By not so much as the quiver of an eye-

lid did he show that he recognized his visitor. He rose to his feet, smiling cordially, hand extended.

"I do not know who you are," he said, "but you are welcome anyway. My house is always open to the passing traveler."

Dick took the extended hand. "I am Richard Varney," he said, "a friend to Dolores Cravat. She told me that if I ever chanced to pass this way I must not fail to call upon her."

"Your coming is rather inopportune," was the reply, "for Dolores is away. I do not know when she will be back. She is a girl of whims, a trifle headstrong. It is too bad that you missed her. She loves company and I know she will be disappointed if she fails to meet you. Perhaps if you are not pressed for time, it might be possible for you to remain a few days with me. At best it is rather lonesome living in such a dreary house. I would be more than thankful for your company."

"After such a delightful invitation," said Dick, "I really can not refuse. Perhaps in a couple of days Dolores will be back again."

"Undoubtedly," agreed Davga, "undoubtedly." He rubbed his hands together with satisfaction, much as a famed chef might do before carving a savory roast.

SUPPER that evening was an elaborate affair of countless courses and varieties. It was served in the Chinese manner.

Davga was a splendid host, an excellent conversationist. He could talk on any subject in an interesting manner. He discussed world politics, literature and science with equal fluency. Under happier circumstances Dick Varney would have been drawn to him. But his experiences had been sufficiently out of the ordinary and harrowing so that he was not to be deceived by a cloak of friendliness. There was no denying that Davga had a magnetic personality. He was ugly to an extreme; the suggestion of great age was like a veneer glossing his face. But his voice had a quality, a drawl to it, that submerged every other thing. All the deficiencies in his appearance were forgotten. In his tone was charm.

When the meal was ended they returned to the library which was his workshop. He had suggested a game of fan-tan, and the repulsive individual who had greeted Dick at the door made up the trio. His name was Yeh Ming Hsin and there was a suggestion of hauteur about him that was unbecoming in a servant. For example, he chose the most comfortable seat for himself. But this was no more surprizing than the fact that Davga offered him a cigar before bestowing one upon Dick Varney. Dick smiled to himself. What a contradiction, he reflected. He had been welcomed to the house like a king, but in the choice of a cigar he was subordinate to a servant.

As Davga took the cards to deal, the massive brass lantern above Dick's head gave way and crashed to the floor. Had it not been for the fact that he was stooping to tie a shoe-lace at the moment he most assuredly would have been killed. As it was he was unhurt, but the table was badly damaged.

Davga sprang to his feet. He was all apologies. "What a pity!" he cried. "What a pity!"

Dick laughed shortly. He was in a bad humor. "Do you mean it was a pity it missed my head?"

"Anyway," said Davga, "I'm glad to see you can still joke. A fellow has to be pretty decent to take such an accident

smiling. Of course I meant it was a pity the lantern fell at the precise moment when my guest was in the path of danger."

Dick shrugged his shoulders. "Why give the matter further thought?" he asked. "If you still wish to play fan-tan I suggest that you deal."

Later, sitting in the splendid room which had been assigned to him, Dick tried to decide on a course of action. He knew that Mortimer Davga had recognized him. That in itself constituted a peril. The fact that he was a friend to Dolores Cravat only served to double it. He knew that unless he was constantly on guard his life in that beautiful, sinister house would not be worth a farthing. The room was in darkness. Restlessly he rose and walked over toward the window. The moon was rising but it was still so low it cast the garden into greater shadow. The tree tops stood out in silhouette, etched sharply against the sky. The garden was a place of wandering wraiths and shadows. Was it only his imagination or was there really a form crouched beneath his window? His room was on the second floor and there were clinging vines ladder-like in strength climbing up the gray façade of the house. It would be quite an easy matter for an assailant to climb into his room and attack him while he slept. He could lock the strong mahogany door that led into the room, but what use would that be if he could not seal the window?

As he gazed down steadily his eyes grew accustomed to the gloom. There was no doubt that a figure was crouching there, though now it crouched no longer. It slowly rose to its feet and mounted the vine-ladder for about a half-dozen feet.

"Master," a voice whispered, "master."

It was the gentle voice of Wing Lo.

(Continued on page 141)

The Man Who Limped

By OTIS ADELBERT KLINE

*The strange and disagreeable adventure of Hamed the Attar,
and how he overcame his perverse hatred of women*

YOU wonder why I limp, *effendi?* You are too considerate to ask, of course, but I, whom Allah, in his infinite goodness and mercy, has already permitted two years beyond man's allotted three score and ten, have learned to read the thoughts of people by their expressions. Serving as a dragoman sharpens the wits.

You will hear the story? So be it. Here is the coffee-shop of Silat where we can rest in comfort, and the tale will serve to while away the time. This cushioned *diwan* is better than the sidewalk stools, and more quiet.

Ho, Silat! Pipes and coffee for two.

You know me, *effendi,* as Hamed bin Ayyub, the Dragoman, for thus it is that I have been known for many a year—subsisting on the *baksheesh* of worthy travelers like yourself, and showing them the sights of the Holy City.

None remain who remember me as Hamed the Attar, for full fifty years have passed since I was a druggist and perfumer with a prosperous shop of my own.

Looking on this gray beard, this wrinkled countenance, and this withered frame, you will scarce be able to picture Hamed the Attar, for in those days I was a handsome youth with a skin as smooth as peach-bloom, a beard as black as night, and a tall, straight body that was the envy of many of my less favored acquaintances.

Most of my customers, *effendi,* were women, and I was patronized not only by the wives and daughters of the middle class, but by many of the great ladies and kohl-eyed beauties of the harems, as well.

Aihee! What a business I did in scents, cosmetics and unguents, in henna, depilatories and aphrodisiacs, so that each day added to my profits, and I was in a fair way to become a man of great wealth.

Each day, also, added to my knowledge of the ways of women, for being prosperous I attracted flirtations from those of little wealth who desired husbands, and being also good to look upon, I received signs, hints, and even plain proposals from those who had wealthy lords but desired handsome lovers.

Many were the kohl-rimmed eyes that signed to me with signs of love—many the slender, henna-tipped fingers that sought to thrill me with their gentle pressures, and many the *yashmaks* that were dropped as if by accident from faces of such ravishing beauty as would have broadened the breast of a sultan.

My father, on whom be peace, was a great and wise *Imam,* and a true and pious believer. "My son," he had told me a hundred times, "beware of women who sign with the eyes and hands—and avoid as thou wouldst the unclean those who, feigning accident or innocence, disclose their charms to thy gaze, for if thou wert to take one of them to wife, Eblis himself could not play thee more falsely, nor wreak more mischief and bring more sorrow upon thee."

His words, perhaps because of their repetition, and also of the great love and respect I bore my father, had made a firm and lasting impression on my mind. Nevertheless, having an eye to business, I feigned ignorance to those who signed

"She reclined on a low diwan placed among potted shrubs and flowers."

or hinted, put off with excuses those who made plain proposals, and turned piously away when aught was revealed that should not be, though I must confess that I was at times sorely tempted, and would perhaps have yielded, had it not been for the timely warning of my father. Thus it came about, that I slowly grew to be a decided misogynist.

For two years this went on, adding to my wealth and to my distrust of and dislike for women. That is, *effendi*, I *thought* I disliked women.

Then I saw *the* woman.

Having grown sufficiently prosperous, I had taken a pretentious, richly furnished house in a quarter favored by well-to-do merchants, and had bought two black slaves to minister to my wants.

So it chanced that, on the evening of the day I took possession of my new dwelling, when my shop was closed and vesper prayers were over, I mounted to my housetop to smoke my *shishab* in the moonlight and enjoy the coolness of the evening.

Scarcely had I seated myself on the cushioned *diwan* which my slaves had brought up for me, ere I heard the soft tones of a woman's voice, so silvery sweet that they might have been those of a *houri* from Paradise, singing a love song of the *Badawin*.

There was that about the voice which thrilled me unaccountably, and I was consumed with a desire to see the singer. Presently, unable to restrain myself longer, I stood up on the *diwan* and looked over the wall. With that look, *effendi*, went the heart of Hamed the Attar.

THE voice, I have said, might have been that of a *houri* from Paradise, but when I looked over the wall it seemed to me that I looked on one whose comeliness would turn a *houri* furious with envy. All unmindful of my ardent gaze, she reclined on a low *diwan* placed among potted shrubs and flowers, singing to a bird suspended in a cage before her. And even as I looked, she finished her song, and the bird answered her with trilling notes of its own.

To this day, *effendi*, I see her in my dreams as I saw her that night, her beauty radiant as the sun at dawn, with hair of spun, red gold, with Paradise in her eyes, her bosom an enchantment, and a form waving like the tamarisk when the soft wind blows from the hills of Nejd.

At some distance from her on a mat, there sat an old slave-woman with folded hands. Presently, with croaking voice, she interrupted the sweet warbling of the bird.

"Salamah Khatun," she said, "you sing so beautifully that the voice of the thrush rasps harshly in comparison. It is perhaps for gladness that you sing."

"What gladness, *Ya Ummi?* I have no reason to be glad."

"Is it not, then, an occasion for great joy that your brave and handsome cousin, Sheik Ali ben Mohammed, comes to take you to wife ere the moon waxes full again?"

"To be his third wife, and thus subject to the rule of the first and the jealousies of the second? I do not so understand the significance of joy."

"I, too, was young once, my lady, and though a slave, I loved and sang for love. You can not fool me thus easily, my pretty."

"Nor do I seek to, *Ya Ummi*, but rather to confide in you. I sing for love, but not for love of Sheik Ali, who forces his cousinly claims on me."

"*Awah!* I suspected as much. Today I saw the blush that suffused your cheeks when the youthful attar gazed into your eyes for but a moment. The *yashmak* could not hide it from my old, dim eyes, yet that young and sanctimonious fool did not perceive it. Or if he be not a fool, then is he like graven stone, and in neither case would he be worth a paring of your nail."

Now when I heard these words of the old woman, *effendi*, though they were not complimentary, my heart leaped with a great joy that knew no bounds, for it happened that I was the only youthful attar in the city, and that I now recognized these two as having come into my shop that very afternoon. I recalled that the young lady had purchased a bottle of my most expensive scent from me, and had blushed when I looked into her eyes for a moment, whereat I had tactfully paid no attention, as was my wont, though marveling at the unusual occurrence. For while signing with the eyes and hands are voluntary, and denote boldness, a blush is involuntary and denotes modesty. It was like finding a nugget of pure gold in a worthless heap of glittering dross.

The old hag continued to vilify me, calling me an "*Akh al-Jahalah*," which means "Brother of Ignorance," and many other unpleasant names which I will not trouble to repeat, but her tirade was suddenly cut short by the girl.

"Enough!" she exclaimed. "I will not permit you to slander him thus. Begone, now, and prepare me a warm bath against my retiring."

The old woman rose, shaking her head sorrowfully.

"*Awah! Awah!*" she groaned. "If

this should come to the ears of the great Sheik Ali ben Mohammed, what calamities will befall us all! Were you to marry this fool of a drug-mixer this very night, the next full moon would find you both dead of his wrath, or you a widow and mayhap a slave; whence I would either be a slave of nobody or a slave of a slave."

"Have no fear, *Ya Ummi*, that I will marry him this night, nor any other," said the girl. "He does not even know that I exist; much less does he care. Go now. Prepare my bath and cease your wailing, or people will think we have a death in the house."

Now, *effendi*, having heard all this, and seeing the girl cooing softly to the little bird, which had grown tired and tucked its head under its wing, I was more than ever affected by the beauty and modesty of this maiden, and the secret love she bore me, and desired her above all my possessions and above all the wealth which it had been my hope to acquire. Yea, I desired her even above my hope of Paradise.

This being so clear in my mind as to admit of no doubt, and I being a man of action, I climbed to the top of the wall and noiselessly let myself down not ten paces from her. So silent was my tread in my *mezz* of soft morocco, that I stood beside her, yet she was not aware of my presence.

Folding my arms, and bowing my head, like a slave awaiting the will of his master, I coughed gently.

She looked up at me, uttered a stifled cry of fear, and sprang to her feet on the other side of the *diwan*. Then, seizing a wrap of flimsy, translucent material, she threw it over her head and drew a corner across her face so that only her glorious, terrified eyes were visible.

"Have no fear, O lady," I said, "and make no outcry, for I will go at your command, but only humbly ask leave to say what I have come to say before I depart."

"Oh, my misfortune! Oh, my sorrow! Oh, my disgrace!" she exclaimed, drawing still farther away from me. "And alas, it is Hamed the Attar who brings this shame upon me."

"Nay, Hamed your Slave," I replied. "Wilt vouchsafe me but a moment to say that which I have come to say?"

For answer, she flashed at me such a look of scorn that I truly felt the very slave I had named myself. Then she turned her shapely back on me and started toward the stairway.

"Wait," I pleaded, whipping my *jambiyah* from its sheath and poising its keen, curved blade above my heart, "or you leave only the corpse of Hamed your Slave behind you."

At this, she turned and surveyed me with a look of concern that flooded my heart with hope. Her words, however, were words of scorn.

"Alas," she said, "that my faith in you has been so rudely destroyed. I had thought you different from other men, and better, yet you violate the sanctity of the *harim* without so much as a single *'destoo'r'* to warn me to veil my face. You, whom I had thought so good and so pious, enter my house like a common thief, to my disgrace and your own unending shame. Now you heap injury upon injury by threatening to take your life here. Take it, if you will, for it is a worthless thing, but pray do so elsewhere."

Humiliated beyond words, I sheathed my *jambiyah*, bowed low, and slowly walked back to the wall over which I had just come. I realized that every heart-stabbing word she had uttered was truth, and that I had committed one of the most disgraceful crimes a believer may commit. I was about to draw myself up on the wall when, to my surprize, I heard her speak once more.

"Stay."

Turning, I saw her coming toward me, and with head bowed and arms folded once more, I awaited her further words.

"I know not why my heart is softened toward you, transgressor and profaner though you are," she said, coming up before me, "yet the deed is done, and may not be undone by your sudden departure. Nor can it be made worse by your lingering a moment longer. I therefore grant you leave to say that which you came to say, providing only that it is honorable."

"O, lady," I replied, "it is honorable in thought and purpose, yet I dare not say it now, with the full realization of the heinous crime I have so thoughtlessly committed, upon me. My only words, then, will be to humbly ask your forgiveness for what I have done."

"Allah does not withhold His mercy from the truly penitent. Who, then, am I to refuse you pardon? Take my forgiveness, freely granted, but pray to Allah for His."

"May He requite you," I said fervently, and laid my hand on the wall to draw myself up.

"Must you go?" she asked.

I paused. There was that in her eyes which somehow reassured me and bade me stay. After all, I had come with a definite purpose in mind, and it was the height of folly to leave without accomplishing it, now that I had the opportunity.

"It lies in your province to say," I replied.

She laughed softly.

"I fear you have an ally, a very powerful aid on which you have not counted," she said. "Woman's curiosity has got the better of me, and it seems that I simply must know what you came to tell me. Take your moment, therefore, and say your say."

I stood awkwardly before her, not knowing how to begin—seeking suitable words with which to describe fittingly the depth and purity of my passion. Finding none, and marking her growing impatience, I blurted it out in a most unseemly and uncourtly fashion.

"I came to tell you that I love you, and to ask you to become my wife."

She drew in her breath sharply, and swayed slightly toward me, but when I would have caught her in my arms she quickly eluded me.

"Your words are no less startling than your manner of entrance," she said when she had recovered herself, "nor are they less unconventional. If what you say be true, why have you not sent *khatibeh* women to convey the message, as is the custom? Surely you are not too poor to employ at least one *khatibeh*."

"Nor a dozen, nor a hundred," I rejoined. "I would squander my all on *khatibeh* women if I might thus hope to win you. No, the reason is to be found in my own foolhardy precipitancy. Tonight, when I heard you singing, I suddenly realized that I loved you. I wanted to be with you, if but for a moment, to tell you——"

"Enough," she said coldly. "You heard me singing, so I presume you also heard what I said to my slave. If so——"

It was my turn to interrupt.

"I heard you talking to someone," I lied, instinctively feeling that her outraged pride would be my undoing, "but as to what was said, I know nothing."

"Allah forgive you if you speak not the truth," she said. "But I will grant you the benefit of the doubt. As to that which you have asked of me, it is that which I have not the power to give, even if I were inclined to give it."

"You mean that you have parents—a guardian?"

"Not that. My parents have been received into the mercy of Allah, and I have no guardian. Being of age, I am legally my own mistress, yet I have a cousin, a powerful and war-like sheik of the Beni Sakr tribe, who has given notice that he comes next month to claim his cousinly prerogative."

Well I knew, *effendi*, the rights which tradition and custom give a first cousin in such matters, and of the affront which would be placed upon him if his priority claim were disregarded. And only too well was I aware of the revenge which a powerful and war-like sheik would take for a transgression of such rights. Yet so great was my desire for this girl that I would have risked my life a thousand times to possess her.

"Such little as I have to offer, in comparison to that which your cousin can give you," I replied, "is yours for the choosing. Only name your will, and it shall be the will of Hamed your Slave."

"I can not answer you now," she said. "I must have time to think."

"So be it," I replied, swinging up on the wall.

"My slave-woman will convey my answer to you," she said. "Meanwhile, send no *khatibeh*, for I would spare you all unnecessary expense, and say nothing to anyone about this, lest it reach the ears of my cousin."

"To hear is to obey," I said. Then I dropped onto my own *diwan* where I spent the rest of the night smoking, and thinking over my strange adventure and what it might lead to, until the *mueddin* called the summons for the dawn prayer. . . .

AFTER prayers and breakfast, I went to my shop, but found it difficult to keep my mind on my business. Being lovesick, I mooned about, with the result that my faculties were not as keen as they should have been, and I lost several opportunities for quite profitable sales. When midafternoon came, I made up a package of choice perfumes, cosmetics and unguents, and sent my apprentice with them to the Lady Salamah, telling him that all was paid, and forbidding him to accept anything for them.

When he returned he told me that an old slave-woman had met him at the door, and had taken the package without so much as an offer of *baksheesh*.

On the following day, I sent a porter with a choice collection of potted flowers and shrubs which I had purchased at no little cost.

On the third, I forwarded by messenger an assortment of delicious and costly sweetmeats.

The next day being *El-Goom'ah*, which is our Sabbath, I repaired to the mosque for worship at the noon call, nor did I reopen my shop thereafter, but spent the rest of the day in holy contemplation, and in selfishly praying Allah to soften the heart of the lady toward me.

The fifth day found me still without word from her whose love-slave I had become, and in the afternoon I purchased a valuable prayer rug on which were depicted the *mihrab*—the tree of life—and the hands of Mohammed, the Apostle of Allah, on whom be peace and prayer. This I sent to the lady by messenger.

On the sixth day I sent a bale of valuable hangings, tapestries and silks.

The seventh day arrived without word from my beloved, and I sat behind the curtains in the rear of my shop, leaving my apprentice to attend to all sales. By this time, hope had so far fled me that my bosom was constricted, so that I no longer had the power of peace. In the afternoon, I rose, and taking with me a considerable sum of money, visited a jeweler, where I purchased an *asawir* bracelet studded with diamonds of great price.

I had resolved to deliver this valuable present in person, but passing my shop on the way, I looked within and was overjoyed to see the familiar figure of the Lady Salamah's slave-woman, evidently awaiting my return.

After I entered, and we had exchanged greetings, I led her into the rear room, anxious to hear what she would have to say.

"My mistress," she said, "sends you the peace, and the wish that Allah may increase your prosperity because of your great thoughtfulness and generosity. She has directed me to inform you that she will accept your offer under certain conditions."

"And what may be the conditions?" I inquired.

"They have to do with her safety, comfort and dignity," she said.

"Then I accede without further question."

"But wait," continued the old slave. "You may find them difficult."

"Well, name them," I said.

"My lady will not be married except in a manner befitting her station in life."

"That can be arranged," I answered.

"But not here in Jerusalem. Remember the question of my lady's safety. A secret marriage she will not have, but a wedding suited to her position would instantly be known over the entire city, and her cousin the sheik would learn of it and come for his vengeance."

"Then how can it be consummated?"

"By marrying elsewhere. Her desire, in brief, is this: that you sell all your possessions here, and take her to Damas-cus, where the ceremony will be performed. Only thus can you hope to escape the wrath of her war-like cousin. You can then set up a new business in Damascus without fear of being molested."

"But how travel in secret to Damascus?"

"Can you not get camels, and a litter?"

"But if we join a caravan the news will travel back to the sheik, and he will follow us, even to Damascus; so it were as well to stay here and have it out with him."

"Are you then afraid to fare forth with my mistress and me, you and your two slaves? If she puts her trust in your strength and bravery to protect her from the *Harami*, are you yourself fearful of them? Are you less brave than a woman? Fie upon you! I will go back and tell my lady you are afraid."

"Stay, and be not so ready to judge me before I have spoken. I am not afraid for myself—only for the danger which she might run. If it is her desire to go, her will is my will. Tell her I will be glad to do all she asks, and only await her final word. Pray convey to her this *asawir*, a slight symbol of my affection, tendered with the hope that she may consider it a token of our pledged troth."

"I go, and will return the answer of my mistress in the morning. . . ."

In the morning, the old woman returned, according to her word, and told me that her mistress would be ready to go with me in a week, that in the meantime she would dispose of her property, except such as might be taken with us. She also told me that her lady did not wish to put me to unnecessary expense and would therefore be willing to ride in an ordinary *shugduf*, or one-camel litter, but she added that if I wished to show true affection I would provide a *takht-rawan* with two camels of easy gait to carry it, as she feared her mistress' frail form would not stand the swaying and jerking of a *shugduf*. This I promised to do, and she departed.

I immediately set about disposing of my business, my house, and other property which I did not have the means or the desire to transport.

Within the week, I had completed all preparations, packed my belongings, and purchased a gorgeous *takht-rawan*, together with brass and scarlet trappings and two gentle, sure-footed dromedaries to carry it. My two black slaves I retained to lead the dromedaries, and purchased also a third slave and four pack-camels to be haltered together and led by him, carrying our tents, provisions, rugs, and other possessions. For my own use I bought a swift-pacing dromedary with a splendid saddle and equipment. Each of my slaves I armed with two pistols, a simitar, and a *jambiyah,* and in addition to this armament for myself, I carried a rifle, slung across my back. The greater part of my possessions I had converted into gold, which I divided into equal quantities and placed in strong bags depending from either side of my saddle.

Thus prepared and equipped, it was with no small feeling of pride and satisfaction that I drew up my cavalcade before the door of my lady's house. She was ready to go—a virtue which I understand is quite lacking with your *Ferringeh* women—and I noticed with satisfaction that she had disposed of all but a few of her belongings, which consisted of the rug and bale of goods I had given her, a small bundle of clothing, her caged song-bird, and her slave.

I assisted her and the old woman into the *takht-rawan*, while the slaves loaded her belongings on the pack-camels, and I reflected that the crafty old hag, when advising a two-camel litter, had probably been quite as much concerned about her own comfort as that of her mistress.

It was early morning when we set out, and coming to the Via Dolorosa—along which walked Sayyidna Isa with the cross, nineteen centuries ago—we passed thence through the Bab es Subat, which the *Ferringeh* call St. Stephen's Gate, and struck out on the Jericho Road, our first objective the Hajj Road which leads from Mecca to Damascus.

HAVING traveled all day with but a short stop for prayers, food and rest, we made camp in a wady, some fifteen miles beyond El Ghor, near Mt. Nebo. We pitched three tents—one for the lady and her slave, one for my slaves, and one for me.

My slaves built a fire, and would have prepared coffee, but my lady insisted on doing this herself, and her old slave, who was busy baking bread, declared that no coffee was quite so good as that prepared by the fair hands of her mistress.

As I watched my affianced at her tasks, and noticed her grace, her skill, and above all, her maidenly modesty—for she continually kept herself veiled to the eyes—I felt that she was indeed worth a thousandfold more than any cost I might be able to bear for her.

The coffee prepared, she tasted it, then, as a mark of special favor to me, stuck a small lump of ambergris in the bottom of my cup, that my beverage might be perfumed with it. I asked her to enjoy it with me, but she insisted that she had purchased this ambergris for me alone, and hoped that her lord-to-be, who being an attar was an excellent judge of such things, might find it good.

One of my slaves, meanwhile, brought me my *shishah,* and I smoked, and enjoyed many cups of coffee while the meal was being prepared. Presently, to my great surprize, I found myself growing drowsy.

My head nodded, and I heard, as if in a dream, my lady commanding her slave-woman to serve coffee to my slaves, as there was more than enough for all of us. Then a strange sensation came over me—a feeling of exhilaration and of lightness, as if I were floating in the air like a bit of down. This was followed by strange and grotesque hallucinations, in which I would, at one time, imagine myself as tall as Mt. Nebo, and at another, as small as the ants that crawled at my feet. A word seemed to be forming itself in my mind. Presently I saw it flash in letters of fire from various points of the landscape. I saw it written on a silvery cloud in the sky above me. The word was *"bhang."* More I do not remember, for consciousness left me. . . .

THE sun had been near to setting when I lost consciousness. When I awoke it had just risen. Moreover, I was no longer in the friendly shadow of Mt. Nebo, but was surrounded by a glittering expanse of rolling sand dunes. My head ached frightfully, I had a feeling of intense nausea, and my muscles were sore and bruised as if they had been pounded. Attempting to move my arms, I found them bound to my sides. My feet, also, were tied together. I turned on my left side, and saw that my three black slaves were lying on the sand, all bound and helpless. Turning on my right side, I beheld two women and a man packing camp equipment and utensils on my kneeling camels. The man I had never seen before, but the women, their faces now indecently unveiled, were the two I had brought out with me. A mule, evidently belonging to the strange man, was tethered near my beasts.

She whom I had known as the Lady Salamah was the first to notice that I had awakened. She immediately called this to the attention of her male companion, and the two walked to where I lay. To my horror, I saw that she was attired in the costume of a common *ghazeeyeh*, a shameless dancing girl who displays herself before all men in vulgar postures and movements, and that her companion was a low and extremely villainous-looking hautboy player with a warty, bulbous nose and a black patch over one eye.

The fellow spurned me with his foot.

"Sit up, O son of a disease," he ordered gruffly.

"Not at your command, O spawn of a pestilence," I replied.

He kicked me again so that my ribs were near crushed in when I uttered this defiance, then swung on the girl. "Build a fire, slave, and heat the oil," he commanded. "We shall see to the case of this thief who robs the homes of true believers."

"Harkening and obedience, master," she replied, and set about building a fire.

"Now, stealer of slaves and profaner of the *harim*," he said addressing me once more. "You know the penalty the Koran and the law of the land impose for theft. Can you give me any good reason why I should not strike off your right hand, which is the legal penalty for the first offense?"

"What mockery is this?" I asked him. "First I am drugged with *bhang* and robbed. Then I am accused of theft."

"First, O father of a calamity, you committed theft. Then you were drugged and bound, but you have not been robbed. I have taken nothing from you but my own property, as Allah is my witness. Yours is untouched, and near at hand."

"Will you be so kind as to inform me what I have stolen?" I asked.

"In the first place, O dog, you stole my slave-girl, Salamah."

"She was represented to me as a great

lady, whose favors were her own," I retorted.

"That does not excuse you, even if true." So saying, he suddenly seized me by my beard and jerked me to a sitting posture. Then he unbound my right hand, and unsheathed his simitar.

"Will you hold out your hand, that I may strike it off?" he asked. "Or must I have it bound across one of your bales?"

The girl, who had placed a small cauldron of oil over the fire, the purpose of which I knew only too well, now walked over in front of me, swaying her hips in the wanton manner of the *ghazeeyeh*.

"Is there no help for it, but that you cut off his hand, my lord?" she asked.

"There is no help," he replied. "Hold out your hand, O sink of corruption."

"It is pitiful for him to lose his hand," she said, "when he has worldly goods with which he may expiate his crime. They can be replaced, but a hand lost is lost forever."

"That is true," he replied. "Offender against the law, how much is your right hand worth to you?"

Before replying, I considered the situation in which I was placed. What he had said regarding the law was only too true, and it was quite apparent that Salamah was really the slave of this villainous musician. The fact that he and the two women had plotted against me to bring this very thing about, might or might not be capable of proof. In the meantime they had not only the Koran and the law of the land on their side, but the well-known "right of might" as well.

I bethought me of the two bags of gold which hung from my saddle, each of which represented nearly half of my fortune. After all, what is half of one's fortune compared to one's right hand?

"There is a bag of gold hanging on the right side of my saddle," I replied. "If

it suffice you not, then strike off my hand."

Immediately he sent the slave-girl to fetch the bag, and when she brought it, he examined and hefted it.

"A fair price for a right hand," he said. Then he turned to my three slaves, who had by this time regained consciousness. "You have heard and seen this transaction, and bear witness that your master has purchased his right hand with this gold," he said.

All assented.

"It is well. The right hand is secure to your master. Now, the Koran says that for the second offense, the left foot shall be cut off. Your master has committed a second offense, in that he stole Marjanah, the slave of my slave. Unbind his left foot from the other, that I may strike it off."

"Is there no remedy, master, but that you strike off his left foot?" asked the girl.

"There is none," he answered. "It is the command of the Koran, which every true believer should obey."

"But if he make restitution, can not his foot be saved to him?"

"Take the other bag of gold, which hangs on the left of my saddle, and have done with it," I groaned.

Whereupon the slave-girl fetched the other bag of gold, and my slaves were duly exhorted to bear witness to the transaction.

"It grieves me to relate," said the mendicant, screwing his ugly face into a look of extreme sternness, "that still another theft has been committed. The song-bird of my slave was stolen—carried out of my house, and into the highways and byways. The Koran expressly states that, for the third offense of this nature, the left hand of the thief must be cut off. Therefore, O my pretty slave, bind his right hand and unbind his left, that I may comply with the command of Allah, the great, the glorious, issued through Mohammed the Apostle, on whom be peace."

"There lie my three slaves," I said. "Take them and leave me my hand."

"Their value is but slight," said the ruffian, glancing contemptuously at them. "Now if you will include the camels, together with their trappings, all weapons and ammunition, and all things which they have carried to this place, your person excepted, then will I consider your offer."

"What! All these for a song-bird?"

"Nay, for your left hand."

"Take them—take all," I moaned. "I may as well be utterly ruined."

"You heard him?" asked the fellow triumphantly.

"We heard, and bear witness," replied my slaves and his, in a chorus.

"Unbind these slaves, girl, since they are now mine," he ordered.

When she had unbound them, and they had stretched their cramped limbs, he said: "Ho slaves! Two of you attend the beasts, and the third come here. I have yet a duty to perform toward this stealer of slaves and violator of the *harim*."

When my former black slave had come up to where I sat, in accordance with the command of his new master, the mendicant continued: "Much as it pains me to dwell on the many offenses of this habitual criminal, there is yet another crime which must be expiated. This villain, who is so crafty he could steal the kohl from off the eyelid, and so depraved he would undertake it, has pilfered, in addition to other property, the cage in which the bird of my slave is confined. He who would steal the home of a bird must be a scoundrel indeed. Now the Koran explicitly commands that when a fourth offense of this nature is committed, the

right foot shall be cut off. Who am I to disregard the commands of Allah, the One and Most High God?"

"It is there you are in error," I corrected him, "for the *Sooneh* law expressly ordains that this punishment shall not be inflicted if the value of the stolen property be less than a quarter of a *deenar*."

"Unfortunately for your argument, and your foot," he replied, "the cage cost me exactly twice that sum. Unbind his legs, therefore, slave, that I may comply with the law."

"Is there no alternative, but that you strike off his foot?" asked the girl.

"There is absolutely none," he replied. "Has he not just told us that he is penniless?"

"Yet he has one thing which everyone has, and which he can give," said the girl.

"What is that?" asked her master.

"His blessing," she replied.

"True enough, yet it does not suffice."

"But it is something."

"It is something. If he give me his blessing, I will only strike off part of his foot."

And so, near choking with rage at the irony of this final humiliation, I called upon Almighty Allah to bless this malefactor, his slaves, his relatives, and his descendants.

Scarcely had I finished, ere he swung his simitar and cut off all the toes of my right foot. Then, while my former slave held me, he plunged the wounded stump into boiling oil, and stopped the bleeding. At this, I swooned dead away. . . .

WHEN I came to my senses, I was alone. There was no sign of the beasts or the people who had surrounded me when I fainted. My hands had been unbound, and in one of them was a note. Gritting my teeth with the pain of my wounded foot, I opened and read the missive:

In the Name of Allah, the Merciful, the Compassionate!

To Hamed the Attar, greeting:

Food, cooking-utensils, water, coffee and tobacco are under the mat behind you. There is sufficient of everything to last you two weeks, but your foot should be well enough to permit of some travel within ten days. It had been spared you entirely, except that, as it is, it will effectively dissuade you from the folly of following me. Follow the path of the setting sun, and you will reach the Hajj Road, where assistance is bound to be forthcoming, and

The Peace.

HE WHOM YOU ROBBED.

I abode in that barren spot for ten days, whereupon my foot was nearly healed as the note had prophesied. Then I slowly and painfully made my way to the Hajj Road, and then, with the help of a kind-hearted traveler who had room for me on his *shugduf,* to Jerusalem.

Being penniless and crippled, I was forced to beg for a living until a certain learned *Ferringeh,* hearing my story, gave me light work to do in his home, and in return for my poor services gave me food and lodging, and taught me your language. My benefactor left, but his teachings enabled me to make a living thereafter as a dragoman.

And so you will conclude, *effendi,* that I became a confirmed misogynist, and never married. Not so. It chanced one day, when I was passing the *hammam,* a well-dressed young lady of pleasing carriage signed to me with her eyes. Not being employed at the moment, I followed her at a distance and learned where she lived. I loitered about the place thereafter when business was poor, and she sat in the window of the *harim* and flirted with me. Several times she made it appear that her veil had slipped out of place, and thereby revealed to me a countenance of rare beauty. I had saved some money, so I sent a *khatibeh* to sue for her hand, and we were married. For forty years she was a true and faithful wife to me. Then Allah received her into His mercy.

They tell me, *effendi,* that you have in your country many women and girls who brazenly expose as much of their persons

(Continued on page 138)

MY FAVORITE TALES IN THE OCTOBER-NOVEMBER ISSUE OF ORIENTAL STORIES ARE:

Story   Remarks

(1)_____   _____

(2)_____   _____

(3)_____   _____

I do not like the following stories:

(1)_____   Why?_____

(2)_____   _____

It will help us to know what kind of stories you want in Oriental Stories if you will fill out this coupon and mail it to The Souk, Oriental Stories, 840 N. Michigan Ave., Chicago, Ill.

Reader's name and address:

_____

_____

_____

The White Queen

By FRANCIS HARD

A chess game was played in the heart of the Arabian desert,
with human beings for pieces and life and death as stakes

IT WAS Bishop Fergus who suggested that his daughter's future should be staked on the hazard of a chess game.

"But that is gambling!" cried Fenworth, appalled. "Why not let Constance decide the matter herself? She is the one most vitally concerned."

Bishop Fergus looked over the side of Granby's yacht and stared meditatively into the Persian Gulf. His massive, nobly molded face and chiseled forehead, aureoled with an ample crop of snowy hair, looked like the carved bust of a Roman senator. Apparently he was lost in contemplation of the sand riffles on the bar that held the yacht fast a hundred yards from the Arabian shore, but in reality he was deep in thought. He twirled his spectacles absently by the black ribbon that held them. With his left hand he rubbed his smoothly shaven chin.

Suddenly he whirled around and faced his daughter, who was gazing at him with a world of entreaty in her eyes. He glanced from her to Fenworth, back to the girl, and looked at Fenworth again.

"Constance is only nineteen," he said. "She can not possibly know her own mind, and she is altogether too young to marry."

"But Father——" Constance interrupted.

The bishop raised his hand and continued hastily:

"No, no, do not break in. Hear me out, for, after all, I am your father and whatever I do will be with your best interests in mind.—Fenworth, you loved Constance before ever you came on board. If I had known that before we left San Francisco, then you never would have started. When old Granby placed his yacht at my disposal for a trip to the Holy Land, and you asked to go as my secretary, you kept to yourself your love for Constance. That was dishonest. Oh yes it was, Fenworth! You knew I never would take you along if I had suspected such a thing. But we had not been on the ocean two hours before I saw how matters stood.

"I like you, Fenworth, in every capacity except that of son-in-law. Now that you have come to me and asked for my consent, I could refuse to give it, but I must have your acquiescence. I must not be opposed in this matter. That is why I am putting it to the test of a game of chess. You have boasted of your prowess. I, too, am a chess-player, although I have not touched a piece in twenty years. There is a chessboard in Granby's cabin. I will play you one game. If you lose, you must break off this foolish love affair at once."

"And if I win?" Fenworth faltered, disquieted.

The bishop shrugged his shoulders impatiently.

"If you win I shall cease to oppose you, but I can't promise to co-operate."

Fenworth scanned the bishop's face, without answering. The bishop averted his eyes, and continued nervously twirling his glasses.

"Come, come," he said at last. "Will you play?"

"But that is gambling," Fenworth repeated again. "You are a bishop."

"Chess is never gambling, no matter what is at stake," the bishop affirmed. "Chance plays no part in it, for it is purely a game of skill. You are a good player, are you not?"

Fenworth did not reply, but continued to stare into the bishop's face.

"Much better than the average, I take it," the bishop continued, with a suggestion of sarcasm in his voice. "A really fine player, perhaps?"

"Father!" Constance admonished him. The asperity in his voice amazed and wounded her.

"An uncommonly brilliant player, I believe?" the bishop continued, not heeding his daughter's interruption.

"Yes, sir," Fenworth answered, nettled. "I think I may say so without boasting, if past achievements prove anything. I am the best in the chess club. I won the intercity trophy two years running."

"Very good, then," Bishop Fergus continued, smiling blandly and rubbing his hands together rather gleefully. "In that case, it would seem that I am taking all the risks, and you none. Bring up the board, my boy. You will find it behind the book-shelf in Granby's cabin, and the chessmen are in the table drawer."

His face beamed as he saw Fenworth disappear. Not for weeks had he seemed so happy.

"He held her before him on the shoulders of his black mare."

"Father, you mustn't," Constance pleaded.

"Constance, please do not oppose me," he ordered.

A HUGE red, green and yellow umbrella was put into place on the deck, and Fenworth sat down in its shade with Bishop Fergus to play for the bishop's daughter. The sky-blue water lapped gently against the sides of the yacht, and the hot sun rained its rays upon the yellow sand of the desert, a scant hundred yards distant. Not a sound broke the stillness, except the droning of the desert flies, for the boat's machinery was stopped.

The position of the stranded yacht had been wirelessed, and help was on the way from Muscat. To the two lovers the delay caused by this side trip up the Persian Gulf had meant merely another week of paradise, but now the bishop had ended it all by proposing his absurd chess game.

Constance watched the movements of the little carved ivory horses and bishops and foot-soldiers with vast interest. She did not understand the moves, but those sinister-looking warriors were fighting out her destiny. A dark red knight on horseback tore through Fenworth's line of pawns and demolished two white foot-soldiers and a saintly-looking white bishop with flowing beard before it was captured and removed from the board. The dark knight looked so evil and terrible and it moved about the board in such an erratic and apparently illogical way that Constance conceived a terror of it. She stared at the two pieces as they stood side by side on the table, after they were removed, the saintly white bishop with a smile on its face and the dark horseman glowering.

She turned from the discarded pieces to look again at the game as the other dark knight was laid low in exchange for one of Fenworth's white knights. Constance felt somehow happier, knowing that the two evil-looking horsemen were removed from the board. Anxiously she studied Fenworth's face. He seemed worried. In truth, the game was going not at all to his liking. Bishop Fergus had forced a terrific attack upon his queen, which could not be rescued without the absolute sacrifice of a piece.

Fenworth sank dispiritedly lower and lower in his chair, desperately pondering his next move. Suddenly his hand trembled and he shot at Constance a glance of hope. He sat up straight in his chair. His heart beat so loudly that he feared the bishop must hear it. He tried to maintain his calm, but only the bishop's preoccupation with the game prevented him from detecting the new hope and anxiety in Fenworth's face.

After carefully studying the board before him, Fenworth deliberately abandoned the white queen to capture and moved his remaining white knight into position for an attack upon his opponent's king. If Bishop Fergus should take Fenworth's queen instead of building up a defense for the king, then Fenworth would win the game within four moves.

Would the bishop see his danger? He considered his next move for what to Fenworth was an interminable time, poising his hand over the white queen as if about to capture it. Fenworth restrained his jubilation, and the bishop withdrew his hand and pondered again. Fenworth raised his eyes from the board and looked across the yellow sand of the desert, seeking even a stunted tree on which to rest his gaze. Only a cloud of dust, probably a mile away. He turned again to the board.

Would the bishop never move? His finely carved head was still bent over the game as he studied the positions of the pieces, holding the edge of his spectacles against his lips. He saw danger threatening him in Fenworth's move, but he did not see the inevitable checkmate that would defeat him if he captured his opponent's queen.

Both players were so intent on their game that they did not hear a smothered exclamation from Constance, who was looking out over the desert, watching the cloud of dust draw rapidly nearer. The bishop's fingers closed over the white queen and lifted the piece from the board.

"Checkmate!" Fenworth shouted jubilantly.

"Checkmate?" the bishop echoed incredulously.

"In four moves!" Fenworth explained joyously. "You should have perfected your defense. But now——"

His sentence remained unfinished, for Constance cried out again, sharply. Fenworth sensed alarm in her tones, and he sprang to her side, overturning the board and spilling the chessmen. The girl's eyes were fixed upon the desert.

Fenworth glanced across the ribbon of shallow water that separated the grounded yacht from the shore. A troop of Arabian horsemen was spurring directly toward him. They were already within a few hundred yards of the water's edge, and riding full tilt for the yacht. The sand flew out in clouds behind them. The little stretch of desert that intervened narrowed rapidly and disappeared under a rush of flying feet and the splashing of horses' hoofs into the warm water of the Persian Gulf.

The troop rode across the shallow water of the sand bar, and in another moment were beside the yacht. They uttered not a sound, these silent men of the desert, but stood on the backs of their steeds and came up the side of the yacht hand over hand, leaving the horses champing in the water.

One of the Arabs seized Constance, who struggled and cried out. Fenworth, recovering from the amazement that had paralyzed him, lifted a camp-stool. Before he could swing it, another Arab deftly twisted his arm. The stool fell to the deck, and Fenworth was quickly thrown and trussed. The crew of the yacht was overpowered with ease. The skipper had not even the opportunity to seize his revolver. The Bedouins bound them each and every one, and passed them over the side of the yacht to the men below like sacks of flour.

SPEECHLESSLY, as they had come, the Bedouins rode away across the desert with their captives. The sun poured down mercilessly, and the cruel thongs cut into the flesh. The bishop suffered perhaps worse than the others, but he had no thought of complaint for himself. He cried out several times to Constance, who was carried by a handsome young Arab with short, silky black beard and prominent forehead, and black eyes that shone brilliantly, like polished ebony. He held her before him on the shoulders of his black mare, and occasionally he lifted her in his strong arms and swung her around so that she could be more comfortable.

The bishop was carried by an old, cruel-looking Arab whose beard was streaked with gray, and who was absolutely indifferent to the comfort of his captive. Fenworth swung precariously across the neck of a swift roan, in front of a tall, strong Bedouin whose mask-like face gave no hint of what thoughts might lie behind it. Before long he suffered acute pain from his uncomfortable and cramped position. The pitiless heat made him dizzy as they rode into the face of the westering sun.

As they faced more and more that

blazing disk, Constance's captor pulled the hood of his burnoose down over his forehead to keep out the sun, and turned the girl more and more toward him to shield her from the glare. Thus the two found themselves gazing into each other's eyes. Frank admiration gleamed in the Bedouin's lustrous black eyes, and he held her very firmly and gently, as the girl duly observed in spite of her fright.

The ground became more uneven, and was cut up by wadies. The troop crossed the dry beds of several, and Fenworth involuntarily cried out at the rough jolting as the horses loped down and up again. But the Bedouin who held Constance lifted her tenderly in his arms as they went across the wadies, and protected her from the jolting.

At length, as the sun was touching the rim of the desert, the troop, at a sharp command from the Arab who held Constance, turned north up a wady, where the going was easier than across the open desert. They followed the wady for perhaps half an hour, then turned westward again at another command and rode slowly up a long hill. The barking of dogs and the cries of children were borne to the ears of the prisoners. As they reached the summit, Constance's captor turned her around so that she could look down.

She gasped in astonishment. Spread out before her in the dusk was no temporary tent-village of nomads, but permanent buildings, waving palms, and a great pool of water. They had been brought to an oasis in the most inhospitable part of the Arabian desert, and a welcome sight it was to the travel-worn captives.

The Bedouins broke their silence for the first time that day, and began to talk excitedly among themselves. They carefully picked their way among a band of sheep, then broke into a gallop and charged down into the oasis.

A mob of dirty children and barking dogs immediately surrounded them, and several youths ran over to the arriving horsemen. A huge black slave, wearing the burnoose of the Arabs, stood motionless before the doorway of the most pretentious of the buildings, fixing his gaze with utmost interest upon the strangers.

To Constance, when her bonds were removed and she was placed upon her feet, they seemed to have arrived in some storied village out of the *Arabian Nights*. A large central building in Moorish style, made out of colored clays, slender beams and curiously cut stone, stood immediately in front of them. Radiating from this were galleries, like the cloister of a monastery. Behind them were the low mud dwellings of the Arabs, ornamented, like the central building, with colored clays and carved wood. A large pool, bordered with date palms, lay to their right, and to this pool the whinnying horses were allowed to stray.

THE prisoners were led at once through the portal of the main building, past the stolid black slave, and conducted into a central court. There they were grouped around a fountain, which flowed slowly through the court. Its waters were carried away to the pool through a stone gutter.

The young man who had carried Constance left them standing by the fountain while he went through an arched doorway into an inner room. He returned almost immediately with a gray-bearded man, whose entrance the other Bedouins acknowledged by profound bows. He was clad in spotless white, and wore about his neck a sparkling necklace from which depended a large black pearl. The deference paid him by the others, the air of mastery with which he approached the prisoners, the whiteness of his garments, all marked him as one who possessed authority. His vivid black eyes looked out upon the world through deep wrinkles, and his expression was the incarnation of curiosity and eagerness. With cautious dread Constance studied his face, bronzed and chiseled by the winds of the desert. He might be either good or bad, for all that she could read in his countenance. Certain it is that his face at the moment looked kindly rather than hostile.

The Arab approached the bishop.

"English?" he asked.

"No. We are Americans," the bishop replied.

"But you know how to speak English?"

"Yes," said the bishop.

"That is good," the Arab answered, a million wrinkles carving his face as he smiled. "You are no longer prisoners, for you were also our allies. I was with Lawrence in the war against the Ottomans. I am the Sheik Ferhan ibn Hedeb, and you are my guests. Smeyr!" he called, raising his voice and clapping his hands thrice.

The black slave who had stood before the entrance came quickly in and prostrated himself before his master in a profound salaam. Sheik Ferhan gave a few crisp orders in Arabic, and Smeyr retreated backward through the door.

"Smeyr will have the women place dwellings in order for you," said the sheik. "He will be the slave of the lady during your visit. I have place for several of you in the palace, and the rest must stay in the dwellings."

Sheik Ferhan glanced around with the pride of possession.

"Now I would know the names of my eminent guests," he continued, "and chiefly the name of this lady, who is a dream of beauty."

He bowed low, and Constance flushed.

"This is my daughter Constance," the bishop said. "I am Bishop Fergus of San Francisco, and this is Fenworth, the young man who is one day to be the husband of my daughter."

Fenworth gave Constance a quick look, and the flush on her cheek became deeper. Sheik Ferhan's appraising glance covered Fenworth from the soles of his feet to the crown of his head.

"Smeyr!" he cried, as the black returned.

He gave further commands, and the slave extended his hands and stood expectantly to one side.

"Smeyr will lead your people to their dwellings, Bishop," the sheik explained. "You and your beautiful daughter will remain here, with your friend. In thirty minutes all will return and take lebben. You are very tired. You will rest here— three, five, seven days, perhaps. Then you will be taken back to your ship. I am most unhappy that my men caused trouble to you, but most happy that you are here. I will show you the hospitality of Bedouins, like nothing else in the world. Do you like lebben?"

"Lebben?" the bishop repeated. "I do not know the word."

"Our goat's milk, soured and fermented. Very good, very strong, very stimulating. But there will also be dates, and my women will prepare sweet goat's milk for the lady. I am told that your women always drink their milk unsoured."

Sheik Ferhan himself conducted the bishop, Constance and Fenworth to their rooms. Smeyr returned shortly, and carried to Constance a huge basin of water. He discreetly withdrew, and knocked on the post of her doorway when he thought a sufficient time had elapsed for her to prepare her toilet. She handed the basin back to him through the curtains that served as door, and the black then carried it to the bishop, and afterward to Fenworth, without changing the water.

A few minutes later Sheik Ferhan called to his guests, and they came out into the court, where they were joined shortly by the remaining members of the bishop's party. Seating Constance on his right and her father on his left, the sheik sat cross-legged on the floor. A bowl of soured milk was placed before each of the guests, and the sheik's women passed around salvers piled high with golden dates. Constance drank a long draft of goat's milk. Sheik Ferhan did not partake, aside from taking a few dates, explaining that he had eaten his daily meal some hours before.

"But in my country we eat three times a day!" Constance exclaimed.

"Three times!" Sheik Ferhan echoed. "Then why do you not become fat and ugly, like the Ottoman women? But no, you are thin and graceful, like a fox. I think you eat very little at each sitting."

He looked well pleased with himself for his compliments. Constance dimpled, and Fenworth looked grave.

After the meal, Sheik Ferhan clapped his hands four times, and the Arabs who had captured the bishop's party came into the court. They bowed low, and then came over to the sheik, bowing once again. The tall, handsome Bedouin who had carried Constance was introduced to her as Zadd. He bowed low before her, and touched her hand with his fingers, pronouncing the name "Constance" very carefully. He was presented to each of the party, and then, bowing low again before the sheik, he and his companions departed.

"Zadd wants the lady to know his great sorrow at your discomfort," Sheik Ferhan explained. "We are all sorry to annoy you, but happy, very, very happy, to have you with us. Every house is open to you. Ask for what you wish, and it shall be yours. If you have coins about you, my people will be glad to have some.

But you must offer them when you enter their houses. Then they are gifts. No Bedouin will take pay for hospitality, but they like coins as gifts. They are very proud, my Bedouins. Two centuries on the oasis have not made fellahs of us. But now you are very tired. You will want sleep. Tomorrow will be time to see my people and my good oasis. Peace to you!"

Bowing deeply, he withdrew. Smeyr conducted the crew of the yacht to their dwellings, and the bishop, Constance and Fenworth went to their rooms.

CONSTANCE lay wide-eyed on the woolen mattress in her room, thinking over the exciting events of the day. She had never met anyone quite so courtly as the old sheik, who had rescued her and her party from the hands of his tribesmen. She thought of the tales of Harun-al-Rashid, and drifted insensibly into slumber. Sheik Ferhan, Harun-al-Rashid and the handsome Zadd were inextricably mixed in her dreams.

Bishop Fergus, his mind relieved by the benevolent protection of the sheik, soon dropped to sleep, despite the soreness of his body after the long ride across the desert.

Fenworth, alone of all the party from the yacht, did not sleep. He had seen the look of admiration on Zadd's patrician face while crossing the sands, and although he was too much preoccupied with his own discomfort and danger to think much about it then, it troubled him now. But what the attitude of Sheik Ferhan might be troubled Fenworth even more. The young American had watched the sheik closely during the meal, and in his face he read shrewdness and crafty cunning. To Fenworth it was obvious that Sheik Ferhan desired Constance. A look of annoyance had darkly wrinkled the sheik's face when the bishop told him that Fenworth was to marry Constance. The look disappeared almost as soon as it was born, but Fenworth had seen it, and it made him tremble.

Another man slept but little that night, had Fenworth but known it. That man was Zadd, for he, too, had looked upon Constance, and he, too, had seen the look of desire in the eyes of Sheik Ferhan. The sheik had promised protection to the party, and henceforth the Americans were no longer prisoners, but guests, and every member of the tribe was bound by the laws of Bedouin hospitality to treat them as friends. But for some reason that he could not explain, some imperceptible insincerity in Sheik Ferhan's manner, or perhaps only an impalpable and meaningless shadow of fear, Zadd was troubled.

CONSTANCE awoke early, and was about to arise when one of the sheik's women came into the room, bearing a basin of water and a coarse linen towel. Her ablutions finished, Constance entered the court. Fenworth was there before her, pacing stiffly back and forth, keeping watch on her door. As the curtain was pushed aside he came forward eagerly and greeted her with a betrothal kiss, the first he had been able to give her since he won her at chess the day before. The bishop joined them a few minutes later, walking slowly, sore and weary from his ride across the desert.

"Happy morning!"

The three turned quickly as Sheik Ferhan entered the court. He was smiling broadly. Three women accompanied him, bearing milk, butter and dates for the breakfast. The sheik again declined food, but sat and talked with his guests while they ate.

"I am a Bedouin," he said. "One meal a day is enough. If I ate more I might become fat, and that would be ugly. I

have great wish to show our oasis to you, and we shall have horses racing. And you must meet my wife. I have but one, although the great Prophet (on whom be peace!) allows four to every man who, like myself, can give the necessaries of life to so many."

He smiled his broad smile, his little black eyes twinkling and little wrinkles radiating good-humoredly from the corners.

"Come, my friends," he said, smiling again, and stroking his grizzled beard, "I will show to you the hareem."

He offered Constance his arm, with all the courtly grace of a Solomon greeting Sheba's queen. Constance laughed delightedly and went with him through the curtains into the secret recesses of the dwelling. Her father followed with Fenworth. A tall woman, arrayed in spotless white, without a veil, waited in the hareem, attended by two women slaves. She evidently expected the visit.

"My one and only wife, Adooba," said Sheik Ferhan, saluting her with a deferential bow.

He added a few words in Arabic. Adooba smiled, and bowed to the three guests in turn. She looked keenly at Constance. Fenworth, watching her narrowly, saw distrust written on that desert-bronzed countenance.

Conversation was impossible; so, after an interchange of formalities through the sheik, they passed the baths of the hareem and went out into the open air, the sheik and Constance leading. Zadd and one other, who served as interpreter, awaited them, and the black Smeyr followed a few paces in the rear. Smeyr never left the party throughout the day.

Zadd's companion, in very bad English, introduced himself to Fenworth and the bishop as Faris, who served with General Townshend's army in the advance on Bagdad. While Sheik Ferhan explained everything to Constance, Faris tried to do the same for the bishop and Fenworth.

"I learned English very good," he explained. "I interpreter at English army. I interpret you oasis. Here big water pool—water tree, goat, sheep, horse, men. Here horse run for you this today. Ten, and ten more, with Zadd on black she-horse. You see, after dinner."

The party completed its tour by visiting the mud houses. The crew of the yacht had already struck up an acquaintance with the Arabs the evening before, through the medium of Faris, who had suggested that they would like gold coins as keepsakes, and was desolated to find that the Americans had no coins in their pockets when they were dragged from the yacht.

All of the Americans—Constance, Fenworth, the bishop, and the fourteen men of the crew — gathered in the sheik's courtyard for the noon meal. Zadd and Faris formed part of the party, and Adooba, who usually ate in the hareem, sat silently beside her lord as a special honor to the strangers. The sheik's women brought heaping trays of dates and bowls of milk, and a huge wooden platter containing the great fat tail of a sheep, surrounded by splintered masses of cooked mutton. Bones and meat were mangled together and boiled without seasoning. Lumps of butter and dough were ranged around the edge of the platter, and bits of liver surrounded the tail of the sheep.

The meal was far from appetizing, and there were no plates from which to eat it. The platter was first placed in front of Sheik Ferhan, who handed it on to Constance and instructed her how to eat from it. He passed a little dish of salt to her, and she dipped her fingers into the meat, salted it and tasted it. She did not like it, and turned her attention to the milk

and dates, while the sheik passed the platter to Adooba. Then he ate from the platter himself, and it was passed in turn to the bishop, Fenworth, and the members of the crew. There was much of the strange food left when it reached Zadd and Faris, and the sheep's tail had not been touched, but they fell upon it like hungry wolves, and passed the scraps to Smeyr.

Bowls of water from the fountain were then passed among the guests, and the party arose and proceeded to the smooth plain at the west of the pool, where the races were to be run.

TWENTY young Arabs rode in the first race, which Zadd easily won on a speedy little black mare. Then came spear-throwing, foot-racing between the youths of the oasis, and pitching of quoits. Sheik Ferhan explained the sports to Constance, and Fenworth chafed at the attentions he paid her, for the newly engaged young man had hardly had a word with his sweetheart all day. He found his opportunity to join her after the races, when the sheik dropped back to chat with the bishop.

"It's about time," Fenworth commented ill-naturedly, as he took the sheik's place at Constance's side. "I thought that old mage was going to stick to you forever. He must bore you frightfully."

"On the contrary," Constance said, "I think he's clever. He is certainly terribly interesting. I believe I like him immensely."

"You're as bad as the White Queen in *Through the Looking-Glass*, who believed six impossible things before breakfast," Fenworth growled.

"Surely you aren't jealous of a nice old Arab sheik," Constance replied.

"Why," Sheik Ferhan was asking the bishop at the same moment, "why is your daughter going to marry that young man?"

"He is really very worthy," the bishop answered. "And besides, he won my daughter in a chess game. They are to be married on our return to San Francisco."

"What a pity!" Sheik Ferhan replied, shaking his head and stroking his grizzled beard. "What a pity!" he repeated, with a look of great shrewdness in his eyes. "So he won your daughter in a chess game."

For a minute he was deep in thought. A merry laugh from Constance broke up his revery, and he raised his head almost fiercely.

"Fenworth!" he spoke out sharply, in a tone of command.

Fenworth looked up. Sheik Ferhan rose and came toward him. His eyes were twinkling, and the little wrinkles at their corners writhed in mirthful exultation.

"You are a player of chess," he said, with a suggestion of contempt in his voice. "Tomorrow you will display your ability. You will play with me a game, and the chessmen will be living men and women, and the pieces will walk across a giant checkerboard marked out on the plain. You and I will direct them from a platform built like a tower at one end of the field. The beautiful Constance will be the white queen, and Adooba will be the dark queen. It is fitting so, for Adooba's face has been darkened by the sun, but the face of the American girl is white like milk. You have seventeen persons in your party from the ship. You will play, and the other sixteen will be pieces in our game. The castles will ride on camels, and the knights will ride on mares, that we may know them as we overlook the checkerboard from our tower. The bishops will be robed in long white burnooses, and

the pawns will walk on foot. Thus will there be a game that will amuse us for half a day."

"But not for a stake," Fenworth interposed. "I won Constance once in a game, and I don't want to stake my fortune again in that way."

Sheik Ferhan's face became terrible, but the cloud passed on the instant and his face wrinkled again in a smile.

"If I wished to have that beautiful girl in my hareem," he said, "I would ask her, and not come to you. A woman loves, or she does not love, and the hazard of a game can not change it. Smeyr!"

He brought his palms together sharply, and Smeyr was before him almost immediately. The sheik gave him orders in Arabic, and he withdrew at once.

"Over there will be the platform," said Sheik Ferhan. "Here will be the field. We will mark the dark squares by rugs and cloths, and the sandy ground will be the white squares. But you would now eat dates and milk. I find the Americans do not like lebben. But dates and milk there are for all. We will now withdraw to the palace that the Americans may eat."

THE repast over, Sheik Ferhan suggested to Constance that they go out by the pool and watch the moon.

"They tell me," he said, "that at Mecca the moon looks just the same as it does here. Do you see the moon in San Francisco?"

As they came into the open and saw the moon silvering the desert, Constance tugged at Sheik Ferhan's sleeve.

"Oh, beautiful!" she exclaimed. "I have seen the moon just as it is now, as I looked across the water from the ocean beach, by the Cliff House in San Francisco, and I have watched it sink lower and lower until it was drowned by the swell of the Pacific Ocean."

"Then the moon must shine everywhere," Sheik Ferhan said, measuring his words. "I do not understand. It is here, and it is there at the same time. Mecca lies across the desert, hundreds of miles south, almost within sight of the other sea, on the other side of the land. And Aleppo is far away, north of the sunset, in the Ottoman country, yet the same moon shines there. And London and San Francisco are at the ends of the world, farther even than Aleppo, and they all have the same moon. My poor brain can not understand it."

Constance laughed. Her mirth seemed to please the sheik, for the crow's-feet around his eyes wrinkled even more than usual, and he beamed ecstatically.

"But you will teach me many things, about the moon, and the ocean, and your country, and I will learn from you each day, oh palm-like stranger from across the water."

Constance looked at him wide-eyed.

"But I am to return!" she exclaimed. "You don't mean—you can't mean you will hold me here!"

"Your beauty is like the palms waving in the moonlight, after a weary ride across the sands," said Sheik Ferhan. "It tells of sweet repose and whispers of cooling waters and fragrant flowers. I am like a wanderer in the desert. I have been lost in the sands, and you are the oasis that tells me I have found my rest. You are not fat and ugly like the Ottoman women, nor dark like my own race. Listen, daughter of strangers. My wife Adooba is very sweet, but you are far sweeter than she. The great Prophet had four wives, which Allah allowed to him. I have but one. You will rule my harem, and the black slave-girls will serve you, and you will be my second and favorite wife."

Constance kept her eyes fixed on Sheik Ferhan during this speech. He hung his head, as abashed as a schoolboy declaring his love. His crafty glance sought Constance's face and shifted again to the ground.

"The great game of chess on the plain tomorrow will celebrate our wedding," he added, thoughtfully.

Then his arm encircled her and drew her to him, and his eyes sought her face. Constance struggled and pushed him away. He released her and gazed fiercely into her terrified eyes, reading there her horror and fright.

"You prefer the weak young man from San Francisco?"

Constance nodded.

The sheik's tone became hard.

"Very well, then. The Sheik Ferhan is refused. The weak young man from across the water is winner. Then let him earn his prize. Let him look well to his game, as we move our human chessmen across the checkerboard tomorrow."

He meditated a minute. His face became tender.

"Let us go inside," he said. "Your weak young man with the white face will be impatient."

He bowed low and motioned to her to precede him.

An excited whispering caused her to turn her head. Two white figures were moving by the date trees at the pool's edge. She wondered if they had overheard Sheik Ferhan's declaration. The sheik saw them, too, but made no sign. The moon shone upon their faces, and Constance thought she recognized them as they withdrew into the inky shadow of the palms. One was Faris, the interpreter. The other was Zadd.

THE shouting of children, the barking of dogs, the chanting of a Bedouin and the hum of voices woke

Constance at daybreak. She arose and dressed, and found Fenworth and her father already pacing the court. She ran to her father and threw her arms about his neck. Fenworth stood by, vaguely troubled, and as Constance told of Sheik Ferhan's proposal the young man clenched his fists in impotent anger.

Two Arab women entered the court with trays of dates and figs, and pitchers of goat's milk. A minute later Sheik Ferhan joined the party and bade them good morning. He seated himself, smiling craftily, but did not partake of the food, as it was far from mealtime for him.

"The workmen are preparing the field," he said. "It will be ready very soon, and we shall have rare sport. With you directing, there will be just enough persons in your party to be pieces and pawns on your side. The fair Constance and the dark Adooba will be our queens. We will have a pretty game, very good to look at."

He clapped his hands, and Zadd and Faris came to his side. Shortly thereafter Adooba joined the group, and they proceeded toward the field, Sheik Ferhan walking with his wife, while Constance walked between her father and Fenworth. Zadd and Faris brought up the rear.

Constance clapped her hands in pleasurable excitement at the sight that greeted her. A huge checkerboard was mapped out on the plain. Rugs formed the dark squares, and gleaming sand the white squares. At the outer edge, toward the desert, and between the opposing groups, was built a platform ten feet high, from which Sheik Ferhan and Fenworth were to direct their human chessmen. Opposite, in the blacker sand of the oasis, the sheik's workmen had sunk a hollow pit, which was filled with water. Beside this stood Smeyr, clad only in a snowy white girdle, his

giant black limbs and body shining in the sun. At a signal from Sheik Ferhan he lifted high a huge bowl.

"This is the water clock, by which our moves will be timed," Sheik Ferhan explained.

He spoke to Smeyr, and the black cast the bowl down upon the pool. It began to fill with water, which forced its way through a hole in the bottom. The bowl settled lower and lower.

"It takes ten minutes for the water to fill the bowl so that it will sink," Sheik Ferhan explained. "As soon as you have made your first move, Fenworth, Smeyr will let the bowl fall upon the water and I will have ten minutes to make my move. If I have not moved before the bowl sinks, Smeyr will strike this brazen gong to show me that my time is used up and I must make my move at once. Whenever a piece is ordered moved, then Smeyr will empty the bowl and let it fall again upon the water, and the other player will have ten minutes to think out his next move, if he wishes to take that long. But let us begin."

He gave a few sharp commands to Zadd and Faris, and soon the human pieces were in motion toward the checkerboard. Camels stood at the board's four corners, awaiting their riders. Next these, on the north and south edges of the mammoth board, were hobbled mares for the knights to ride—white mares for Fenworth's side, black mares for Sheik Ferhan. Bishop Fergus and the skipper of the yacht, in long white burnooses, took their positions on the squares next to the mares, to be the white bishops in this strange tourney. On Sheik Ferhan's side two patriarchal Bedouins with gray beards were the bishops.

The sheik himself escorted Adooba to the queen's square, and Constance, mistaking her place, walked to the white king's square, from which Fenworth laughingly shifted her to the queen's square adjoining. The pompous cook from the yacht, with an improvised crown on his head, stepped to the king's place. In front of each of the opposing lines of pieces, after much laughter and confusion, were at length ranged the pawns—the eight remaining members of the yacht's crew on Fenworth's side, and eight young Arabs on Sheik Ferhan's side.

Then the sheik and Fenworth, accompanied by Zadd and Faris, made their way to the platform. A small checkerboard was placed between the two players on a little table, with ivory and ebony chessmen, that they might direct the human pieces by their mimic counterparts. Zadd and Faris stood on the platform with folded arms as Sheik Ferhan and Fenworth took their seats.

Then Sheik Ferhan spoke. His voice was calm and even, and bore no trace of the passion that guided his words. Fenworth, watching him intently, read his feelings only in the narrowing of his eyes. Zadd, uncomprehending, stood impassive, but Faris, the interpreter, started, and on his face were dismay and consternation.

"Young man with the weak face," said Sheik Ferhan, softly, "last night I offered the American girl the honor of ruling my hareem as my second and favorite wife. She refused. You, and she, and all of you, are my guests, by my own act, although my men hoped to hold you for ransom, when they captured you. I could have kept you as prisoners, but I did not. But the American girl has hurt me—here!"

With a theatrical gesture, he struck his clenched fist upon his heart.

"However," he continued, quickly recovering his tranquillity, "I shall not force her into my hareem. But I can not forget the hurt. I am a Bedouin, and therefore proud. Young man with the weak face, if you love this girl you must fight for her. You must prove your right to her in this chess game. Listen well to me, and hear my offer.

"If you lose, then you, and she, and all of you, will be sent into slavery among the lost oases. Your Europeans' maps do not show them, and your travelers have never visited them. Your consuls and your soldiers can never find you. You will disappear, and be heard of no more. And you will be separated from the American girl. She has refused the honor of becoming my wife. I accept this fate, but she will grace the hareem of some sheik in the lost oases.

"But if you win, then you, and those of your people who are not captured in our friendly game of chess, will be sent back to your ship, with all the gifts my little wealth can provide. If you still keep your white queen uncaptured, then you can take her with you. But if she, or her father, or any other of your people are removed from this great checkerboard, then they will be sent as slaves to the lost oases, and the rest of you will return to your ship. Do you understand?"

Fenworth set his lips tightly together. An unwonted pallor blenched his cheeks. He looked steadily into Sheik Ferhan's eyes, and the old man's gaze fell before the American's stare.

"Come, young man with the weak face," said Sheik Ferhan, "I will be fair. I tell you that the American girl will be sold into a hareem if you lose her in this game, but I offer you Adooba if you remove her from the checkerboard in our game of chess. What is fair to me is fair to you. Win the game and capture the dark queen, then you may take Adooba away to your ship. And if I capture the white queen, then you lose the American girl. I warn you that I am an excellent player. Many nights I played with the English officers and beat them badly. Let us begin."

Z ADD raised his hand at the sheik's command, and Smeyr struck the gong. A brazen note rolled over the plain. The chess game had begun.

Fenworth carefully advanced the pawn in front of the dignified cook from the yacht, who stood in haughty majesty, with his mimic crown, for all the world like a real king standing before his throne. The gong sounded again, and Sheik Ferhan ordered his own king's pawn into the center of the board. Zadd shouted his orders in Arabic, and the black, who had cast down the water clock upon the pool, picked up the bowl and emptied it. Sheik Ferhan's move was duplicated on the field, and Smeyr cast the empty bowl upon the pool.

That part of the Arab population not engaged in the game crowded around the mammoth checkerboard and watched in fascinated but uncomprehending interest the progress of the play. Women and children elbowed and jostled one another as Zadd and Faris ran among the living figures of the game directing their movements according to the moves made by Fenworth and Sheik Ferhan with the carved ivory and ebony pieces on the platform.

Again and again Smeyr struck the brazen gong, emptied the bowl, and cast it down again upon the pool. Cautiously the two players maneuvered their black and white pieces, and Zadd and Faris duplicated the movements on the field, sometimes shouting out the directions, and sometimes leaving the platform and going out among the human pieces. The women laughed as the hobbled mares lumbered over the squares, bearing the knights on their backs, and the children

clapped their hands in gleeful excitement. But Fenworth sat silently, with mouth tightly compressed and eyes glued to the board in front of him, only raising his glance from time to time to make certain that Faris had properly repeated his move among the human chessmen on the plain. He castled, and a camel lumbered to its feet under Faris's blows. The children shouted as the ungainly beast, rocking from side to side, moved to the spot just vacated by Bishop Fergus, who had been shifted to the center of the board.

Then Sheik Ferhan moved out Adooba, using her to launch an attack against Fenworth's queen. Fenworth gazed fixedly at the position in front of him, as if to verify the danger in which the white queen stood, then shot a quick glance toward Constance. She blew a kiss to him and smiled radiantly, ignorant of the danger that enveloped her. Fenworth fixed his attention again upon the board, and blocked the sheik's move. Faris descended from the platform and duplicated the move upon the plain.

Sheik Ferhan darted one fierce glance at Fenworth, and set himself to the task of capturing the white queen and removing Constance from the field. He forced an exchange of knights, and the children shouted again as the hobbles were removed from the mares' legs and the riders dismounted.

The benignant smile faded from Bishop Fergus' face and he muttered an angry exclamation, for two Arabs from the sheik's household set upon the sailor who had been riding the mare as Fenworth's queen's knight, and bound him and laid him down upon the plain a prisoner. A murmur ran through the crew of the yacht, and the faces of the rest of the concourse expressed genuine surprise. Zadd stood for a moment stock-still, as if unable to trust his eyes.

He expostulated with the two Arabs, but their explanation seemed to satisfy him, and he strode back to the platform. Smeyr struck the gong again and cast down the bowl upon the pool, and the play was resumed.

Now the two antagonists settled down to a terrific duel. Fenworth used the full ten minutes allotted to him for each play, but Sheik Ferhan made his decisions rapidly, moving the ebony pieces on the board almost as soon as Fenworth's moves were completed, and sending Zadd post-haste to carry out the maneuver on the field. Two of Fenworth's pawns were exchanged and set bound beside the sailor, and Zadd, still uncomprehending, remonstrated with the sheik. But Ferhan spoke sharply to him, and he descended from the platform to carry out the instructions of his chief.

The game was turning slowly in the sheik's favor, and Fenworth, trying desperately to save Constance, found himself open to a strong attack upon his king, an attack that seemed certain to win the game for Sheik Ferhan. But the Arab's reckless attack upon Constance had overreached itself. It exposed the sheik to the loss of a piece, and with it the game, for the players were too evenly matched for Sheik Ferhan to expect victory if Fenworth had the absolute advantage of a piece. To force the exchange and gain the piece, however, Fenworth would have to give up Constance in exchange for the Arab's queen.

Bishop Fergus saw the desperate plight of Fenworth's game, and realized Sheik Ferhan's treachery. The attack upon the white queen made him fear that the sheik planned to take Constance into his hareem if he captured her in the play. He saw Constance's danger and knew that he was the buffer that must be interposed and exchanged to prevent an interchange of queens. He thrust two fingers into his mouth and whistled shrilly to attract Fenworth's attention.

Fenworth was conscious of a vast irritation. This was *his* game, not the bishop's. In that moment he hated the bishop for distracting his attention from the pieces before him. Had he not proved himself the better player by winning Constance from him? Why, then, did the bishop not keep out of it?

If he protected Constance by interposing her father, then only the flimsiest chance of winning remained to him, for the position against him was very strong. Slavery threatened all of them, and Sheik Ferhan had said that he and Constance would be sold to tribes quite far apart. He looked out over the field and saw that the water clock was slowly sinking. The minutes were creeping on, and beads of sweat stood out on Fenworth's forehead as he fought to decide his move within the time allotted to him.

If he should accept the exchange and surrender Constance to a temporary slavery, would not a rescue be possible? Most of the party would return to the yacht, and the American government would surely punish the sheik and find those whom he had sold into the lost oases. Had it not rescued an American citizen from the Moroccan bandit Raisuli? The skipper of the yacht was an Englishman, and the British government possessed great influence with the Bedouin tribes, because it had actively aided the Arabs in their struggle for independence. The British government could surely force the return of the prisoners. But if he protected Constance now and lost the game thereby, then all of them would be enslaved and no news of their fate would ever reach the outside world.

The cries of the Arab children had ceased. Everyone sensed some important decision to be made, and the throng hung upon the event with breathless interest, even though the spectators did not understand the maneuvers.

Hardly more than the rim of the bowl still showed above the surface of the pool. Fenworth scowled in silent rage. If the water clock would only give him more time to make up his mind! How could he think with that sinking bowl speeding away the seconds, and Bishop Fergus shouting at him?

He stared sullenly, unable to withdraw his eyes. The last few seconds seemed hours. What had that bowl to do with him, anyway? He experienced a strange anger at it.

And now the bowl swirled, and sank from sight. The huge black lifted his shining arm and struck a blow on the brazen gong. It seemed a full minute before the club in Smeyr's hand touched the gong and the harsh sound boomed discordantly through the air, but it was in reality only a small part of a second.

Fenworth's world seemed to fall away from him. He moved the ivory bishop to protect his queen, and Faris hastened to the field to duplicate the maneuver. He had made his decision and taken the fighting chance.

Sheik Ferhan without hesitation lifted the ivory bishop from the board, and sent Zadd to direct the removal of Bishop Fergus to the group of prisoners who sat, with arms bound behind them, near the water clock.

Now Faris, returning from directing Fenworth's move, encountered Zadd. He told him what Zadd already half suspected, and it made the tall Arab's handsome face become for the moment distorted with strong anger. Sheik Ferhan, from his place on the platform, called to him to hasten. Zadd gave Bishop Fergus over to the two Arabs

from the sheik's household, and they tied his hands behind him. Smeyr cast down the bowl, and the game was on again.

Fenworth gnawed his thumb-nail and tried to see daylight through the gloom that enveloped him. On the board before him, as on the field beneath him, with carved or with human pieces, he saw defeat and slavery. The net drew tighter, and Fenworth struggled vainly, as the water clock again told off the seconds against him.

Zadd and Faris returned to the platform, and the handsome Bedouin spoke to Sheik Ferhan in low, measured tones. Fenworth, who knew no Arabic, nevertheless felt the restrained feeling that surged beneath Zadd's words. He saw the determined visage of the tall Arab, and the clenching and unclenching of his left hand as he spoke, and he saw the eyes of Sheik Ferhan narrow to mere slits.

Slowly the ancient sheik rose to his feet. As slowly as he had risen, he extended his right hand and grasped the hem of Zadd's burnoose. Speech poured from him in a flood, beginning low at first and swelling in angry volume as his voice rose higher and higher. Zadd closed the fingers of his powerful left hand around Sheik Ferhan's knuckles and wrenched his grasp from the burnoose. Then he deliberately pushed his chief to one side.

Raising his voice until it carried clearly across the giant checkerboard and rang out over the pool of the oasis, Zadd addressed the Arabs. He had uttered but a few words before Sheik Ferhan smote him upon the neck and tried to pull him from his perch.

Meantime Faris broke his silence and tried to explain to Fenworth what was happening.

"Zadd say Sheik Ferhan break Bedouin law. You no prisoner, you friend.

Sheik must be friend to guest. Zadd say sheik break hospitality, make all you prisoner. He say Sheik Ferhan no more sheik."

Zadd broke the sheik's hold and sent the old man spinning into the board, knocking the pieces over. Sheik Ferhan crashed through the little table and fell from the platform to the ground, ten feet below, for there was no railing to break his momentum. He struck his head sharply against a corner post of the platform, and lay still on the ground.

The knights and castles and bishops and pawns came running swiftly across the sand to the base of the tower. Faris leapt the ten feet to the ground, and was first to reach his fallen chief. Zadd stood with folded arms, while Fenworth sat in his place amazed at the sudden passage of events.

Sheik Ferhan was dead. His neck had been broken as he fell head foremost from the platform. And now Zadd addressed the Arabs, vehemently at first, then more slowly and with more measured accents. What he said was gathered, bit by bit, from the hotchpotch of English that came from the willing but ineffectual lips of Faris.

"Your sheik has shamed you," said Zadd. "He made these strangers his guests, and by immemorial custom their persons were inviolate thereafter. He abused the sacred privilege of host and made prisoners of his guests. He proposed to sell them to the lost oases. He broke the law of hospitality, which is the worst crime a Bedouin can commit. Thereby he forfeited his right to the title of sheik. And now he lies dead. Peace be with him."

Silence greeted Zadd's solemn words, broken only by a stifled sob from Adooba. The dark queen of the oasis sincerely mourned her fallen lord. But on Zadd's heart also there lay a shadow, for his face was eloquent of gloom.

He conferred at once with the other leaders of the little tribe, and it was decided to send the Americans immediately to their yacht, in the half-day that remained before sunset. Zadd rode beside Constance, in silence, for how could these two converse, since neither knew the other's tongue? He threw over her shoulders a snowy white burnoose to protect her neck from the rain of heat rays, and he set a leisurely pace on his coal-black mare, so as not to weary the American girl.

He seldom looked at her, but Constance stole frequent glances into his finely formed face, with its strong nose and chin and short black beard. Fenworth rode immediately behind her, with an Arab escort, and the bishop rode third, beside Faris. Two by two, the party moved slowly across the desert.

THE sun had set and the moon cast deep black shadows upon the yellow sand before they came within sight of old Granby's yacht. Still Zadd maintained the immobility of his countenance, and Constance gazed more and more often into his face. On the deck of the yacht several faces were seen, and a boat, with steam up, lay alongside. It was the relief boat from Muscat.

The Bedouins dismounted at a sign from Zadd, and Fenworth helped Constance to the ground. Faris again endeavored to convey his apologies for Sheik Ferhan's breach of hospitality. Then Zadd crisply ordered his followers to horse, and they rode away, each leading one of the horses that had brought the Americans back to the yacht.

Zadd was left with Constance. Diffidently he extended his hand in farewell greeting. She grasped it, and smiled into his face.

O. S.—**3**

"Constance," he said, tenderly, and repeated the name carefully, several times: "Constance, Constance, Constance," as if to engrave it into his memory.

Her face betrayed the sadness of her heart as she scanned his features. He kept her hand in his and gazed fixedly into her eyes as the moon shone upon her upturned face. Then the girl kissed him on the mouth, in view of Fenworth and her father and the crew.

"Good-bye, Zadd, my sheik," she said, and her lips trembled.

Ashamed to let him see the moisture in her eyes, she turned away and strode to the water's edge, where she awaited passage to the yacht.

Zadd mounted the snow-white stallion that had brought her from the oasis. Leading his own coal-black mare, he loped back into the desert. Constance, looking from the deck of the yacht a few minutes later, saw silhouetted against the horizon two horses, and on one of them was a rider. They lingered for a little, and she tried to call to him.

"Good-bye, Zadd," she cried. "Good-bye!"

The silhouettes disappeared beyond the ridge, and Constance laid her head on Fenworth's shoulder and wept.

Flower Profiles

By HUNG LONG TOM

How many times through countless hours
Have I heard Li Kan describing wondrous profiles
Of the girls he paints on vases and fans
And white bits of old ivory.

The profile of a golden girl
Against a soft blue screen is finer far
Than any cameo yet carved,
Loveliest of pictures lying 'neath the sun.

Now through my garden
I walk and dream and smile.
Has one not noticed the profile of a flower,
The lovely clear line of a tea-rose
Laughing in the sun,
Or of a pale pink peony
Lush with morning dew?

Is there a music more exquisite
Than the perfume of a rose?
Or a sweeter profile
Than a simple garden flower?

Strange Bedfellows

By S. B. H. HURST

The clash of Russian and British interests in Islam—a fierce Afghan of the Durani Clan—the slave region of Ruba el Khali— and the adventurous secret-service man, Bugs Sinnat

THE sunlight drenched the forward deck of the old steamer where the pilgrims for Jidda were making themselves comfortable. A group squatted about Ben Mohamet, a big Afghan of the Durani Clan, laughing delightedly at his Rabelaisan stories. Very popular was this Ben Mohamet.

"Now, when the Sultan came home that night . . ."

He paused. A battle-scarred veteran of many pilgrimages got up and left the group to help a blind man from the rail to his mat.

"Ah," said Ben Mohamet, "we have, I see, many of God's afflicted with us. Blind and lame men! But there is one more unfortunate than all the rest—this deaf and dumb man at my side. For consider, brothers—he can not hear my delightful stories!"

The group laughed at this typical hill wit. Ben Mohamet told another tale. Then a pipe was passed around. It looked like a coconut with a hole in it, the bowl stuck in on the top. Ben Mohamet drew in the awful smoke without a shudder. He was used to it. For years this most remarkable of India's secret service men—Sinnat, 006, known among his intimates as "Bugs"—had lived and moved among Mohametans. A rumor of another Mahdi, Mohametan Messiah, had decided him to make the dangerous pilgrimage to Mecca. Another Mahdi meant a Holy War — a *jehad* troublesome and perhaps dangerous to British rule in India. . . .

"Who is this poor man to whom God has given a silent tongue and ears that hear not?" Bugs asked the group about him.

Nobody knew. The deaf mute was a stranger. But nearly all were strangers to one another. The group demanded the tale of the Rajah of Swat, who was a man of strange emotions. . . .

So the day went by. At the time for evening prayer they all faced in the direction of Mecca and went through their somewhat gymnastic devotions.

Bugs lay down on his mat. He had been watching the deaf mute intently ever since the steamer left Bombay. He had helped him at every opportunity, as the other well pilgrims helped the blind and the sick. And he was distinctly puzzled, for he was convinced that the deaf mute could both hear and speak, if he wished, as well as he could himself.

"He's not a native, either," thought Bugs. "Now, what's he doing here, aping that difficult part? Who the devil can he be? What's he pretending to be a deaf-mute Mohametan for—a pilgrim going to Mecca?"

Bugs went to sleep. The stars passed overhead. The pilgrims snored and tossed uneasily on the hard deck—somewhat cooled by the eight knot progress of the steamer through the oily swell of the Arabian Sea. A blind man talked in his sleep, quoting the Kuran. Another growled in the dream memory of some old fight. Every half-hour the colashe

"The Nubian beat him frightfully."

sailor struck the bell on the forecastle, and howled mournfully, *"Um decta hi!"*, which told the officer on the bridge that he was keeping a good lookout. The sea muttered, whispering uncannily to the iron plates of the steamer that disturbed it.

Morning. On the forward deck was an open cookhouse where the pilgrims prepared their food. There was no squabbling. Grim men cared for the afflicted as if trained all their lives to that end—helping them with their food, finding them soft wood for their teeth cleaning.

Bugs—Ben Mohamet—loudly expressing sympathy for the deaf mute waited on him, anticipating his needs.

Small stores, or extras, could be bought from the ship's steward; and about five the next afternoon Bugs walked aft and interviewed that gentleman. He spoke to the steward in rough Hindostani, and said that he had "found" an English sovereign. He was not accustomed to using such money—how much was it worth in rupees? Because he wished to trade it for coffee and sweet things—which the steward sold.

The steward, an elderly Scot, grinned. He spoke excellent Hindostani, with a Gaelic accent!

"Ye *found* this bit of money?" he asked, grinning. The steward knew well the sort of pilgrim that travelled on that old steamer.

Bugs grinned in return.

"Between friends," went on the steward, "what was the name of the jail superintendent from whose pocket this money —fell?"

Bugs laughed. "English names are difficult to me—I am from the hills. But I think the name of that Englishman was McGregor!"

"That's not English," growled the steward. "That's decent Scotch, ye puggle! Would ye call a Bengali by the name of an Afghan chief?"

Bugs bowed gravely. "How many rupees for the money?"

"How about eleven?" asked the steward.

The change in Bugs was startling. One moment a polite if somewhat dirty Mohametan, the next a fierce Afghan looking for trouble. No race in the world can beat the Afghan at bargaining, who proudly claim descent from the Children of Israel.

"Fifteen," amended the Scot quickly.

He was no coward, but he wanted no trouble with Bugs and his fierce friends. It is not generally mentioned, but a small steamer was once captured by her pilgrim passengers.

"Sixteen!" said Bugs with cold ferocity.

That happened to be the correct exchange. The Scot growled agreement.

"What do you want to buy?"

Bugs smacked his lips over a list of the sweetest and stickiest things he could think of. Such are very dear to the Afghan stomach. And coffee. A sovereign will buy a lot of such things on a pilgrim ship.

The steward began to fill a clean flour sack with the stuff. . . . The warm salt wind blew into the storeroom.

"The coffee is in the lazarette below," said the steward. "Wait here while I get it."

Bugs, who knew the ways of storerooms, sat down on his haunches, and the steward went down the ladder. With the quickness of a conjuror Bugs brought out a metal hypodermic case from among his clothes. From among the tubes containing various drugs he selected a tube of morphine sulfate. He hid this in his turban, and returned the case to the belt next to his skin.

The steward came puffing and perspiring up the ladder. "Those blasted boys never stow things where I can find them!" he growled.

The coffee was terrible, but that did not matter, as Afghans love it so strong that its only flavor is its bitterness. And Bugs had accomplished the reason for his generous spending. He had the morphine in his turban. On deck among the pilgrims he dared not take the chance of selecting the drug. There was no privacy among the pilgrims, and no lights were allowed at night. . . .

"*Salaam,* McGregor," said Bugs politely.

"Lindsay is the name, but *salaam,* all the same," replied the steward.

Bugs went back to his friends. Much merriment resulted. Purple shadows were spreading over the Arabian Sea when that popular story-teller, Ben Mohamet, began passing around the coffee he had so gratuitously prepared. The officer on watch had sent a *secunnie* [quartermaster] to tell the pilgrims that all lights and cooking-fires must be out in an hour. The *kassab* [native storekeeper] had given out the rations guaranteed by the steamship company. It was a restive scene of twilight when Bugs, in due order and ceremony, presented coffee to the blind, then to the cripples, and last to the deaf mute.

"Now you big roughnecks," he shouted to the hale and very hearty remainder, "take your coffee! Are you not weaned, that I must feed you? Come on—fill your ugly bellies with the sack of sweets! The afflicted have been fed!"

The pilgrims patted Bugs' shoulders with heavy fists. They drank with polite regards to him, and the roar of happy Moslems went heavenward.

EVENING prayers. The dark, and sleeping-mats. The steamer went its lazy way through the oily swell. The engines hammered out the rhythm of some new jazz time.

Bugs had thrown his mat down by the mat of the deaf mute, which by this time had become the proper thing for him to do. And of all the snoring that disturbed the air of night the snoring of Ben Mohamet was the most jagged and tremendous. . . .

Presently the deaf mute began to snore —deeply and heavily.

"The stuff seems to be working," thought Bugs. "I gave him an awful dose, to make certain. Was a bit afraid it might make him sick, but the bitter coffee stiffened his stomach, besides hiding the taste of the morphine. Another proof he is not a native—opium affects him too easily."

Bugs laid a hand rather roughly on the deaf mute. As he did so a swift thought momentarily halted him.

"What a lovely bit of drama if this chap has outguessed me! But, yet, he can't do a thing. . . . I don't know, though! If he lost his head we might feed the fish together. I'd have to do some quick shooting, and then. . . . Oh, forget it! The chap is the same as he would be under an anesthetic—almost!"

With his sensitive fingers Bugs felt under the deaf mute's clothes. He sought, first, for papers. There were no papers. Some money in a belt. No gun or other weapon.

"Is he a secret service man of some other nation? He is establishing an iden-

tity with this tough gang to make himself safe from suspicion in Mecca. . . . So, that's that! The rest remains to be experienced. . . . We travel together. Now let's all go to sleep!"

In the morning the deaf mute was puzzled. A bad taste and a headache. But Bugs was as far beyond suspicion as the battle-scarred man. In the end the deaf mute blamed indigestion.

THE voyage passed peacefully. Daily Bugs became more attached to the deaf mute. The pilgrims were loud in in their praises. . . . The steamer went by Aden and into the Red Sea. Along the coast to Jidda—a mile-long town of queer smells, bad water and Turkish rule.

The talk of the Mahdi had grown. The eyes of the pilgrims gleamed when they spoke of the Coming. . . .

And Bugs, more loudly than any, bragging of what the world of Islam would do to the world of Christianity when the Messiah came to lead the Faithful. . . .

"I know!" he would shout, while his friends listened admiringly. "The Mahdi waits, as he did a thousand years ago! He is waiting at Mount Radwa, guarded by a lion and a panther, and fed by the angel Gabriel!"

The cry of creed answered him.

". . . la ilaha illa-llahu, Muhamad rasul allahi!"

THE crowd off the Nurani rested a day by the old Medina gate. The next day it would leave for Mecca. Bugs began chaffering the argot of the camel-drivers with the owner of two of those useful beasts as soon as morning prayers had ended. . . . He and his deaf friend, neither of whom had been there before, needed a guide and a driver of camels. This was a polite beginning to rough bargaining, for with that crowd a guide was not needed for the forty-six miles of worn trail.

He examined the camels. They seemed respectable—they were too old to be otherwise.

Bugs said this loudly. It raised as big a laugh among his friends as any of his tales. The owner of the camels glowered inwardly but he was too good a business man not to join in the laughter.

Bugs explained that he was a very poor man, and that he was glad the two camels had been honored by Noah, who took them with him into the Ark—for such antiquities were all he could afford.

"Only for the rich are the pure-blooded camels with feet like the wings of the morning, who can almost cross the Sahara between two suns!" wailed Bugs loudly. "And my friend has no money at all!" Thus the bragging Afghan, advertising his charity. "So, if the price is right, I will hire these two beasts of an age long past both desire and delight!"

The camel-owner came back sonorously. He was angry, but he would not pass up a chance to make money—and perhaps get even.

"The protector of the poor afflicted speaks with the wisdom of the sages," he shouted. "Not before have my ears heard such discourse! My soul trembles with joy at the prospect of hearing thy melodious voice, oh Ben Mohamet, all the way to Mecca—and, I trust, back again! Eastward toward the sun one march to Bahra will I drive my camels, entranced! At Bahra we will rest, although I would rather listen to the sweet voice of Ben Mohamet, who has hired me, than dream delicious dreams! And on the second march the rough hills of the Madi Marr will resound to the music of thy conversation, oh Ben Mohamet—and we will wander in ecstasy through the maze of the valleys! . . . Shabash! I am hired!"

"Hired—maybe! Maybe, elder brother of Abraham," howled Bugs, and his audience howled with him. "Hired, maybe thou art, oh man who carried pitch for the building of the Ark—to caulk its seams so it would not sink and thy camels be drowned—for you loved them even then! Behold, I am a Durani, and a friend of the poor. But first tell me—who in hell would hire either thee or thy beasts if he could afford better-looking creatures?"

This brought down the house—and also the price of the camels. But the driver demanded money in advance. He had hired his unhappy and smelly beasts to other Afghans in times past.

Finally, to the delight of the crowd—which swore it would forever love this remarkable humorist—Bugs agreed to pay one forty-sixth of the hire in advance, the balance in forty-five other payments on the way to Mecca—a payment every mile.

"Then if thy camels die—I will not lose," shouted Bugs. "And if my money gives out, as it probably will, you can try to make me walk!"

The badgered and swearing driver agreed, and Bugs knew himself to be beyond suspicion on the most hazardous trip he had ever taken in disguise. His identity as a bullying Afghan was firmly established. . . . The mute was helped on board his shaggy and moulting steed, and the camels began their undulating march to Mecca.

It was not a pleasant ride. The ancient route, camel-flattened centuries before Mohamet made the district famous, spewed dust in the riders' faces. Dust of millions! It was vilely hot, the water was rotten. But the pretended mute suffered more than any one. He was white, but not as tough as Bugs; he could not relieve his feelings by swearing and he was oppressed by the continual strain of acting a difficult part. And he was driven nearly crazy by the ostentatious attentions of his solicitous friend the Afghan Ben Mohamet.

THE Medina road, where the troops of the Prophet had massed before storming the city, the shouts and the prayings, the arguments with the cameldriver. The rest at Bahra for one night— a place like the stable of Hercules before the god got busy! A smelly tapestry of action and religious emotion. . . .

In a flurry of dust, in a fervid mob, in a clang of voices like a hundred thousand beaten cymbals of brass—Mecca, the Holy City of Islam. Bugs took the mute— and six of the original gang of the steamer went along—to one of the *ribats* which provide lodging for the poorer pilgrims. They were tired out and lay down to sleep at once.

Evening prayers had been said three hours before. The strange hum of the city gradually grew less. Bugs tossed and turned. He was too tired and sore from the camel ride to sleep. The deaf mute tossed and turned also. . . . Bugs wondered if the mute was sufficiently tired to talk in his sleep—and so betray himself. With that thought a sudden notion came to him. . . . Not morphine this time but crude opium, which no native would refuse, and the deaf mute would hardly dare refuse—perhaps not wish to. . . .

Bugs got up and walked to the opening arch of the *ribat*. Mecca breathed like the huge, mysterious animal of a fairy-tale. Over the Great Mosque a crescent moon hung appropriately, and a few stars twinkled with desert nearness. At the opening a blind old man slept. Bugs wakened him gently. The blind man had one trade—he made a living selling opium to the tenants of the *ribat*. Bugs bought two small portions of opium, and the blind man blessed him.

Bugs returned to the mute, and gave him a piece of opium. The mute swallowed it.

"I admire you more all the time," thought Bugs. "You know that a native would not refuse the stuff, so you take it."

He lay down and began to snore. And presently the deaf mute snored. . . . Some time later he began to turn restlessly. Bugs waited tensely. Then, softly:

"*Sunu. Sunu. . . . Sunu, Dini. Gorodu. Utro!*"

A long pause of deep breathing. Then, endearingly, "Sonia!"

"My Russian is limited," thought Bugs, "but I know that *sunu* means sleep. *Dina* is day. *Gorodu*, town. *Utro*, morning. Sonia of course is the name of a girl. . . . This very clever man is a Russian secret service man. Now, why has he come to Mecca?"

THE swift dawn crossed the desert, and the city awakened to a fervor of religious emotion. . . . That the Russian was trying to lose Bugs in the delirious crowd was obvious, but Bugs stuck close to him. It was the day of Arafa, when not even sickness was an excuse for missing the essential ceremony of Dhu'l Hijja, when to miss the Wouf would be to miss the pilgrimage.

The crowd swirled to the mosque of Ayesha, then like a turbulent stream to the sacred Caaba. Then, under the noon sun, a maddened mob to Omra, just outside the Holy Territory, shouting "*Labeykak! Labeykak!*" . . . Then the throwing of seven stones at the devil in the name of Allah, after the hot walk along the Mecca Taif road to the cairn at Mina. . . . The clamor around the Hill of Mercy. . . .

The great day. After it, Bugs returned to the *ribat* with his charge. He complained loudly of being very tired. But he shouted texts from the Kuran and boasted loudly of being, at last, a Hadji.

"The greatest day in the life of a man!" he shouted. "The day of Arafa! But I am tired. . . . I am so tired that I will kill the man who disturbs me this night!"

He threw himself down on the floor. He grunted artistically. Then he began to snore. But it was nearing midnight when the Russian moved cautiously, and strolled casually into the *ribat* yard. He paused there, listening and watching. But no one was awake. A sea of snoring, uncouth, unpleasant. The Russian grimaced, but the first smile for a long time creased his face. The strain had been terrible. He had good right to be proud of the way he had carried out his assignment.

He looked back. No one moving!

"Ben Mohamet will have a boastful fit," he thought. "What a kindly damned nuisance he has been! Yet he came in handy!"

He began to walk swiftly, his bare feet making hardly any sound. And he disappeared among the ancient stone houses —often five stories in height—unchanged since before William of Normandy conquered the English.

But a shadow followed the Russian.

Behind the Caaba is a narrow street in which live the real rulers of Islam, men of immense wealth. The Russian walked fast. The street was silent and deserted. Only the high old walls and the bars of the windows. And shadows. . . .

Almost directly behind the sacred place is a narrow alleyway that leads to the yard of the tall house standing there. Like a cloud the Russian melted into that alleyway. . . . And that house, as all the world knew, was the house of Abu Ali Al Hassen, the most powerful man in all Islam. . . . No wonder Bugs, blending with the dark, was startled!

His quick wits gripped at many theories, but, after all, the only way to make certain was to go and find out. But to follow the Russian was remarkably like walking into a den of hungry lions. To enter the house of Abu Ali Al Hassen uninvited at any time was dangerous. To do so in the dead of night! . . . In that house now was a secret agent of Russia. He would be welcome. That house had been his objective during all the weary nerve-racking days since the steamer left Bombay. . . .

Presently there swaggered into the narrow alleyway a truculent Afghan, with an excellent excuse on the tip of his tongue if one was needed! But would that excuse save him? His gun would not save him. He had it handy under his arm, but the first shot would bring hundreds of fanatics swarming over him like enraged hornets. . . .

It was very quiet in the alleyway. What danger lurked there? Bugs hardly breathed. The truculent Afghan had become a shadow again. . . . The yard of that mysterious old house was deserted!

And then Bugs understood. That house was safe unguarded. Its powerful owner was, as it were, *tabu*. Also, expecting the Russian, and desiring no curious onlookers, Abu Ali Al Hassen had given the servants who usually slept in his yard a night off. And what better night for a holiday than the night of the day of Arafa?

How exquisitely had the Russian dovetailed his movements! Only the expert can thoroughly appreciate the expert. . . . In the Russian Bugs saw a master of the Game.

But the clever arranging helped Bugs. Softly he crossed the yard. He slipped into the house!

It was no time to investigate. The Russian had probably been taken upstairs. To try to find him would be suicide. . . . Somewhere on the ground floor would be the room of the parting guest—where the guest and his host sip a final cup of coffee and smoke a final pipe before the guest goes his way. . . .

Bugs walked stealthily along the hall. Ah, there was the curtain—the guest room. Bugs slipped into the dark place. . . .

The rest of the night passed without sound. The dawn rose behind the minarets of the great mosque. It showed a comfortable room—divans, water pipes, a place of Arab luxury. Bugs lay down behind a divan, by the wall opposite the door. . . . The muezzins began calling the Faithful to morning prayer. . . . Mecca awoke to a new day. . . . Sweetmeat sellers crying their wares. . . . The chanting of a hundred thousand pilgrims. . . .

Footsteps in the house. Servants coming and going. Then a voice giving orders. The same voice again, at the door of the guest room, speaking courteously in Arabic:

"I beg you to pass in before me, and I will shut the door!"

Bugs cautiously watching from the end of the divan.

The speaker was a tall old man. On both his cheeks were three parallel scars —the "Tashrit," which indicates a man born in Mecca. Abu Ali Al Hassen. With him was the Russian.

"This was by far the best way of making our arrangements known to one another," Abu was saying. "As a deaf-mute pilgrim you can go anywhere without suspicion, and men will help you, whereas to have trusted our plans to the mails would have been risky. The English spies are everywhere. This was the best way. Difficult for you, but how well you have performed your task! I again congratulate you."

"The English know a Mahdi is about to arise," said the Russian.

"Of course they do," Abu laughed. "But they are all at sea concerning him. He is necessary. When he says to the Mohametan world that a Holy War is proclaimed—then the English will be driven out of India. With your country smuggling in arms and ammunition through the Khyber Pass, and money through many channels—the result is not in doubt. The English are too few. . . . A Mohametan emperor will again rule India, as Mohametan emperors have ruled India in times past. . . . You have the papers setting the times of action, and my letter, in your belt. God go with you, for my prayers are yours. The time is written down when I will give the new Mahdi his orders. The plan is all arranged. The English will be baffled and outnumbered. . . . You have done well, for only through your wonderful work could our communications be arranged with your government!"

"Thank you," said the Russian. "The spoils in India will be immense—far greater than ever before in history. . . . Russia has always seen India as the weak link in the English chain. We will strike there, when you strike. The result is not in doubt . . . oh Abu Ali Al Hassen!"

There was a sudden and very startling yawn. . . . For a petrified moment the Russian and Abu stared at the divan from behind which the yawn had come. Then from behind it rose the head and face and body of a big, sleepy-looking Afghan, who, before Abu could move to have his servants take him, shouted joyously.

"Why, there you are! All night I sought thee! But the poor fellow can not hear me!"

And Bugs jumped across the room and embraced the Russian tenderly.

"Reverend sir!" he now addressed Abu

Ali Al Hassen, "this poor afflicted man has been in my care since we left Bombay. I missed him last night, and sought, and sought, and sought. A friend, who was with us in the agboat, said he saw this poor man come into this house. So I followed. But I saw no one. I did not wish to be rude, so I did not wander about the house to seek my charge. I should have got lost, anyway, for never in my life did I see such a house as this —so fine, so large. . . . It seems that you have cared for this poor man in thy charity. I slept behind the divan. I thank thee for taking care of my poor friend!"

It was all said so naturally that even the wily Abu believed him. The Russian had spoken about the somewhat tiresome care of Ben Mohamet. . . . This was excellent. Now, again, Ben Mohamet should see the Russian safely on his journey. But Abu was not going to be anxious about it.

"Who are you," he asked grimly, "that dares sleep uninvited in my house?"

"My name is Ben Mohamet, of the Clan Durani!" Bugs stood very straight and stared fiercely into Abu's eyes. "I am a Hadji, and a man of the true faith and no liar but a fighter, as are all my race! Did I come into your tent at night? What of it? I sought a friend! Have I stolen?"

The last words were shouted angrily.

"Nay, nay," Abu spoke soothingly. "To seek an afflicted friend is a sacred quest. . . . I thank thee! For this poor man is my cousin! . . . I am glad you have come. I will reward thee to take care of my cousin again . . . to take him back to Bombay!"

"The poor fellow," said Bugs tenderly, but not declining the reward. "He can not speak, and can not hear. I tell good stories, but he can not hear them. . . . Would you like to hear one?"

Bugs' face expressed the inevitable de-

light of the superstitious and illiterate Afghan seeking applause.

"I regret," said Abu politely, "that I have to go on some business." He went on hastily, because Ben Mohamet seemed about to launch into a story whether he wanted it or not! "Here, take this purse. Buy good lodgings for my cousin, and what is left over is thine!"

The Afghan forgot stories. He grabbed the purse.

"You will take care of my cousin?" asked Abu Ali Al Hassen.

"Without your asking!" exclaimed Ben Mohamet grandly.

"But not without my gratitude," smiled Abu. "I pray thee to guard him well. He is witless and without speech or hearing. But charity is charity and he is my relative, and dear to me because of his affliction. . . . Take this—can you use it?"

He handed Bugs a revolver, a thirty-eight.

Bugs laughed.

"The Amir's officers tried to teach us how to shoot these baby guns—but I could not learn. We Afghans are not good shots—as thou knowest! Give me the sword, and, when I fight, the hacking and the sweating and the . . ."

Abu interposed tactfully. What a swaggering turmoil this Ben Mohamet was! "Come back to me, please, when you have safely seen my cousin to Bombay! I need a fine, brave, big, strong man like you—and much pay will be yours!"

"Shabash!" shouted Ben Mohamet, gratefully. "I will guard your cousin as if he was my right eye!"

Abu Ali tenderly embraced the Russian. He sent for more coffee. They all drank with noisy ceremony. With grave courtesy Abu Ali Al Hassen escorted his guests to the street.

"God go with you!"

Bugs bowed ceremoniously. The Russion made a guttural noise and bowed clumsily to the ruler of Islam. Bugs took his charge gently by the arm. . . . They crossed the street, Abu watching them. They kissed the sacred black stone of the Caaba, which tradition says was given to Abraham by the angel Gabriel. The sunlight shimmered on its ancient binding of silver bands. . . .

They walked back to the *ribat!* No Afghan of Ben Mohamet's class would waste money on decent accommodation. The Russian raged inwardly at such penury. . . .

ANOTHER night on the floor where the fleas tormented. The owner of the camels that had brought them from Jidda came to them after morning prayers. He wept—being an adept at the easy art of tears. Bugs inquired solicitously after the health of the camels. Such wonderful beasts! Only their extreme manginess showed their extreme age. The camel-driver wept some more. Ben Mohamet, he said, had ruined his business.

"Men deride me! Thy fame is abroad in the land, Ben Mohamet! When I try to find a hirer for my camels men laugh and offer to rent a forty-sixth part of one and a thirty-second part of the other. For, they say, my camels are so near death from old age that it is too risky to hire either of them in full—and that the only valuable part of a dead camel is his hair, which mine lack entirely! How am I to get custom back to Jidda—from which place you lured me, Ben Mohamet?"

"You specter of indecency!" shouted Bugs.

The camel-driver began again. Finally Bugs hired him, for the same price as before, which was the intent of both before the argument started. It had lasted half an hour.

They left Mecca. There was hardly any one on the road—the pilgrims were enjoying the city, lured by the variety of its unspeakable vices. The Russian and Bugs rode, the driver walked.

About eight miles out the driver turned the camels off the main road to a trail among the hills.

"Why?" asked Bugs.

"Softer for the feet of my 'poor old camels,' and saves half a mile," the driver growled uneasily.

"Turn back to the main road!" snapped Bugs, suddenly suspicious.

"As you desire," growled the driver. "As soon as we get around that small hill ahead of us!"

It seemed somewhat silly to suspect the camel-driver, yet Bugs felt certain that he was planning something. He examined the revolver given him by Abu Ali Al Hassen. The camel-driver would not expect an Afghan to carry a revolver. Turning swiftly to look at his companion, Bugs saw suppressed alarm in the Russian's face.

One of the camels coughed—as a horse snorts when alarmed. The driver spoke to the camel. His voice showed excitement. They had reached the small hill. Suddenly the driver stopped the camels. Two men leaped from behind the hill, shouting and waving old muskets.

Bugs fired. One of the robbers dropped, dead. The other threw himself face down on the sand.

"Now," growled Bugs, "before I send you to Jehanum, where thieves go who rob poor pilgrims—tell me the truth! Why this?"

The prostrate robber was babbling in terror. "He said you were an Afghan and a big-mouthed fool. To attack an Afghan is bad, but our guns, which shoot evilly, seemed too much for thy knife. . . . But, behold, here is a gun and an Afghan!"

The driver, who had been afraid to run, or else had fatalistically decided that it was no use running, swore.

"So," said Bugs, "thou art the culprit! You hired these robbers!"

The driver did not answer. Bugs turned upon the robber.

"Well?" he growled.

"It was not my fault, Afghan," howled the robber. "The driver hired my friend, and my friend hired me! Had I known so big and fine and brave a man as thou art awaited us I had never attacked thee!"

"Of course not! Go on!"

"This driver said we could have all the money we found on thee! You had insulted him and his camels. . . . He is the half-brother of the man you killed!"

Bugs turned to the now trembling camel-driver.

"Before I send thee to hell also—the truth!" he demanded.

"He has told it! You have made me a byword and a mockery. Why would I not try to regain my face? . . . You win! I had not counted on you having a gun. You shoot well, Durani!"

The camel-driver faced Bugs defiantly. His fatalism had gotten the better of his fear.

Bugs laughed. He did not at all blame the owner of the camels.

"Face about!" he ordered.

He was obeyed.

"I kill neither dotards nor babies," laughed Bugs, "but they are a nuisance when one has other things to think about! I will let you show me how fast you can run! It will amuse me! Run, now! Toward Mecca!"

The robber started immediately, floundering awkwardly in the soft sand.

The driver stared at Bugs. He could not believe his ears. Was this Afghan an utter idiot? To let him and his accomplice go free! Did he not know that they would be revenged? That the dead man on the trail would have to be accounted for? Kismet! And Allah had made the fool Afghan mad!

The driver ran after the robber. Bugs shouted, and then fired after the two men. He did not try to hit either of them, but he made it seem that he did. As his last shot missed and the robber and the driver disappeared behind a small sandhill, Bugs threw away the revolver.

He turned suddenly to the Russian on the other camel, saying, "Abu should have given me more cartridges! Now that gun is so much useless weight to carry—so I threw it away!"

A typically Afghan speech . . . but the Russian showed no understanding of it. Bugs had acted the Afghan splendidly since the robbers attacked, but the Russian had acted the deaf mute of very limited intelligence quite as well. . . .

"Too bad you are on the other side," thought Bugs as he prodded the reluctant camels. "What a man you are! . . . Logically, I should have shot both the driver and the other robber—to have two such fellows crying 'murder' against one is damn dangerous in this country. . . . Yes, I should have shot them! . . . But before they can do anything I will be back in Jidda and on some steamer."

He kicked the camels forward, and continued to drive them hard, without any rest at Bahra. With the strain and irritation of the driving there grew on him the realization of his mistake. He ought to have killed the robber and the driver. With so much at stake he had no right to indulge in mercy. . . .

B UGS drove the tiring camels hard. He wanted to put the Red Sea between himself and the land of Arabia. . . .

Through the night and the heat and the dust, and in his tired brain the dancing mockery of his folly. . . . Too well had he acted the braggart Afghan! By this time the revengeful driver would have collected fifty witnesses to an unprovoked slaying of his half-brother. . . . Would the camels last the distance? They had done well. How he had maligned the poor beasts!

He watched the Russian closely. That gallant man swayed from weariness, but uttered no sound. Bugs, an unusually powerful man, was almost all in. How his game antagonist must have suffered! . . .

The strain and fatigue became almost unbearable. And Bugs, blaming himself harshly for his foolish mercy, prayed for day and Jidda. . . . It was during the dark hour before the dawn that the poor camels collapsed. Bugs helped the worn-out Russian to his feet, and half dragged him into a walk. The Russian said no word. Occasionally he muttered, as a deaf mute mutters in protest.

Those last few miles were a nightmare. They met no one. They staggered and tripped over small rocks. The road seemed to fight them.

JIDDA as the dawn came. Bugs felt new strength come to him as he half carried the Russian to the waterfront. . . . The sun rose. Bugs groaned. There was not a steamer in sight. . . . Some few Arab dhows. No other ships. What was he to do?

He could not stand there thinking. A dozen ideas flocked to his mind. All had to be molded by his plan. And the plan was to get a copy of the papers the Russian carried without letting the Russian know he had done so, then to "lose" the Russian in Bombay, so that he would carry the plans to his government, not knowing that the British had a copy of them.

He thought of going to the British consul, and identifying himself—a simple matter. There, under the British flag, he would be absolutely safe. The camel-driver and his friends and the Turkish police would never think of looking for him there. Safety, yes—but failure.

An Afghan is not a British subject. The clever Russian would see through everything, and the plan would fail. An Afghan who put the power of the British government at his service, by merely saying a few words, would seem too strange.

Bugs could, of course, take the papers from the Russian by force, either in the consulate or right there on the waterfront—and leave the fake deaf mute to his fate. Hiding would be easy then, even without troubling the consul. . . . To get rid of the Russian would set Bugs free of an encumbrance, and of an associate with whom his identity since landing in Arabia had been fixed in men's minds. . . . But all that would be folly. The papers Bugs took from the Russian would become worthless papers. To allow the Russian to carry them to Moscow, while Bugs' copy went to the government of India—that was the plan. At all hazards that plan had to be carried through. The danger of death, brutal imprisonment for years without a trial, of being sold into slavery—such dangers could not be allowed to weigh against the plan. It would be nice to have a bath and a decent breakfast, and comfortably safe in the consulate after all the strain—but the plan came first.

Bugs led the Russian toward the lowest part of Jidda. He hoped to find some sort of hiding until a British steamer, carrying pilgrims from Mecca back to Bombay, was ready to leave Jidda.

But swift camels, carrying revenge-filled men, had traveled faster than the poor beasts of Bugs' reviling.

Tremendously impressed by the

Afghan's fighting qualities, although they had seen from behind their hill his throwing away of the revolver—the camel-driver, the robber and two friends had gone to a *cadi* with their tearful tale. The *cadi*, to whom the splendid injunctions of the old Law of Mohamet meant nothing, inquired, first, concerning the wealth of the accused Afghan. When assured that he was a poor man, the *cadi* accepted money from the accusers, and ordered six men to arrest Ben Mohamet. . . .

Even then the tales of his prowess were in evidence, and the six men, with the four accusers, jumped Bugs and the deaf mute as they entered a narrow street. Bugs struggled only enough, for he knew that resistance would be worse than useless. He could have shot his way out, but that would have been worse still. That gun under his arm was his ace in the hole—to be kept unseen until circumstances compelled its use. He might have escaped from the ten men, but not from the hundreds the *cadi* would summon if he did so.

They were marched before the *cadi*, an increasing and derisive crowd with them. Above all the abusive voices rose that of the exultant camel-driver.

"Thief and murderer! Robber of the poor!" And the Arabic equivalent of "He who laughs last laughs best!"

Arabia, or that part of it, still conformed to the old and very fine law of Mahomet in the appointment of *cadis*. Such judges were ecclesiastical appointees, although not allowed to sit in judgment in mosques. But the splendidly ethical formula of appointment often failed lamentably in the men picked for appointment; and the *cadi* of Jidda was, to put it mildly, rotten.

He stroked his beard with portentous gravity.

"Who charges these men, and what is the charge?"

The exhausted Russian faltered, and would have fallen but for Bugs' supporting arm. Jubilantly the camel-driver stepped forward.

"Ah!" drawled Bugs. "The old creature himself. He who cleaned the filth out of the Ark for Noah, and who carried in the pigs and attended to their needs—because no decent Mohametan would do it!"

The fickle crowd cheered. And its enjoyment of the joke was not at all affected by the fact of Noah's antedating Mohamet and his religion by about two thousand years.

The *cadi* nodded gravely. "I observe that the prisoner does not love the accuser!" he said.

"He mocked me, he made me to be the scorn of men by his vile tongue. And then he slew the son of my father by his second wife. And then, trying to escape the law of the prophet and the justice of his *cadi*, he stole all my property—my camels. And, still trying to escape, he killed them by overwork! I call on God to witness that I speak truth! And I ask judgment on him, oh just and honest *cadi*!" shrieked the camel-driver.

"Stand farther away," Bugs spoke quickly. "Stand away—lest thy foul breath and many lies make the *cadi* sick!"

Another large laugh at the expense of the camel-driver.

The Russian leaned heavily on Bugs. Bugs, calling on his last ounce of will and strength, spoke gravely—playing what seemed to be his only card.

"I am the man of Abu Ali Al Hassen! This poor afflicted one is the cousin of Abu Ali Al Hassen, whom I am taking to Bombay!"

A roar of derision greeted the statement. A dozen voices roared that Ben

Mohamet did not know Abu Ali. That he was an Afghan, and that the deaf mute had come with him from India.

"A liar as well!" exclaimed the *cadi*.

The voice showed Bugs that he had blundered. He could not understand why. The *cadi* was corrupt, the entire hearing was a farce—but such conditions were common enough. Why had the great name of Abu Ali been of no avail, and done harm?

"I have heard enough," said the *cadi*. "Thou art a liar as well as a thief and murderer! I judge you guilty, Ben Mohamet! . . . Take him away to prison. Let him lie there while I meditate on his sentence!"

Bugs laughed insultingly. He never in all his life had found it so difficult to laugh. But he had to play the proud Durani to the bitter end. A poor but proud Durani, under whose clothes it was no use looking for money. That gun must not be discovered.

"*Cadi*," and his voice rose sonorously above his weariness, "*Cadi*, thou art more of a fool than a knave! Abu Ali would not have thee for his dog. I am his man! God help thee when he hears of this!"

The crowd gasped at this loud insult.

"The sun hath made him mad," droned the *cadi*. "Put him in the lowest cell, where the heat of the sun can not trouble him. I will meditate on his sentence!"

Bugs and the tottering Russian were marched to the filthy jail. As they went the *cadi* beckoned the camel-driver.

"I think you lied also," he drawled. "If it turns out he spoke the truth concerning Abu Ali—who will protect thee then?"

The camel-driver shivered.

"Get what money you can, and I will do my best for thee," said the *cadi* in matter-of-fact tones.

The *cadi* meditated, but not upon the sentence of Ben Mohamet. He had decided that long ago. Even if he had given the weary Bugs a chance to explain why he had killed the "son of my father by his second wife," such explanation would have made no difference. He did not think for a moment that Bugs had told the truth about Abu Ali and his cousin, but he would have liked to believe it was the truth. For Abu Ali Al Hassen, far above graft and petty *cadis*, had, after many tales about this particularly rotten one, sent word that his days as a judge were done.

"You may plead that you are no worse than many others," the message had run, "but they go also! Lest it hold the office of *cadi* up to the scorn of the people more than thou hast done thyself—I give thee the chance to leave Jidda and never again show thy face there. Be gone after tomorrow's judging!"

The *cadi*, who had made hay for years, was making hay frantically while the sun still shone. His power held until midnight. After that hour began the Mohametan sabbath. . . . There were a hundred wretched prisoners in the jail. They lacked a sufficiency of both food and water. Their other conditions can not be described. . . . At nine that evening the poor creatures, broken in mind and body, were called out into the yard two by two. There a ring was welded around their necks. A chain was attached to the rings. There was one chain to two rings. Thus two prisoners were chained to one another, and so on. Fifty helpless couples, after the fashion of slaves. . . . Two men ringed together can not do much, or escape. And a gang of a hundred men so ringed can be herded, if necessary, until they fall in a strangling mass.

A smith did the work, but two huge, bestial Nubians bossed the job. Then into the dark of Jidda the prisoners were marched, their necks strained, the chains jangling.

One poor wretch called brokenly, "God help us, my brothers! They take us into slavery—toward the Ruba el Khali!"

One of the Nubians jumped forward and brought his heavy whip down on the poor fellow. The man fell. The Nubian beat him frightfully. Then he kicked him until he managed to struggle to his feet and continue the march. His companion had of course fallen with him, and was almost choked by his ring.

"Let that teach you!" yelled the Nubian. "No talking. Hurry, now!"

The Nubian was slightly nervous. Of course the *cadi* was responsible, but he knew the *cadi*. If trouble resulted from this last, semi-legal act of the *cadi's*, then would the *cadi* thrust all the blame on the Nubians. . . . And the Nubians were themselves criminals of the lowest type, whose word, they believed, would never prevail against the *cadi's*. He "had it on them," so to speak. They did not know that the *cadi* was himself an outlaw after midnight.

Bugs helped the half-dead Russian. He had shuddered at the shouted words of the poor prisoner. For the country of the desert, Ruba el Khali, is beyond the ken—more so than uttermost Siberia. No European has ever explored that country. . . . Slavery for what time life lingered —of the worst and most hopeless sort. . . . But, even as he shuddered, Bugs made up his mind to "get" that Nubian when opportunity offered.

THE pitiful march continued through the night, by unfrequented ways. Many of the prisoners had been hurt by the smith when he put the rings around their necks, or by the stocks of the whips in the brutal hands of the Nu-

bians—"to keep them quiet." . . . Bugs had not been hurt. His tough reputation had helped him with the cowardly blacks. The suffering Russian had been chained to him. During this business in the jail yard Bugs might have got away. That terrible trigger finger of his. Got away— by force. But to have done so would have meant abandoning the Russian. This would have wrecked his plan—the plan it was his duty to put through, black as the prospect looked. And with this had been another reason, a strange one. The weary Russian could not have escaped with him—he was all in. Bugs felt that he could not leave him. He had become fond of him. Admiration of his gameness and his cleverness had grown into respect, then fondness. . . . Bugs would do all he could to copy the papers, to beat the Russian in the great game—but even had this been accomplished he felt that he could not have left him to the brutalities of the slavers. . . . And the faith that had carried him so well through the years was still strong—another chance would come.

They were marched until dawn, southward along the coast. The lordly Nubians rode in an ancient auto truck, which carried also the scant amount of dates for the prisoners' food. Water, or what answered to that gracious word, would be obtained if found along the route.

During the day the Nubians took turns to keep awake under the awnings of the truck. They had old-fashioned rifles. The prisoners crawled wearily about a sand-hill, seeking what shelter from the pitiless sun it afforded. Bugs slept but little. He had found a small piece of flint, and was already busy filing at one of the links of the chain binding him to the Russian. It would be a long job, but to attempt escape without separating himself from the Russian would be suicide.

As he worked he thought carefully over the matter of this speechless companionship. He could speak to the Russian in French, and the astonishment of the Russian would break his disguise. Then they could call it a truce and the Russian would become a help instead of a hindrance. Simple enough, and Bugs longed to do it. But the plan intervened. If Bugs revealed himself as Sinnat he could never copy the papers without the Russian's knowledge. Another drug would be too suspicious. The plan would be wrecked. The loneliness and the dragging acting of the deaf mute were terrible—but the plan had to go through.

Every day saw them farther south. Somewhat north of the Protectorate of Aden they would turn inland. No white man had ever been inland more than a hundred miles. . . . The protectorate is British. If Bugs, still Ben Mohamet, could get the Russian into Aden—then would the plan be a success. They could continue to Bombay, and the Russian would never know Bugs as anything but an Afghan. . . . To get away, after filing the chain, in the auto truck of the Nubians. . . . To Aden.

But half-way down the coast, after ten of the prisoners had either died or killed themselves, a complication arose. The *cadi* arrived in a very good car, driven by another Nubian. Evidently he had arranged for the sale of his slaves, and was going to make delivery himself. He raged furiously when he heard of the deaths. . . .

South, march by march. The heat, the filth, the thirst, the starvation. . . . And Bugs, like Bayard or Sidney, giving the Russian part of his own scant food. And the Russian suppressing his showing of gratitude. A strange drama of a conflict of human wills. Two men who would

willingly have died for one another, who had grown to love one another like brothers—divided by duty and the rigors of the service they so luminously served.

They arrived, after many weeks of indescribable hell, at the last march along the coast line. Bugs had worn the connecting chain so thin that he could easily snap the link, weak as his once powerful hands had grown from the unspeakable diet. Next day they would turn inland, and his chance would be gone. They were closer to British territory than they would be again.

At that his was a desperate chance. To get the Russian into the truck, and drive it across the line—even farther, since the *cadi* would never stop pursuit at an imaginary boundary. To get the *cadi's* better car was impossible—it was parked by the *cadi's* tent too far away from the prisoners. All Bugs could expect was the chance of a sudden rush to the truck, in which one of the Nubians slept. The neck chains would make action difficult, even when the connecting chain was severed. And, what was worse, Bugs had to chose the hour before the dawn for his escape. That desert road was no place for night driving at speed; for, naturally, there were no lights on the truck.

To do all this as Ben Mohamet, never to let the gallant Russian know he was anything but that Afghan.

The night seemed to pass very slowly. Bugs lay down by the Russian—indeed strange bedfellows—the Russian who had so long acted the half-witted deaf mute that Bugs often thought he was no longer acting—that the strain had made the part real, and no wonder. . . . The poor prisoners moaned in their fitful sleep. He would have to be careful not to waken any of these. They would yell for him to take them with him. He would have liked to, but could not. He had a better plan for them. . . . It is very easy to persuade a British colonel to step across the border for a few miles—to stop slavery. And there was an English garrison in Aden.

The hours passed. Now and then a distant jackal barked. The heat was sweltering, for the heat of that locality is well-nigh unbearable by Europeans. The low-hung stars passed slowly overhead.

At last Bugs twisted the worn link. He was separated from the Russian. He shook the Russian gently. The Russian started into a sitting position, but he made no sound. He was still the deaf mute.

Bugs got to his feet, lifting the Russian with him. The Russian understood. With a stealth equal to Bugs' own he followed Bugs to the truck. No man heard or saw them go. Bugs had put the end of the chain into the Russian's hand. It did not jangle. . . .

They crept to the truck in which the solitary Nubian snored. Bugs was ahead. He had his revolver out, but not to shoot. With all the force at his command he brought the butt down on the head of the brutal Nubian. He meant to kill the creature, and he did. There was some slight noise of crunching, but that was all, save a slight dying gasp.

Bugs swiftly thrust the gun back under his left arm. He did not want the Russian to see that gun. Afghans do not carry revolvers under their arms.

Bugs put his hand under the Russian's arm and helped him. The helping was unnecessary, but not even at that moment of trial was Bugs taking the chance of wrecking his plan by becoming anything but Ben Mohamet, who had taken money to see the cousin of Abu Ali safely to Bombay.

Bugs followed. He started the car, but he could not do that without a noise. In that heat the engine was almost hot, but that old truck made a fearful racket in the quiet desert night. The prisoners awoke, some yelled. Bugs gave her the gas, and started along the coast toward Aden.

The darkness was lightening to the dawn, and he could see fairly well. The roaring of the truck drowned all other sound, but Bugs did not need to look back to find out what was going on behind him. The pale light showed surprize in the eyes of the Russian—but why should an Afghan not know how to drive a truck?

THE road was very bad, and Bugs drove carefully, knowing that the pursuing *cadi* would do the same; but as the dawn came strong Bugs gave the old truck all she had. As he did so a rifle bullet whizzed past his head. . . . It was about twenty miles to British territory. The *cadi* would catch the truck within a very few miles. Bugs had counted on that. Even if he had had the speed of the other car he would not have used it. He wanted the other car to come close enough for his gun. The *cadi* and the other rotten Nubian were going to die, and Bugs was going to kill them. They defiled the decent earth on which they continued to exist. He was no longer the calm and collected Sinnat, but a man with a lust for fight, a desire to kill. If he was caught he would be beaten until nearly dead, then beaten again.

So, with the first rifle bullet, Bugs got out his revolver. . . . Neither the *cadi* nor the Nubian could shoot straight. . . . The old truck swerved and jumped. Suddenly Bugs stopped the truck. As he did so one of the *cadi's* bullets made a lucky hit.

The Russian fell forward, shot through the head.

And then Bugs forgot everything but the lust to kill. The gallant Russian was dead. Bugs' great plan was dead with him. But it was not the plan that roused Bugs. It was grief. He had come to love his strange bedfellow.

The *cadi's* car came alongside the truck, its brakes screaming. Bugs shot the Nubian dead. The body toppled on to the road. The terrified *cadi* fired his rifle, but he was too scared in his cowardly soul to take aim.

"Drop it, and reach up with your hands!"

The *cadi* obeyed the terrible ferocity in Bugs' voice. Bugs turned on the chauffeur.

"You, too, get out of the car!"

The shivering *cadi* and driver stood on the side of the road, their trembling hands held skyward.

"This is an execution." Bugs was mad with rage and grief. "I could easily have shot you, without troubling to talk. But this will hurt you more! I wish I had rope to hang you. . . . I have never done such a thing before!"

He walked a few yards away. Then he fired at the *cadi's* head—missing him by deliberate inches. Intentionally. He fired again. The terrified *cadi* went through hell with every shot.

Suddenly it came to Bugs that he, a white man, was lowering himself to the *cadi's* level by this brutality—much as the *cadi* deserved such a death. He put his next bullet through the *cadi's* head. Then he spoke to the chauffeur.

"Got a gun on you?"

The chauffeur went down on his knees. He had no weapon at all.

"Go to that old truck," commanded Bugs. "In it you will find the dead body of a very gallant gentleman. Carry that body over here to this car. Be reverent. You are greatly honored in ways beyond your vile comprehension! . . . So, very gently now! Rest him on the cushions of the back seat. Compose him! Gently now, with reverence! So! Now, worm of hell, get back to your driver's seat, and drive ahead—to Aden. And be careful! If you hit a rock and disturb this dead gentleman I will put a bullet through the back of your head, and drive the car myself!"

The chauffeur obeyed. He drove as if on the edge of a precipice. . . .

Bugs looked at the dead Russian. He took the dead hand in his, and shook it respectfully.

"I shall never know your name, old man," he said gently. "But as I am quite sure that you are watching me from somewhere on the 'other side,' may I tell you that you were the best man I ever met! We are enemies—according to the laws of our countries. But we became brothers, you dear strange bedfellow—by the law of God. Good-bye, old man. We played a great game together. It ended in a draw, for the papers you so gallantly gave your life to deliver to your government are useless to me now. . . . So, the game is over. A draw. . . . Somehow I am glad—I would not have liked to have won from so gallant a man. . . . Good-night, old man. Good-night!"

Bugs wiped a hand across his eyes and looked ahead. Over to the right, in the morning refraction of the steaming Red Sea, was Perim Island. And, bearing to the left, was Aden and the flag in the morning breeze.

Another gripping Bugs Sinnat story will be published in our next issue.

The Tiger's Eye

By PEARL NORTON SWET

'A strange curse followed the killing of a tiger with a blue eye—a weird story of Bengal and a disastrous tiger-hunt

THE first time that Wynne Carson saw Marie Pilotte, the singer, on the terraces at Monte Carlo, pink and white under a lacy hat, he mentally called her a professional beauty, and dismissed the thought of her frivolous daintiness.

The second time that Carson saw the singer was at the Lido, a year later. At that time she was more beautiful than ever, and Carson's eyes strayed to her more than once, as she sat on the sun-drenched sands in her green and gold bathing-suit, her black hair spread over her shoulders, rippling and uncut. By chance he was introduced to her; began to find her company very pleasant; learned that she was English, not French, as he had supposed. She said the season being over, she was going out to India, where her brother was stationed at a place called Judhpore.

Then, being a pawn on the great chess-board of the press, the master-finger pushed Carson into Delhi, the very next year, and so he saw Marie Pilotte again.

It happened this way. Carson was at a table in the shady courtyard of the Hotel Metropole, sipping cold drinks and watching the kaleidoscopic effect of the passing crowds, when he saw a native slowly approaching, wheeling an invalid's chair. And pacing, with the erect, easy carriage of the king's men in India, a man in the uniform of an English officer strolled beside the chair.

As they came opposite Carson, the officer's face lighted with recognition. He stopped and motioned the native to bring the chair up to Carson's table.

Carson arose and held out his hand. Captain Rawlins was known to journalists from Siam to Finland. Many a story of Rawlins' travels and explorations had secured for the men fortunate enough to get them, that particularly genial expression of editorial pleasure for which the correspondent is ever striving. So Carson was brought out of his lazy contemplation of the crowds, into an attitude of animated greeting.

The captain turned to the occupant of the wheel-chair: "My sister, Carson." And to the invalid: "Marie, this is Wynne Carson—*the* Wynne Carson, you know, of the *News-Eagle,* New York City. He can make celebrities go through their paces for the public."

Carson saw a woman apparently years older than the captain—shriveled, wrinkled, her graying hair drawn smoothly over her ears. When she looked up in greeting, Carson saw that her eyes were wondrously, beautifully blue and youthful, yet filled with a strange, hunted expression. Carson experienced a shock of surprize. The woman was Marie Pilotte! And yet he had seen her but a year before, radiantly beautiful and young and in glowing, perfect health.

She extended a claw-like hand, the hand of an old woman, and spoke in the soft contralto voice that Carson knew as that of Marie Pilotte, the sweet singer.

"Oh, but we've met before, haven't we, Mr. Carson? The Lido?"

"He spoke hysterically, pointing to the dead tiger."

Carson's power of speech seemed to have left him. He bowed over the wrinkled hand; smiled. And she went on, "I never used to forget the press men—the big ones like you, I mean. It meant a write-up, and if it was favorable——" She laughed a low, rippling laugh, youthful and sweet. A man, in passing, looked at her shriveled old face in surprize.

"Come around and see us, won't you?" the captain invited. "We've a bungalow. Been stationed here only a short time. I came down from that hole in the ground they call Judhpore." He laid a visiting-card on the table and penciled an address on it. Then the chair was wheeled away.

Carson sat for some moments in deep thought, after they left his table. Marie Pilotte an old woman—and she not yet twenty-five, if reports were true! And she had spoken of her career in the past tense; had said, "I never used to forget the press men." What could it mean?

ABOUT a week later Carson went to dine at the captain's bungalow, set in a swirl of trees and shrubs on a road out of Delhi, a road called by the natives "the Road of Siva's Bull."

Marie Pilotte, gowned in white, had the appearance of a woman past sixty. It seemed to Carson that Captain Rawlins was watching his sister furtively during the courses. The native servants came and went almost noiselessly. Instinctively Carson awaited something—he did not know just what. His sixth sense—the queer sense that belongs to the Fourth Estate—was awakened to some new adventure.

It was a sultry, Indian night. The room where the three sat seemed charged with some powerful element that might at any moment strike them in a terrible, unknown way.

The captain's sister laughed and talked, to be sure, yet to Carson there was an undercurrent of nervous dread in her beautiful, youthful eyes that illumined her colorless, old woman's face. From time to time she glanced across the room toward an open window, and it was then that Carson fancied she paused, faltering on a word, seeming to be waiting. Her eyes were widely open, her lips thin and with the parched look of fever.

The servant had just put coffee before them and left the room, when Marie Pilotte suddenly sat erect in her wheelchair. Only a moment before she had forced a jest about the wheel-chair at a dinner party. The words had hardly left her lips when her thin, dead-looking hands gripped the arms of the chair and her wide eyes widened still more, filled with utmost terror.

Rawlins sprang to her side, his face tense with pity. He held her rigid body against his steady arm, patted her shoulder, as one would reassure a terrified child. He seemed entirely oblivious of their guest. Carson sat quietly, helpless, ignorant of what it meant.

In a few moments the thin figure relaxed, drooped, fell limply back against the cushions of the chair. Her eyes were closed. Her bony hands lay inert in her lap. Exhaustion and the mark of swift age was upon Marie Pilotte, who had been but a year before the loveliest woman at the Lido.

The captain rang. A native woman came in and wheeled her mistress away, the rubber wheels making no sound over the polished floor. The captain went to the door with them, kissed his sister tenderly, whispered a few words to her, and came back to his chair.

He poured wine. Carson noted that his hands were trembling and that there were great beads of perspiration on his forehead. He drank his wine in one gulp. Leaning his arms on the table, he faced Carson seriously.

"You are wondering what it is all about, Carson? Well—I wish I knew what it is about. I don't know what it means. She is not ill."

Carson put down his glass. "You don't know—you say your sister is not ill?"

The captain shook his head. "No. It was not illness you just saw. It was a terrible, devilish fear that comes to her."

"Fear? Fear of what?"

"She can't tell . . . doesn't seem to know. That's the worst of it. It's killing her. There's a long story to it. . . . I think I'd be relieved to tell someone—someone who isn't a medic. All the doctors seem to think we're crazy when we tell them. It wouldn't bore you?"

Carson, remembering the lovely face of Marie Pilotte and the hours they had idled away together on the sands at the Lido, replied emphatically.

"Bore me? Why—why, man alive, why should it? I—I can't help remembering——"

"All right. Let's get out of this beastly hot room. It's a bit better on the veranda."

They went out through the swinging doors to comfortable chairs in the dusk. A low, golden half-moon shone through the trees.

"Mother India, eh?" Carson stretched out a wide arm to the darkness about the house.

The captain grunted. "Damn queer mother she is to the white ones in her care. Blisters us with sun. Chokes us with dust. Drowns us in the monsoon floods. Crazes us with her magic and her superstition. Huh! I don't talk like an Englishman and an army man, at that, do I? Well——"

THEY lit cigarettes and the captain began talking in a low, even voice. Carson listened, with occasional glances toward a smear of pale light across the lawns.

"My sister, after her last season, came out to Judhpore where I was stationed. Awfully rum place, but she wanted to 'see India.' Then, shortly after she came, I got a long leave and we went to the hill country for a vacation with friends. We were there perhaps a month, or more, and were on our way to see the sights at the capital when we met a hunting-party at the hotel. They were agreeable English people—I'd met some of them before—and they urged us to join them.

"The tiger season was on. Every coolie was talking about the unusual number of tigers that year. Of course, you know a native wouldn't kill a Bengal tiger. He'd let said tiger chew him up first. That's just what the tiger does, eventually. Well, my sister thought a tiger hunt would be thrilling and I was a bit enthusiastic myself, so we made our preparations and joined the party.

"In the jungle country we saw a new India. One can never forget that jungle country, once he's seen it—and smelled it.

"We were in luck. I should say, the tigers were unlucky. The fourth day Marie begged to be allowed a gun. I never dreamed she'd have the courage to use it, much less even kill a cat.

"But toward evening that very day we heard a great cat pad-padding through the twigs and leaves that led to the stream near the ambush. The wind was right, so that the beast suspected nothing, but bent his big, tawny head to drink. There was a flash, a report, a waft of smoke, and the tiger reared and fell beside the water. My sister proudly held up her gun. She had shot a tiger.

"Natives helped us examine the huge beast. He was shot cleanly through the heart. There was scarcely a spatter of blood on his black and orange hide. Suddenly one of the natives cried out in di-

alect to the other, who sprang away from the tiger. Then he spoke hysterically to me, pointing at the dead tiger.

" 'The lady-sahib has killed a tiger of the blue eye. It carries the soul of Ramayana. A thrice sacred tiger and with the curse on the one who kills it. Ai-ai-yah!'

"Then he began to weave to and fro, intoning the weird singsong of the ancient curse of Ramayana. It went like this: 'She will die slowly. Her body will be shriveled up like the grass in the time of the great drought. The Great Terror will steal upon her unawares, and she will have the Great Fear in her heart till her life is sucked away. Ai-ai-yah! It has been written.'

"We gathered around the fellow, all talking at once. He understood English, but we could not shake his reiteration of the curse that followed the killing of a tiger of the blue eye. We examined the beast again and again, of course. Its right eye was of a clear and beautiful blue, more like a human eye than the eye of a jungle beast."

The captain paused a moment, and the silence of the Indian night surged about the little bungalow. Carson looked out at the light far across the lawns.

"I've got to pinch myself to realize that you're sitting right there telling me things like that. Why, a fellow might dream a thing like that, but it hardly seems——"

"There are a lot of things in India that don't seem true, but *are* true," interrupted the other. "Shall I go on?"

At Carson's assent his even voice took up the amazing story again.

"You know, we English are slow to believe such things. Marie, of all the party, showed the only signs of agitation. But we were so insistent that the whole thing was native superstition and the blue eye of the tiger a biological freak, that she was, I believe, more than half convinced and ashamed of her fears.

"It was only when the native guides were near her that she became unquiet. The brown fellows acted in a strange way whenever they came near her. They made, if possible, wide detours to keep out of her way. I caught them eyeing her with furtive, fearful glances.

"My personal servant, sitting outside my tent one morning, cleaning my gun, sprang aside suddenly as my sister passed by him to enter the tent.

"What is the matter, Durah?" she asked. For answer he pointed to the strip of sun-lit ground before the tent where he had been sitting. His voice fairly hissed at her. 'Your shadow, lady-sahib, it is cursed—and it fell upon me as I sat by the doorway . . . the Great Fear will stalk me. Ai-ai-yah!'

"He buried his head on his knees, giving his cry of fear and despair. I heard him, and coming out, saw my sister standing rigidly erect, staring straight before her. She looked as a sleepwalker does, her eyes glazed and wide. The servant was watching her with fearful fascination. As I stepped toward him he slipped away into the shade of the big trees.

"To my questions Marie gave no answer. Her face was ashen and drawn. In a moment she relaxed, and looking very tired, she went to her tent.

"After she had rested a while she told me that there was nothing that she could explain, except that a horrible fear had gripped her suddenly, a fear of she knew not what, but a terror so intense as to paralyze her for the time, seeming to suck away her very life. She only sensed a foul breath of air that approached her and enveloped her and laid its clamminess over her.

"I tried to comfort her, and finally, somewhat reassured, she fell asleep, while her native woman, trained in the missionary school at Delhi and seemingly free from the native fears, fanned her and crooned to her.

"AT LUNCHEON she was very quiet. At about three o'clock, in the heat of the day's powerful sun, instead of resting, like the others, my sister paced her tent. Finally she came to my tent and held out her hand without a word, without any seeming emotion. The hand was quite brown and wrinkled, the soft finger-tips turned calloused and claw-like, the wrist bony.

" 'You see,' she said, with a fatalistic calm. 'The natives are right. The man Durah says the souls in the care of the sacred tigers must always be replaced by the souls of their slayers. He must be right. This shriveled hand is but the beginning. If I were in England it would be different, perhaps. But this is India, and all things are possible here.'

"In vain I tried to remonstrate with her, as did the rest of the party. We insisted that the maimed hand was the result of some poisonous insect bite or the touch of a poison plant. She only shook her head and smiled.

"Near noon of the next day, I observed Durah, my servant, squatting in the shade, inspecting his features in a small hand-mirror. The man's absorbed attitude was a strained one. His dark, young face was anxious as he scanned his reflection.

"I went to him. At my approach he sprang to his feet. It seemed to me, at a glance, that his lean cheeks appeared sunken, the flesh hanging loosely about his mouth. He crept near me like a fawning animal.

" 'Sahib,' he whispered. 'It has come, has it not? I, too, am marked.'

" 'What's that you say?' I asked, not understanding.

" 'The curse, sahib. It is on me, also,' he mouthed, his lips twisting grotesquely. 'Her shadow fell across me as I sat by the doorway—the lady-sahib's shadow.'

"I tried to laugh, in spite of the creepiness that came over me at his words. 'Nonsense, Durah,' I told him. 'You know that's nothing to do with us English people.'

"He clutched at his scrawny throat with long, brown fingers and fairly hissed at me.

" 'You laugh, sahib. But I tell you it will take only time to tell which of us will outlive the other.'

" 'What do you mean?' I asked, for a second wondering if the fellow was hinting at murder.

"A corner of his mouth twitched. He bowed low and answered respectfully, seriously, so that I was impressed by his words.

" 'It is only that I was the first on whom her shadow fell and so there must be a struggle, soul against soul—a race against death, sahib. If I am overtaken first by the Great Fear, your lady lives and will be young again—and beautiful. If she is taken, then I am free, and the curse is removed. It is very simple. It has been so written and it will so happen.'

"His face was the impassive, mystic face of all India, as he bowed and began to slither away toward the natives' quarters.

" 'Wait!' I cried, but he moved swiftly away and was lost among the thick shrubbery.

"I stood quite still, I remember, and went over his words, one by one. Then I went to my sister and told her. I found her as she was usually to be found the past three days, lying on her cot, with the native woman at the side fanning and crooning.

"When she heard Durah's story she raised herself with some animation. 'If that is true,' she said, 'I have a chance, then. Is that true, Ashan?'

"The woman, Ashan, nodded. 'It is true, lady-sahib. Even I who know about the English God, know that to be true. My mother has told me.'

"My sister looked at her wrinkled hand. 'Well,' she said, 'we will be going back soon. The hunters have had enough —six tigers and the blue-eyed Thing. I can't call it a tiger. If it's a race with death, I have a chance. I am as young as Durah almost. He is twenty, they say.'

"AND so, in time, we returned to Judhpore. Marie had to cancel her next season's contract, for every day there were signs of the terrible thing that had come to her—her lined, drawn, old face; her graying, lusterless hair; the tottering step of advanced age. It was terrible.

"We had every medical aid. They were skeptical. They were of no help to us. Carson, she *is* under a curse. It has been more than six months since the tiger hunt. Her time is drawing near. I feel it. But what can I do—in India?"

"Well," said Carson, "people say there is no such thing as curse, as the powers of the evil eye, of things like this—but how can we tell?" He added, suddenly, "What of Durah?"

"That's the other side of this horrible thing. Durah stayed on with me as my servant, though it was not many weeks before he was unable to do much work. It is as he said it would be, he is failing, failing rapidly. My sister has never seen him since the tiger hunt. I could not allow it. As it is, the thought of their terrible race is with them always."

"I'd like to see this Durah," said Carson. "Do you suppose——"

"That's his little place down there through the trees. You see the light? It seems strange that in six months Durah has changed from a strong, young man to a dim-eyed, trembling wreck. I—I—sometimes I've thought that Durah has gone the farther on the road to death. Durah's eyes did not escape, as did my sister's. Perhaps—I wonder if it would be silly to think that because *her* eyes were blue—like the tiger's——"

He broke off abruptly, rose, and said, bruskly, "Come. You shall see Durah, too."

They walked leisurely across the lawns to Durah's little pagoda-like house which the captain had provided for him. The captain opened the screened door and they entered a dim room, lit faintly by two sputtering candles.

A word in native dialect was spat at them from a corner. The captain answered, "It is I, Durah," and struck a match, lighting a kerosene lamp which swung from the ceiling.

The yellow, wavering light showed a man lying on a high bed with netting hung about it on a wire frame. The old, wrinkled face, the squinting eyes, the toothless, half-open mouth gave Carson a feeling of pity and of revulsion.

"Water, sahib, please," asked Durah, and held out a claw-like hand.

He drank thirstily and then sat up in bed, hunched, shaking as with an ague.

He wore a loose, white garment that fell away from his wasted limbs, so that he looked like a dark skeleton in grave clothes. He pushed back the bed-curtains and touched the captain on the sleeve with a plucking movement.

"Sahib," he whispered, hoarsely, "did you hear it as you came in?"

"Hear what, Durah?"

"The pad-pad-pad, sahib . . . the tiger of the blue eye—it is coming for me, sahib."

"You're nervous, Durah. You ought to go to sleep. In the morning, perhaps, you'll be better."

Durah shook his head. "No, sahib. I shall not be better in the morning. You don't understand. It is coming for me. I—think—I lose—the race, sahib."

He touched his brown breast with his trembling, claw like-hand. "Its paw . . . its very soft paw . . . here on my breast, sahib." Then, eagerly: "Perhaps *she* has heard it, too . . . the lady-sahib, yes?" His breath came panting; his eyes peered into the captain's face.

"No, I think not, Durah. She has not heard—yet."

Durah made a pitiful cry in the dialect. "Ai-ai-yah! Then it is I! Ai-ai-yah!"

He buried his head in his thin arms and rocked back and forth, then suddenly raised his head in a listening attitude.

"Hear, sahib?" he breathed.

The captain said nothing, looking at the poor fellow in pity.

There was a shriek in the still night. Durah pitched backward on the bed, clutching at the curtains and pulling them down with him.

The two men sprang to his side, but Durah was already dead, his wasted face twisted in an agony of fear, his bony hands spread out grotesquely on his breast.

At that moment Carson could have sworn that something passed him, something resembling a current of fetid air. It passed, and he felt his face clammy with the starting sweat of vague, paralyzing fear. Only a second it touched him and was gone.

In the silence that followed the death of Durah, they left the little house. Several natives, hearing the shriek, had come running to the door. In a few quiet words the captain told them that Durah was dead. They heard him in frightened dumbness. Only one wailed and he was hushed by the others.

Carson and the captain went back to the bungalow. Carson could scarcely keep step with the other man's stride.

"If she gets well, Carson—if she gets well, we can no longer ignore the power of mystic India. But it is no place for an English woman. I've always said that."

Carson had his own thoughts, so he merely nodded, scarcely hearing what Rawlins had said. He sat rigidly erect in a bamboo chair on the veranda, while the captain went up to his sister, taking the stairs three at a leap.

He was down in a few moments, his eyes shining in the lamplight, as he stood at the screen-door.

"Carson—she is sleeping—like a child. And there is color creeping into her lips and cheeks again. Go away, now, Carson, like a good fellow. I'm not being rude, but I've got to be alone a while—to think this out."

Carson was the sort that would understand that. He rose, held out his hand. "Don't try to explain, Captain Rawlins; I think I get you. And—if you feel fit tomorrow, come over to the Metropole for lunch."

"Yes, thanks—about one, then, tomorrow," answered the other, and sat down in a big chair, almost forgetting Carson.

Carson went toward his hotel in the silence of the Indian night, and there was in him an exultant thankfulness that Marie Pilotte in her health and beauty would live to be young again. Yes, he would see her again. She wouldn't pass out of his life this time.

But arrived at the hotel, he found a cablegram, and so, with his regrets for the captain left at the desk, Carson was well on his way to Calcutta by noon the next day.

After Calcutta, it was London, but through the months Carson did not forget Marie Pilotte.

IN A London season, less than two years after the death of Durah, two men trained glasses on a box at a certain theater.

"Who is the beauty who just came into the left box over there?" asked one.

His companion answered, "The woman in silver? Oh, don't you know? She's Marie Pilotte, the singer. But I have heard that she is recently married—to an American newspaper correspondent."

A Hair perhaps divides the False and True
Yes; and a single Alif were the clue—
    Could you but find it—to the Treasure-house,
And peradventure to THE MASTER too;

Whose secret Presence, through Creation's veins
Running Quicksilver-like eludes your pains;
    Taking all shapes from Máh to Máhi; and
They change and perish all—but He remains;

A moment guess'd—then back behind the Fold
Immerst of Darkness round the Drama roll'd
    Which, for the Pastime of Eternity,
He doth Himself contrive, enact, behold.
                    —Rubáiyát of Omar Khayyam.

Eyes of the Dead

By LIEUTENANT EDGAR GARDINER

Mahbub, the Afghan hillman, went far to avenge the death of his kinsman, Yar Khan

"SALAAM, Sikar Bahadur!"

Officer Trowbridge turned swiftly at the sound of the familiar voice. Through shrewd gray eyes he took in the form of the gaunt, emaciated hillman who stood in the doorway. The voice was as familiar as this apparition was strange.

"Now is my heart sad, Trowbridge sahib, oh my friend! For we two have spoken together with naked hearts and our hands have dipped into the same dish and thou hast been to me as a brother! Yet now thou knowest me not! Ahi! Ahi!"

The Englishman started from his seat: "Mahbub, by God!"

"By Allah, the Dispenser of Justice— by Allah-al-Mumit; it is I." The tall hillman seated himself wearily upon the cloth he spread upon the floor.

Trowbridge looked upon him with pained eyes. Was this the smart, trim native officer to whom he had given permission to leave the Thana [police station] on private business six weeks before? He looked into the burning, sunken eyes, glowing restlessly—had the man slept at all since he left? He eyed the soiled, travel-stained garments— never had he seen Mahbub in clothing so filthy or so disordered! Was this indeed the officer who had been the pride of the Thana; was this his trusted right hand who would follow a criminal even to the gates of Jehanum?

"I am returned, as was my promise to the Presence."

Trowbridge nodded slowly.

"And now, I pray you, give me permission to depart from the Presence. Great honor has the sahib shown me."

"You would now leave the service of the British Raj, Mahbub?" Trowbridge asked slowly, his eyes upon the lean figure before him. The Afghan shook his head.

"Nay, oh Trowbridge sahib. I am weary. The way was long, my brother. My clothes are fouled because of the dust upon the Great Road. My eyes are sad because of the glare of the sun. My feet are swollen because I have washed them in bitter water, and my cheeks are hollow because the food was bad."

Commissioner Trowbridge tapped a bell beside his elbow. To the fat Bengali servant who appeared he gave a few short swift orders. Presently that mountainous one reappeared bearing a tray whereon reposed two tall tinkling glasses, their sides beaded with moisture. He set the tray down upon the flat-topped desk and unobtrusively withdrew, casting one long sharp glance at the ragged, dirty figure sitting impassive upon the floor.

"He knew thee not, Mahbub, save as an Afridi. He is new here with me since thy going, oh my friend." Trowbridge picked up one of the glasses and stretched it out toward the Afghan, who shook his head in firm negation.

"Drink! It is but the chilled juice of mangoes." The hillman took it from him, sipping the cool contents slowly.

"And now, before I give thee permis-

"It was dark when he first saw those glowing eyes."

sion to depart, what of thy quest, Mahbub? As thou hast said, oh my friend, we twain have talked together with naked hearts; we have eaten salt and broken bread together."

"In the name of Allah returning thanks, thrice!" Mahbub intoned as he drained the last cooling sip from the glass in his hand. "My mouth is dry for straight talk. When the grief of the soul is too heavy for endurance it may be eased by speech. Moreover, the mind of a true man is as a well, the pebble of confession dropped therein sinks and is seen no more. In my chest burns a fire that is like the fires of the Pit itself."

A long space he paused while Trowbridge waited patiently.

"Yet before I tell thee of my quest, oh my brother, oh my friend, bid thy servants of the Thana lock safely away that one whom I brought with me."

Once more Trowbridge's keen eyes darted swiftly over the disreputable form before him.

"It shall be done at once, Mahbub," he said at last.

"Again I give thanks to the Presence," Mahbub said softly when the native constabulary had roughly taken the filthy bundle of rags that sat stupidly on the broad veranda without the Thana and had locked him safely within a cell.

"He is one the Presence urgently desired—it is Kundoo who slew Yar Khan."

"What!" Trowbridge started from his chair in his excitement. After a pause, "So that was your quest, Mahbub, was it? I should have known."

The other nodded.

"There is a reward," Trowbridge began.

"Nay, oh my friend!" protested Mahbub. "The fire burn your money! What do I want with it? I am rich and I thought you were my friend, but behold! you are like all the rest—a sahib. Is a man sad? Give him silver, say the sahibs.

Is he dishonored? Give him money, say the sahibs. Hath he a wrong upon his head? Then give him filthy gold, say the sahibs. Such are the sahibs and such art thou—even thou! . . . Nay! I beg thee to forget my foolish words. Forgive me, oh my brother! I knew not what I said. I shall pour dust upon my head, yet I am an Afridi! Because of my sorrow I revile thee, oh my friend—even as a Pathan!"

TROWBRIDGE sat immovable. Across his face shone no flicker of emotion now; it was the calm visage of a Buddha —or a poker player. After a pause the Afghan went on:

"To Delhi my quest first led me, Protector of the Helpless. From that stinking city I sped swiftly to the west to Bahadurgath and Rania, led only by a Voice. Smile not, oh my friend. That Voice was a djinn calling to me from out the hot parched earth. There are no devils, oh Trowbridge sahib? Smile not, for I have seen them pass before my face. I have heard them calling to each other in the parched Rechna as a stallion calls to his mares.

"Yet always before me fled him whom I sought. I came unto Fazilha and passed through swiftly, sleeping not, eating not, while the fire within my breast flared like the flames of the Pit itself. A dancing girl of the bazars told me he whom I sought had gone to Okara with a caravan of horse-traders. Like a leopard on a hot scent I followed, even to the rail that runs to Montgomery, and there the Voice bade me turn upon the road from Jhang, Samundri and Gugera until I came to Sahiwal.

"The one I pursued stood before a sweetmeat stall but the crowd moved thickly to and fro. When I pushed my way to the place where I had seen him he was gone. Did he see me or no I knew not; perhaps a djinn whispered in his ear. Once more I hurried on, past the sandy wastes of the Rechna where devils called and rioted in the evening winds. Though I went swiftly, yet the one before me was winged by the terror of Death that rode upon his crupper.

"The Jehalum was in flood. I forced my mare into the ford, for I would not wait. But the river god was angry. My mare was washed away and so would I have been also save for that pearl among elephants, Ram Pershad, and his mahout, who drove the great beast into the tawny flood below the ford and so rescued me. But he whom I followed was safe upon the further shore, having crossed twelve hours before I came.

"Thrice the sun rose before I could go on. Ahi! Alghies! Ahi! In the light of the third morning I was paddled across that muddy stream, for the ford was yet too deep to travel. I must retrace my steps a long weary way from where the river god's resistless might had driven me.

"The Voice led me to the Salt Hills and on to Shapur, and there again I heard tidings of him I sought. He had sold horses to a sahib near Pindigeb. Though I was far from the Great Road that leads past the cantonments and the iron road that runs to the south which, as the Presence knows, is the winter path of the dealers, I journeyed fast to Sialkit.

"I thanked Allah that we twain would soon be among the mighty hills and the little matter between us would be settled according to our own hill custom. But a Jullalee [Evil Spirit] must have whispered to him. At Sialkit he had doubled back upon his own track toward the south where men are rats and trulls the women. A fit place for such as he! And the flame within me burned the hotter now for I must remember my oath and bow before the Law. Ahi! Ahi!

"Long was the way of my quest but at

the end thereof I found him that I had followed so long and so tirelessly. I have brought him before the Presence as I had given my word to do. And now the Presence would offer me money, even as any sahib! I am the sahib's friend. I have drunk water in the shadow of his house and he has blackened my face! What more is there to do? Will the sahib give me an anna to complete the insult?

"I crave permission to depart, oh Trowbridge sahib. Upon my valley lies the bloom of the peach orchards like henna on a maiden's flesh, the pleasant winds sweep through the mulberry trees, the streams riot with the white snow waters and I may be among men once more.

"I can go in peace. The fire within me will die slowly to cold ashes, for, Trowbridge sahib, my friend and my brother, thou shalt promise me that Kundoo shall pay to the British Raj for the crime he committed."

Long minutes Trowbridge sat motionless.

"Mahbub, oh my friend, I give you my word that I shall do all that I can. But what proof have I that Kundoo did indeed commit that murder? The ways of the white sahibs are not as the ways of the Afridi. Had I his own talk with which to confront him and confound the lies he will assuredly tell before the court —Mahbub, my friend and my brother! I talk to thee once more with naked heart as an own blood-brother. No other among those at this Thana could have done the deed that thou hast done. I shall not again offer thee money after the way of the Anglesi, but the finest mare or the fleetest stallion in all the bazars is thine and a Bokharan belt of finest workmanship. Nay! It is a gift of friendship I would offer thee!

"Yet, Mahbub, is my heart heavy.

How may I confront Kundoo with his misdeed? How may I out of his own mouth make him confess to that which we both know? Canst thou show me a way?"

It was Mahbub's turn to pause, to consider, his chin bowed upon his breast. Trowbridge, watching him, felt a thrill of compassion for this Afghan who times innumerable had stood manfully at his side regardless of all odds. Between them lay, the ceremony of blood brotherhood.

Mentally he reviewed again that tireless, merciless chase. Like a mongoose after a cobra, Mahbub had trailed his quarry; against stupendous obstacles he had carried on, until he had brought the culprit in to the Thana. A six weeks' chase. And as if that were not enough, now he was asking the impossible of Mahbub once more. How could Mahbub, or any one else, force from the prisoner's lips the confession of guilt? The Afghan raised his head.

"Trowbridge sahib, it is an order?" he asked.

"Not so, Mahbub. I ask in the name of friendship. You have done well. I could not have asked of any man what you have done unbidden." Trowbridge's voice betrayed his sincerity.

"Then is my heart made fat and my eye glad," Mahbub exclaimed. "An order is an order until one is strong enough to disobey. But the desire of a true friend —Holy Kurstad and the Blessed Imans! I will do what I can. First, I ask of the Protector that he awaken Kundoo." He smiled fleetingly. "That degraded Mussulman sleeps soundly yet. There was no other way to bring him before you. I but gave him bhang."

"It shall be done at once," Trowbridge responded. "And then?"

"Let none others come near his cell save myself, Bahadur—or Sunua Manji."

Mahbub rose swiftly, all traces of his weariness apparently forgotten, and left the Khana.

Trowbridge looked somberly after his departing form as he telephoned for the doctor. He had wondered not a little how Mahbub had managed to bring in his countryman a prisoner without blood-letting.

Yet he had himself seen that Kundoo was unharmed, though he was sluggish, seemingly with no mind of his own. His brows knit into a frown as he thought of that even greater task he had but now set for his underling. It would be a calamity indeed if, after such an epic chase, the wily Kundoo should go free for lack of positive evidence or through the efforts of lying paid witnesses.

He half wished that Kundoo had gone beyond the border in that grim, long-drawn-out pursuit. Had he done so, Mahbub would have returned alone and the Empire would have been saved the cost and trouble of a trial. That Mahbub would have dealt hill justice to Kundoo before he turned back Trowbridge was as sure as he was of Kundoo's guilt.

The little doctor bustled in, pompous as a bantam cock, and after a few desultory words with the Commissioner, passed from Trowbridge's sight. Trowbridge gave strict orders for all to keep away from Kundoo's cell; then, as an afterthought, he ordered them to admit Mahbub, whom they all knew, at any time he might choose to come. Those matters attended to, he hurried out and was immediately immersed in the multiplicity of routine that made of him the most overworked official, perhaps, in all that populous district.

K UNDOO awoke slowly from his drugged sleep as the shadows lengthened in the evening. He gazed stupidly about him at the clean bare room, the narrow bed on which he lay, the high window with its close-set grating. Hazily he remembered the caravanserai where he had talked with the stranger countryman. That one seemed overjoyed at meeting one from his own valley, he had retailed all the petty gossip of the high hills and, best of all, had insisted on paying the reckoning.

Though Kundoo had cared little for the other's news or his company, yet he was not one to refuse free entertainment. Kundoo's financial standing, always precarious, was just now even more so than usual. A little affair that had promised well in the beginning had in the doing turned out quite the reverse. Jewels and money—much money—he had thought to obtain through it. Instead, he got a beggarly handful of silver for his trouble and had, in addition, been forced to leave precipitately for other parts. Kundoo was beginning to think that perhaps his sudden flight had been ill-advised. He should have stayed and faced it out instead of running. Reluctantly he was beginning to feel that the pursuit he had so dreaded was only a figment of his own imagination after all.

The closer he neared the border the more sure he was that his entire course in the affair had been wrong, and he had turned back before he reached it. There were other unsettled matters beyond that border that counseled prudence, matters more serious than the one from which he fled. No, they were not greater, but justice over there was a personal matter and it was swift and sure. On sober second thought Kundoo had decided to retrace his steps.

If he had been followed, a fact that he now doubted quite as strongly as he had believed in it before, his devious doublings and turnings must assuredly have put such followers hopelessly at fault. And insistently the South called to him, where the gains for such as he were better than in the poorer northern provinces, while the hardy tribesmen who followed fast and far to avenge a personal wrong were almost unknown in the Southlands.

Kundoo had eaten sweetmeats innumerable since that other countryman paid for them, he had drunk heavily because it cost him nothing. Had that countryman paid also for this room, Kundoo wondered? He raised his voice, shouting loud and long. There was no answer. He staggered to his feet and essayed to open the iron-barred door. The door was locked!

Kundoo sat down suddenly. The riddle was clear to him now. That vaguely familiar face of the other Afridi, that insistent hospitality—everything was clear. He had been drugged!

This was no caravanserai lodging! The stout-locked grille that did duty as a door, the high narrow barred window, all were as clear to Kundoo as the long ugly nose upon his unprepossessing face. While he lay helpless in a drugged stupor that unknown had brought him to this unknown place that was surely a prison, a Thana. Kundoo was a prisoner! The long arm of the British Raj had reached out just when he had fancied himself safe; he was in the clutches of the Law!

For a brief interval blind panic seized him. He beat futilely against the stout door, he shouted himself hoarse, without avail. Yet by degrees his native cunning returned to him. The Law could prove nothing. On the other hand, with bribed witnesses, he could lay so convincing a web of lies that he would surely be freed from whatever charge might be laid against him. But to do that would take money, more money, he feared, than the little that was left from that unsavory

affair of six weeks since. He felt in his wide belt for his purse.

Once more fierce imprecations poured from his lips. He called aloud on the Prophet and all the Blessed Imans; he called upon the multiplicity of Hindoo Gods, cursing that unknown countryman, root and branch, to his last ultimate ancestors. Kundoo had been robbed as well as imprisoned!

The little room grew swiftly darker. Kundoo peered watchfully into the corridor through the narrow-gratinged opening. He was hungry. Every fiber of his drugged body called for water. His unholy rage over his predicament had left him spent. No one came; no one paid any attention to him. Outside the building he heard the noisy gabble of natives about their trivial evening affairs.

It was dark when he first saw those glowing eyes—Kundoo was sure they were eyes—staring unwaveringly at him. He retreated hurriedly to his bed and threw himself upon it. He closed his eyes tightly. When he could hold them so no longer he peered through the blackness of that narrow room, looking all about him save where he had glimpsed that apparition. At long last he looked beyond the grating to where they had first appeared.

Cold sweat started out upon his face. The eyes were still there, glowing with cold malevolence. He shrieked and covered his face with shaking hands. At his continued uproar a light appeared far down the corridor, footsteps approached rapidly. Kundoo looked into the face of Mahbub, trim in his spotless uniform. In a flood of words the shaken wretch poured out the tale of that fantastic, unbelievable thing.

Mahbub smiled his disbelief.

"Fool's talk," he sneered. He swung

the light about. "See? There is nothing here!"

Kundoo looked with wide eyes at the bare, freshly whitewashed wall.

"Gampati! [God preserve us]" Mahbub went on. "You must be drunk! A Mussulman! Chapper-band! [Robber] Boh! [Bandit] It must be the eyes of one whom you have killed and who was not avenged that you see. Be quiet now, or must I beat thee with a stick?" he added as he picked up the light and retreated down the corridor.

Partly reassured by that scrutiny under the glaring light, Kundoo lay on his bed and pondered over this absurd idea. Absurd! Was it? Could it have been the eyes of that one—— Involuntarily he glanced out past the grating. His body stiffened, his tongue clove to the roof of his mouth in his terror. The eyes were glaring at him once more.

THE long night dragged endlessly through its age-long length. Whenever he looked, Kundoo could see that cold unwinking glare fixed upon him. He fancied he could even make out the menacing form of his last victim in the velvety darkness. His terrorized shrieks brought him only beatings from the tall Mahbub; the light reappearing time and again showed the corridor bare of every living thing. In vain Kundoo begged that the light be left with him. To all his pleadings and entreaties Mahbub turned a deaf ear.

As the hot morning flamed, a cowering, shaking wretch begged piteously for Trowbridge sahib. Mahbub reviled him and spat contemptuously upon him:

"What can such a louse as you want of the gorra-log [white man]?" he demanded. "Trowbridge sahib sleeps. No djinns disturb his rest. The dead do not glare at him all the night because their deaths are unavenged. In this cell you must stay day after day until the wakils [lawyers] shall argue before the Raj."

At the prospect of endless nights with that nameless terror Kundoo grovelled upon the floor. Piteously he begged to be taken away—anywhere at all! He threw himself at Mahbub's feet. The dapper Afghan's face was hard as flint.

"You did not fear Yar Khan when he lived. Why do you fear him now when only his eyes seek you out in the darkness, calling ever for justice? So shall his eyes follow you ever while life exists in your miserable carcass. Thou crow! Jackal! Dung-beetle! Pathan!"

He stalked majestically toward the door.

The wretched Kundoo shrieked the louder.

"Only for one thing will I call the Kumar Bahadur [Son of a King]," Mahbub said as he opened the door. "If you wish to tell the sahib how and why you killed Yar Khan I shall ask him if he will see you and try to stop that uneasy dead one from troubling you until the Raj takes your worthless life."

Eagerly the wretched Kundoo begged that Trowbridge sahib be sent for.

The noonday sun stood high overhead.

Commissioner Trowbridge had given orders to have the shaking, nerveless wretch removed to another cell and closely guarded, had promised him a light burning ever during the long night hours. Kundoo's full confession, properly attested and signed, was in his hands; he tapped the folded sheets thoughtfully against his opened hand. He looked curiously about the bare little cell. Mahbub held the grating door open for him to leave.

"It is done, Trowbridge sahib, oh my brother," he said softly.

"It is done, indeed, Mahbub; though how it was done, I know not. Perhaps the Gods of Hind—perhaps the Holy

Imans——" He stopped. His eyes were fixed upon the corridor wall. With a curious fingernail he scratched idly at the two little discolored spots that marred its white surface.

"Fungus! Phosphorescent fungus! Foxfire!" he breathed. "How did this get here, Mahbub?" he asked sharply, swinging upon the trim officer. "This wall was whitewashed but three days gone!"

Mahbub shrugged.

"Servants are careless," he retorted.

"Nonsense!" the commissioner retorted impatiently. "This is a jungle fungus that grows only on rotten wood. Mahbub, what dost thou know of this thing? By the blood brotherhood between us I ask thee to speak the truth from naked heart."

Mahbub closed the grating behind his superior with a clang.

"I know only that Yar Khan, son of my mother's brother, shall not die unavenged," he answered as he preceded the Commissioner down the corridor toward the Thana office.

The Desert Woman

By RICHARD KENT

A modern Thais came out of the Great Desert and attempted to lure a priest, with strange consequences

THIS is the story of a woman, a very beautiful woman; a woman as perfect as an orchid, as seductive as hashish. She was as tall and slender as the most graceful of the houris in *The Thousand and One Nights*. Her eyes were as black as jet in shadow; her hair was of the same intense blackness, which only served to bring out into more startling prominence the prime-ivory whiteness of her colorless cheeks.

At the tiny oasis city of Wadi-el-Gibli, far back from the coast of Tripoli, many strange, weird stories were told of the desert woman, Mes'oodeh. Some will tell of how Kasseeb, one of the richest Tuaregs of Ghadames, disappeared from the haunts of men. Then came a day, two years later, when a caravan from the far Soudan, laden with ivory, ostrich-feathers, and gold dust, brought back the broken body of the once famous Kasseeb. Mes'oodeh, on the back of a groaning camel, rode into the village, softly weeping by his side. What became of his great wealth, nobody ever knew, but many condemned Mes'oodeh.

"The woman was a friend to Kasseeb," said one, "and 'if friendship is without money, it is not equivalent to the weight of a grain.' And Mes'oodeh was a very good friend to Kasseeb."

"She has no soul," declared another. "Allah had no power over her birthplace. If her face matched her heart, it would make one shudder just to gaze upon its horror. And yet she is more beautiful than the rarest flower, a flower whose touch is poison. But the law of unity is weirdly odd; a viper's fangs may be contained in a cloth of gold."

Such were the stories which were circulated throughout Wadi-el-Gibli about Mes'oodeh, the woman of the desert, and yet nobody knew from whence she had come. She spoke French fluently, and

English with a slightly foreign accent, but when the people asked her nationality, she smiled wistfully and replied, evasively, that it was good to be born in the desert. "The desert," she would continue, "is symbolic of the world. It contains nothing but what we bring into it ourselves. It is not a power of good, nor is it the abode of evil. It is not the garden of God, as the Arabs imagine, nor is it the possession of Satan. When it brings peace into a man's soul, it does it primarily because its marvelous silence, mystery, and unity draw his mind from other subjects. It is the condition of a person's mind that helps to create the impression. Ofttimes small things are magnified; the great ones overlooked. Some of us have eyes that see; others have but the limited vision of a sand-blind man."

Thus spoke Mes'oodeh, the desert woman of Wadi-el-Gibli; Mes'oodeh whose beauty was famed from the Soudan to Ghadames; Mes'oodeh, the gorgeous flower with the artificial perfume; Mes'oodeh who boasted of her far-seeing vision, and yet who was in reality stone-blind, as blind as Ali, the Berber, who begged for alms in the Arbar-Asat at Tripoli, or Khanoff, the marabout who preached with fanatic vehemence at the Wells of Wadi-el-Gibli.

2

MONSIGNOR ANDREA GIOVANNI, the Genoese priest of the Christian Mission, dwelt all alone, save for one Arab servant, in a tiny adobe house in the southern part of Wadi-el-Gibli. The window of his study faced the Great Desert, and sometimes when he had grown brain-tired from his endless toil in the sun, he would stand by the window gazing out over the reposeless billows of sand which glistened in the dazzling glare like chips of glowing bronze. And as he gazed out into the far silence, he would dream, dream of the days which were to come when the desert had been reclaimed, when the mantle of sadness would be lifted from the Sahara, and the great ocean of sand would come into its own.

Andrea Giovanni was about thirty-five, though his thin, colorless face, sorrowful, idealist's eyes, and simple black robes seemed to betoken a greater age. To him only the finest things in life appealed. He had never met Mes'oodeh. The two lived lives as completely apart as though they dwelt on different planets. But Mes'oodeh, the desert woman, had heard of the esthetic priest and it suddenly dawned upon her that here was a field for conquest. If she could get Andrea Giovanni to fall violently in love with her, it would be a distinct novelty. For a priest who had consecrated his life to God to fall in love with a woman who did not acknowledge that God, seemed to Mes'oodeh the very acme of humor. So she went to the simple house of Andrea Giovanni.

"Father," she murmured wearily, "my soul is a chaos of discordant emotions. I am soul-tired. Can you tell me how I can find peace?"

As Mes'oodeh spoke, she turned her great black eyes full upon Andrea's face. But he did not seem to appreciate her beauty. Softly he took her hand, as though she were a child, and led her to the window. He pointed out over the restless, whirling sand, the burning heat waves which seemed to merge the earth and sky into one great mass of molten metal, as he said, "Yonder is the desert. Go out into the Sahara and pray, for in prayer alone can you find peace."

And Mes'oodeh went out into the desert and knelt in prayer in a spot where Andrea Giovanni could gaze upon her from the window.

"By prayer alone can she find peace," he repeated wistfully.

Out in the desert Mes'oodeh, kneeling in apparent prayer, smiled cynically, as she whispered tensely, "In time, I know that he will come to me."

3

A WEEK later as Andrea Giovanni walked through the mellah of Wadi-el-Gibli, he overheard two old Jewish merchants speaking of the desert woman, Mes'oodeh.

"She has disappeared," said one, "and the city is well rid of her. She had no soul; her only God was Self. Now she has vanished and I am as glad at her going as I would be at the passing of a plague. But where she has gone is a mystery."

"She was last seen riding out alone into the desert," declared the other. "Her disappearance is but another mystery added to the multitudes which have shrouded the desert for ages. She has probably lost her way out there among those rolling sand dunes, and perished as she deserves. Truly it seems that God has purposely caused her to go away in order to purge our city."

"And yet," hazarded the first speaker, "it is a terrible death for a woman. Imagine how she must be suffering, plunging blindly, desperately about among those sand dunes; her lips cracked and broken, her tongue scorched and blackened, her eyes dried into glistening balls of heat, all sense of direction dead within her. Even a rabid dog of the streets deserves a better death than that."

"The people of Wadi-el-Gibli think differently. They say that by arriving at such an end, she does but get what she deserves. It is not their intention to go in search of her. Not a single person will enter the desert on such a quest. They say, 'It is the Will of Allah!'"

THAT evening Andrea Giovanni rode off alone into the desert. The night was exquisitely silent, not a breath of sound shattered the wondrous web of solitude. The moon glowed down upon the desert, creating a glorious brilliance almost as light as day. Not till it had set did he dismount from his camel, utterly worn out, and throw himself at full length upon the burning sand-mattress of desolation. Sleep came almost instantly; a dreamless, profound sleep which comes only to a man who is utterly exhausted.

Dawn had painted the eastern skies with silver before he again opened his eyes, and probably he would not have awakened even then if it had not been for a dull, ominous, moaning sound which seemed to roll to his ears from far off over the desert. Curiously, he rose to his feet and surveyed the far horizon, and there, away off to the south, a great grim wall of dense smoke seemed to be rushing toward him over the desert. In less than fifteen minutes he was engulfed in a raging yellow sandstorm. He threw himself face downward upon the sand, drawing his baracan about his face. The desert seemed to have become alive. Waves of sand surged and roared about him, while the air became so crowded with fine particles of molten dust that the sky disappeared utterly, swallowed up in the dense pall of gloom. As the storm increased in violence, the sand grew as hot as a lava stream. Particles of burning dust even penetrated through the thick folds of his baracan, blinding his eyes, parching his throat and even seeming to burn deep into the flesh of his face. The heat intensified so frightfully that it seemed as though he were being scalded in a cauldron of glowing metal, as though his body were being gradually, torturously burned alive. And yet in spite of everything, he did not sweat; every drop of moisture had evaporated from his body, until only a parched shell of fire remained. Ever and anon he was forced to burrow his way out of a mound of sand which had grown up above his head as though the grim Spirit of the Desert were bent on burying him alive. For hours the storm continued, raging as terrific as a tornado in the China Seas.

But bad as was the storm, its immediate effects were even worse, for when the horizon had cleared again, Andrea found his camel dead, and every drop of water evaporated in the water-bag. To describe the events that followed, one would have to be endowed with the genius of a Hugo. He was almost parched to ashes as a result of the storm, and yet he was a score of miles from Wadi-el-Gibli, with no promise of help in sight. The thought came to him that his position was as precarious as that of Mes'oodeh, of whom he was in search.

He laughed deliriously as he plunged indefinitely deeper into the desert. The sun grew hotter and hotter. It poured down upon his head, a torrent of liquid heat, until his very brain seemed bursting into fire. And then to add to his misfortunes, his helmet suddenly blew off, and as he pursued it drunkenly over the surging sand dunes, he lost all track of time. Sometimes it seemed almost within his grasp, but as he put out his hand to seize it, it would whirl beyond his reach. Insanely he plunged forward; reason had left him, only a dull determination to reach the hat remained in his mind. To his smarting, inflamed, sun-scorched eyes, the desert presented naught but a seething, blinding maze of light.

Eventually the end came. One lone man can not fight against the remorseless-ness of the desert. Suddenly everything went black before his eyes, the desert seemed to whirl dizzily about him. With a moan he crumpled up into a limp heap upon the sand, mercilessly trodden down by the sun which gives vent to its wildest passions in the intense solitude of the desert.

4

THREE hours later, a woman, journeying over the desert alone, came upon him. Dismounting from her camel, she bathed his poor blistered face with a soothing balm, brushed the sand from his hair and tried to force a few drops of deliciously cool water through his cracked, blackened lips. Then abruptly she stooped and crushed her red, burning lips to his brow.

"I knew that he would come to me," she whispered, smiling cruelly. "Priest or no priest, I knew that he would come."

But what Mes'oodeh did not know was that Andrea Giovanni would have entered the desert to save her from death if she had been as black as ebony or as horrible to gaze upon as Ali, the blind Berber who begged for alms in the Arbar-Asat at Tripoli.

FOR three days Andrea Giovanni lay semi-conscious and Mes'oodeh remained with him. By the hour she crooned love-songs which blended well with the strange stillness of the desert. Sometimes she twined her arms passionately around his neck and held her lovely face close to his.

"Kiss me!" she murmured tensely. "Kiss me!"

And Andrea would kiss her as a child might kiss a parent. His brain seemed numbed by fever; he could not remember what had happened. He lay in a sort of semi-stupor.

A great joy flooded the heart of Mes'oodeh, for she thought she had not failed in the task which she had set herself to do. But as suddenly as happiness was born to her, it was crushed back into death, for one morning Andrea awakened to full consciousness. The past blazed out before him in as startling detail as though cast upon a screen.

Mes'oodeh bent over him, and lowered her lovely face to his.

"Kiss me," she breathed with half-closed lips.

A look of intense surprize came into the eyes of Andrea Giovanni. "You know not what you speak!" he cried.

"Kiss me," repeated Mes'oodeh languorously.

Andrea closed his eyes. "I can not," he said wistfully. "My life is consecrated to God and the Church."

At his words a terrible fury convulsed the face of Mes'oodeh as she realized that he was slipping from her. For one brief moment her expression was a mirror reflecting her true character. She threw back her head and laughed in a jarring, mirthless manner that seemed to strike a discordant note in the wondrous peace anthem of the desert.

"God?" she sneered. "God? Of what use is this God of whom you speak? It was I who saved your life when you were lost in the desert, not God. It is the material which sets the balance of life. The spiritual has no weight."

Abruptly she arose and walked with heavy step out into the desert. She felt as though her brain were bursting with hatred, hatred of the religion which held Andrea away from her, and as she walked slowly among the sand dunes she realized that she had lost, that for the first time she had failed utterly.

It was evening before she returned, and now all trace of anger seemed to have left her, leaving a soul saddened by the weight of her sorrow.

She poured a cup of water from the goatskin bag.

"Poor Andrea," she murmured as she held it toward him. "For the first time since we have been together I have neglected you."

With trembling hand he took the cup to his burning lips and drained it to the last drop. A few moments later he fell into a fitful sleep from which he did not awaken until far into the night. The moon had risen when he again opened his eyes and the whole desert seemed splashed with silver. By his side sat Mes'oodeh, crooning a desert love-song which floated weirdly upon the intense solitude.

Andrea lifted himself upon his elbow. "Water," he gasped. "Water. My body seems as dry as though I had been eating sun-scorched sand."

Mes'oodeh held up her lips.

"Kiss me," she whispered.

"Water," he gasped. "Water."

The desert woman laughed harshly. "Let your God bring you water," she jeered. "Truly he would not turn a deaf ear to the prayer of his humblest servant."

She placed her full-red lips to his ear.

"Do you know that you are dying?" she said. "Can your God save you now that I have poisoned you? I emptied three drops of a certain Eastern drug into the water I gave you to drink, from which no power in heaven or earth can save you. The Berbers call the liquid soul-poison because, although it kills, no trace of it can ever be found in the body of the dead."

As Mes'oodeh spoke Andrea closed his eyes and his head slipped back to the sand. So still he lay, for the moment she thought he was dead. But finally he opened his dreamer's eyes and gazed into her face. In his expression there was no trace of anger, only a great pity for the poor soul-blind woman of the desert who laughed in the face of God.

"Mes'oodeh," he said, and his voice was so faint, it sounded like the echo of a dream, "the Arabs say that the desert is the Garden of God, that in the desert is heard the Voice of God—Silence. . . . I am dying, my fingers are growing cold. . . . You often declared that the desert was empty, that it was filled only by our own creations, the things which we bring into it ourselves. . . . But you were blind; you could not see, you could not understand."

A great light came into his eyes as he spoke, and—it is hard to explain—somehow the light seemed to reflect into the eyes of Mes'oodeh, bringing her Vision at last. Slowly her head slipped down to the sand. "Mercy! O God!" she cried. "Mercy!"

But even as she prayed and moaned and pleaded, the soul of Andrea Giovanni slipped from his body, away off there in the Garden of God. And Mes'oodeh, the desert woman, prayed, prayed as she had never prayed before in her life. Softly the shadows of evening slipped down over the desert. A cool breeze rose sadly from the south and brushed against her cheek like the softest caress. And Mes'oodeh knelt there alone in the desert by the body of the young priest. All about her on every side stretched a limitless plain of utter desolation. Nothing but a glorious faith in God remained to her, a faith made doubly beautiful by the fact that it had grown up in a soul that had once been a region of doubt. The miracle of love had been performed anew. It left Mes'oodeh a broken woman; but it left her a *good* woman. Thus did love come to Mes'oodeh, the soulless woman of the desert, crushing her beneath the terrible weight of its sadness, for love and sorrow are closely akin. Slowly she raised her eyes, dim with tears, toward the heavens, and a look of exquisite peace stole over her face as she beheld the glorious light of the Southern Cross lifting slantwise into the sky.

At BAB-EL-LANI, a little desert-town far to the south of Wadi-el-Gibli, near the Soudan, they tell of a strange veiled woman who goes about among the sick and the dying, shrouded in white. No one knows the name of this woman of mystery. The crippled beggars of Bab-el-Lani call her the White Mother of the Desert. And every night she creeps to the heights of the city and looks wistfully out over the desert toward Tripoli. Sometimes it seems as though she whispers a single name, "Andrea, Andrea, Andrea."

Back at Wadi-el-Gibli, the people wonder what has become of Mes'oodeh, the soulless woman of the desert. Some say that perhaps she has gone to some other town more abundant in riches than Wadi-el-Gibli. But always, Doctor Ripley, the American missionary, shakes his head.

"Perhaps," he says, "she has heard the Voice of God out in the desert and has been born anew."

"Such women," declared Lacroix, the French importer, "can never reform."

"You forget the Magdalene," replied Doctor Ripley softly, and he gazed thoughtfully out over the desert.

Now the New Year reviving old Desires,
The thoughtful Soul to Solitude retires,
  Where the WHITE HAND OF MOSES on the Bough
Puts out, and Jesus from the ground suspires.
                    —*Rubáiyát of Omar Khayyam.*

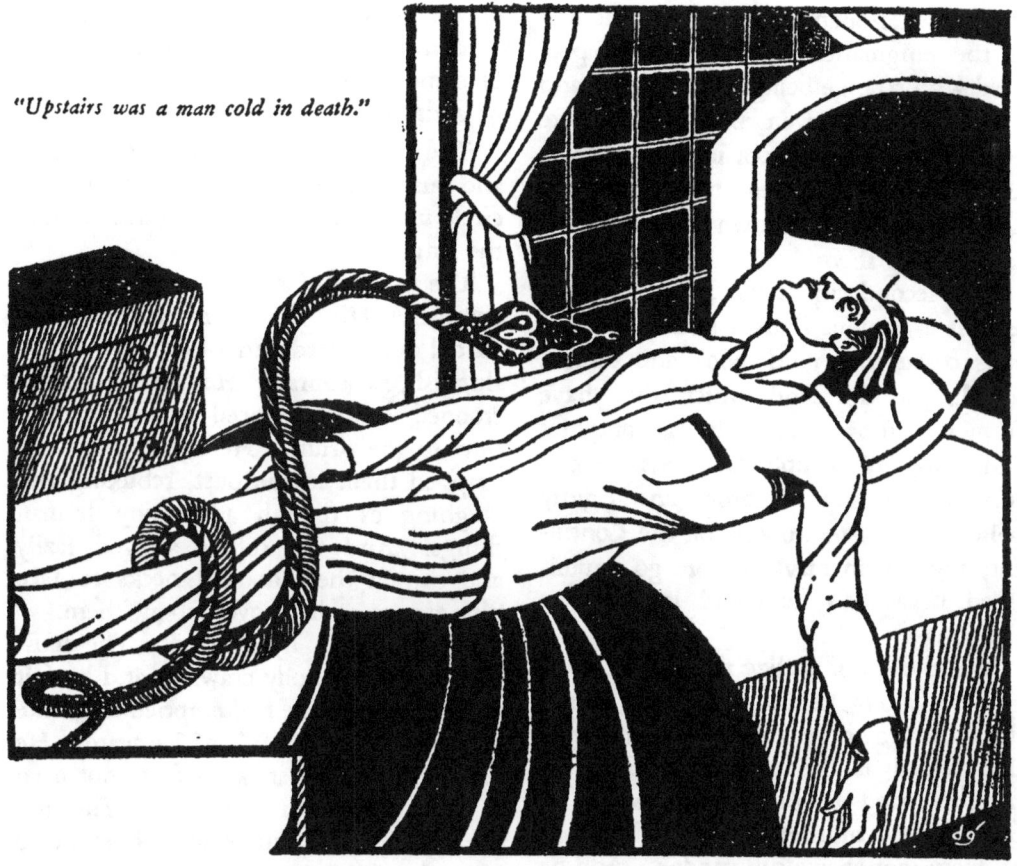

"Upstairs was a man cold in death."

The Cobra Den

By PAUL ERNST

*Venomous snakes and a wild adventure among
the Arabs of Northern Africa*

WHEN Edwin Weiss came to Kairouan, one of the thin trickle of tourists who pass through that grimly dirty city, he made several mistakes that would have seemed incredible had not one remembered that never before had he lifted his shiny, pointed shoes off the pavements of New York.

His first mistake was when he landed from the overland touring-bus that had carried, among the twenty or so others, the dark-haired woman with the lights in her eyes who was the wife of Dancherman. He looked around him then, glanced furtively into the face of the woman, gazed again at the fairy-tale wildness of surrounding city and plain— and decided that in such a place a man might take in his own hands any laws he chose and break them with impunity!

Now, Kairouan is two cities. The first is the enigmatic Arab stronghold peopled with strange beings and mystery and age-old dirt. Seven pilgrimages here equal one trip to Mecca itself; and even as in Mecca the citizens have their own harsh laws and their own discrimination in enforcing them.

The second city is not so much a city as it is a tenuous human stream of travelers come with guide-book and camera to glimpse the land which they have formerly known only in geographies and company pamphlets. This second, smaller city is as decorous and rigidly policed as any metropolis on the Continent; and a man may no more go unpunished here than he could in Paris or London.

Weiss did not realize this. He trailed gingerly along behind the guide, noted the dark brown eyes and light gray eyes that stared at the party with indolent hatred, gazed fearfully into caverns of bazaars, saw murder written in the face of every inoffensive rug-vendor. And he glanced again at Dancherman's wife.

As they went, the guide told stories of violent deeds done in the secretive-looking buildings that lined the alleylike streets. Achmed spoke English with an Oxford accent, and spent his time out of tourist season in Vienna; but now he was dressed in burnoose and fez, and inspired repressed horror in the lady tourists when he came too close to them. And Weiss' sheltered nerves quivered and his delicate, musician's fingers tingled to their tips.

In the market-place, where the wares of the meat stalls hang flyblown and glistening in the African sun, a crowd was collected. Snatches of one-sided conversation floated over the circle of heads, as though someone were talking to himself in the coughing, explosive manner of the Arabic language. This was succeeded now and again by a thin wailing of some musical instrument and the beat of a drum.

The guide led the way to the crowd and pushed aside a segment of the human circle until his tourist flock could see into the ring.

The magnet of attraction was a snake-charmer. His thin, dirt-crusted arms darted out toward and away from several sluggish, fat cobras. He talked to them, crooned to them, danced around them in time to the drum. He lifted them and dragged them in the dust, rebuking and laughing as though addressing human things. And the cobras swayed lazily and turned their hooded necks to face him always as he moved about them.

Weiss stared, hypnotized. The muscles of his soft body crawled, and he felt as though someone had emptied his white skin and poured it full of ice water. He had never seen a snake before, not even in the zoo of his habitual city. The supple, dirt-colored things were horrible to him—horrible!

When the snake-charmer's bare hand touched the repulsive flesh, his own hand ached from the vicarious contact. As the performer clutched one of the wriggling things just under the head, Weiss could feel fire running through his body in anticipation of the poison fangs that might be sunk next instant into the charmer's arm. Once when the largest cobra shook off its drugged coma for an instant and made a lightning dart at the figure that danced about it, Weiss too drew back as though his own body had been threatened. And as he bumped hysterically against the big man beside him—a cattleman on a vacation—the big man smiled with tolerant disdain.

But the musician's newly discovered fear of snakes didn't numb his mind to the growing feeling of outlawry that was instilled in him by the stark mystery of Kairouan. When the performance was ended and the charmer put the cobras and the livelier, non-poisonous wood snakes back into their gunny-sacks, Weiss was plumbing ever deeper into wells of barricaded desire; and he was planning, planning.

He stared at the sacks, moving with their deadly freight. He glanced furtively at Dancherman—less furtively at Dancherman's woman. And Kairouan was off the face of the civilized earth, with policemen and law courts a thousand miles away.

A child should have been more subtle than Weiss.

WITHIN an hour every Arab in Kairouan knew that the undersized little tourist with the shallow chin and the soft brown eyes had bought one of the charmer's cobras. The house-boy saw him carrying a gunny-sack toward Dancherman's room, holding the sack away from him at arm's length, his face gray with fear of the thing he carried. And everyone noticed how he kept Dancherman's wife downstairs by the tinkly piano until long after Dancherman had gone to bed.

As Weiss played on and on, obliging with some of his own popular song hits as well as with the frankly better tunes of others, he began to get uneasy. His fingers trembled on the keys; though to hide this he played louder and louder.

Upstairs was a man cold in bed; beside him a writhing thing that splayed its hooded neck and crawled across the stiffened limbs. . . .

He cringed, and missed a beat in the neat syncopation of the piece he was playing. Where had Dancherman been bitten? Or—had he seen the coiled form under the blankets in time to avoid it? This was unlikely. He would have been down again long before now, telling of the narrow escape, a little suspicious, perhaps, but unable to make any accusations in this land of snakes and wildness.

No. The snake must have done its work, because Dancherman had gone into his room and not come out again. But —Weiss missed another beat as this fact, too, began to seem threatening—surely he must have felt the stab of the cobra's fangs. And surely he must have become aware of the slowly moving coils the instant he got into bed. Why, then, was there no uproar—no rushing about and poking into other beds to see if there were more of the deadly things in the house?

He looked at the watch on his wrist and noted that it had been over an hour since Dancherman had left the room. And now, beside him, the woman with the little glints in her dark eyes must be told that the hints she had thrown him during the trip had borne fruit—that she was free to take the man she had seemed to prefer to her husband.

Three elderly men poked out the stubs of their cigars at about the same instant, and rose to leave the lounge. Weiss watched them go, their figures blurring in his sight as they filed out the door and left him alone with Mrs. Dancherman.

He stopped playing and turned to her. It didn't take long to describe to her some of what had happened. She guessed a part of it from the look on his face; and before he was half through with his mumbled story she had risen and was looking at him as though he were loathsome in her sight.

Under the look, Weiss drew into himself, and he swayed on the stool as he saw her throat swell to a scream. He foresaw the end of all things for himself in that alarm—confused crowds surrounding him, eyes growing harder as they stared at him, a tale of self-confessed murder, retribution!

But the outcry never came. Her throat choked over the attempted sound. Her eyes showed white, and she crumpled to the floor.

She had hardly fallen before Weiss was up from the piano stool and racing for the door. In his mind was no plan, no course of action—only blind haste to get away before she should regain her senses and repeat his story to the others. And as he went he raged against a woman who should lure a man on and then turn against him when he had given her the highest proof of his love—never admitting to himself that she had lured him on only in his own opinion.

In the effort to get away from the hotel, go anywhere before the woman could recover and accuse him, he promptly lost himself in the Arab section of town. It is not good to wander alone at night in the native quarters of such towns as Kairouan. And, rushing hopelessly down one street and another, he was numb with fear of his surroundings.

For the first time the enormous stupidity of the thing he had done came crashing home to him. An alien in a wild and hostile land, unable to speak the language, unable to ask for help or shelter, hunted by every European—or soon to be hunted—with death waiting for him if he were caught! Tears of self-pity welled in his eyes and fell salt to his lips.

The darkness was appalling. Never a light in a house, narrow alleys ending in blank walls into which he often bumped blindly. Now and then a puny street lamp planted determinedly by the French government, but placed usually in such a way that the crooked outjutting of building walls cut off the light within a few feet. Darkness and quiet — the dark and quiet of a great storm about to burst, and in the center of its threatening, the little man, Weiss!

A shadowy, white-robed figure appeared suddenly before him, seeming to have risen from the stones of the street. It may have been the glint of starlight on a knife blade, or merely the reflection on one of the crescent silver pins worn in that land; but, not stopping to find out, Weiss jumped back and ran down the nearest open way.

One of the white, savage desert dogs leaped snarling from the tunneled darkness. Weiss heard the fabric of his trouser leg rip, and felt teeth in his ankle. He kicked out and was rid of the brute.

Finally—lights ahead! The low doorway of an Arab café gleamed like a dim moon in the blackness of house walls, and he went toward it cautiously. A few yards away, however, he observed that the men in the café were gathered about one of their number, and all seemed to be talking excitedly. The central figure was the snake-charmer! He appeared to be describing some incident—the sale of one of his cobras, perhaps?

Another shadowy figure rose in front of him as he turned to skulk away from possible discovery. This time there was no retreat, and he mouthed a prayer to the God he had never before acknowledged, feeling already the slash of a knife in his belly. The figure, however, bowed servilely and spoke in broken English:

"*M'sieur* wish to see the night things of the *ville*, perhaps?"

Weiss could have cried on the man's shoulder with the relief of it. He tried to speak without losing his last shred of self-control and babbling incoherently.

"I am not looking for sights. I want an automobile. A motor-car. *Vous savez?* Automobile. I want to go away from here quick. God—there's probably no such thing as a car here!"

There was, it developed. A friend of a friend had a very gorgeous and beautiful automobile. Very fast. Very fine.

But—so late at night, with a wind whipping up that would bring sand from the desert a few hundred kilometers south—he might ask a great deal for the use of it.

Weiss dragged at his wallet, and the beady black eyes gleamed as he opened it in the distant light of the café. Yes, yes! For all that he could have the so beautiful machine to drive him away at once. The shadowy, white figure sank into the street's darkness.

As he waited for the man's return, Weiss tried to form some kind of a plan. He would be driven to Tunis. Ought to reach there before noon of the next day. Then some kind of a disguise, some vague manner of getting on a boat bound for Mexico or South America. But the main thing was to leave here at once and get to Tunis. In Tunis were coffee-skinned gentlemen who spoke English and would surely hide him and get him a passport of sorts in exchange for the balance of the franc notes he had in his wallet.

Two figures suddenly stood beside him. Again the broken speech of the man who had gone for the car. He was informed huskily that the street they were in was, of course, too narrow for an automobile to negotiate. Would he please follow?

He stepped on the heels in front of him in his haste. The other man was the driver and owner of the car. He could speak no English, and stalked aloof in dirt and dignity. He would be told, through the first, where he was to go. Tunis? But certainly!

THE walk was a long one. Then, as though chopped off with an ax, the town abruptly ended and open country stretched before their eyes. In front of him, Weiss saw the so beautiful motor-car—an unstable-looking, sand-scoured, ancient Renault. The man cranked it,

proving either that the battery wasn't strong enough to turn the engine, or that the starter was out of order. Weiss wondered if anything else were out of commission.

The motor suddenly caught with a nerve-filing grind of bearings. Cars do not last long down there. Each wind raises clouds of fine sand and sweeps north from the father of sands; and sand is not good for bearings. As the machine wheezed off to a start in the direction of Sousse, it shuddered and clanked as though its heart had long since been eaten out by the grit and it was now running entirely by the will-power of the man who huddled behind the wheel.

Over the howl of worn parts, Weiss asked the driver how long it would take to reach Tunis. Then he remembered that he couldn't reply. The bar of language raised a new horror during the night ride. It was as though he were being driven by a ghost—a surly ghost that mumbled to itself in Arabic, and turned to look at him with light gray eyes that seemed like holes leading down into knowing darkness.

An hour out of town, Weiss looked back and cursed. Far behind, a pair of headlights bobbed up and down over the rough road, and moved forward even as they moved, so that an even distance was kept between them. He punched the driver in the shoulder and waved ahead, trying to indicate that he wanted more speed. The driver nodded, sank lower in his seat, and the pound and shriek of worn bearings reached a higher key.

The acceleration was too much. A final pound, as though the motor had kicked itself through the hood—and there was a silence that was startling after the noise of flight. Something had broken.

The driver got stolidly from his seat

and raised the hood. Then he shrugged helplessly.

Weiss swore at him, less afraid of him than of the car behind, which was nearing them by the second. Thinking the man was pretending so that he might return home to his bed, he offered more money. Again the stolid shrug. Even bribes can not move a broken connecting-rod.

The other automobile was now so near that he could hear the whine of its engine. He visioned it as full of men with guns, searching for him. Dead or alive. The phrase came to him from some dimly remembered reading. Dead or alive! They probably had orders to take him that way.

With a last helpless look at the stalled car and the wooden-faced Arab bending over the motor, he turned and raced away from the road—into the dark, unfenced fields about him.

COMPARED to the real desert, the land around Kairouan is a fruitful paradise. But it is that way only by comparison. Bare, hard-baked dirt that supports a few scrubby olive groves and tough dry brush, it is desolate enough. To the man from the sleek pavements of New York it seems like the outer stretches of hell itself.

While the breath in his lungs lasted, he ran into the dark, staggering over loose stones and tripping in the scratchy brush. Then, when his chest was a burning ache and his heart pounded in his throat, he fell over something large and soft and warm that made a rasping bark and snapped at him with yellow teeth. Around him were other large, dim shapes. It was several minutes before the prosaic explanation soothed his wildly jumping nerves—merely camels, hobbled to keep them from straying too far

afield. He got up and walked forward, his hand pressed against his heart.

An hour before dawn, he sank down in the gritty dirt of the plain, entirely exhausted. Too done in to think, he could only lie and suffer from the cold as the sweat of his fear and effort dried on his body. If only he could find some kind of shelter that would protect him from the cold night wind, and help to hide him through the daylight hours of the morrow!

As though in answer to a prayer, he suddenly noticed an irregular triangle, darker than the surrounding darkness. It looked like the door to a very low, peak-roofed hut—some kind of shelter, probably for the herdsmen. On hands and knees he crawled toward it.

With a ragged sigh of relief he lunged into the opening. . . .

Instantly he was falling! Down he plunged, his hands scraping over smooth, damp stones as he tried to check his descent. His head hit a projecting stone and consciousness was snapped out.

It was probably not more than a few seconds before he came to his senses again; but it was long enough to force on him the feeling that he had died and been reborn—into a new and terrible world where nothing lived and light was not yet created. So strong was the impression that for minutes he lay motionless on the rock floor, without thought, without conjecture of any kind.

A sharp pain stabbed his wrist. He moved it tentatively, and cried aloud at the hurt of it. Probably broken. Into the welter of more poignant emotions crept the realization that he might never play the piano again.

Gently he moved his legs, finding them unhurt. He must now dismiss the crazy notion that he had been transported into another and more terrible universe, and discover what kind of a pit held him prisoner.

He did not know it, but he had fallen into a cistern constructed by some worthy Roman colonist nearly two thousand years ago when north Africa was the granary of Rome. It was deep, with sheer rock walls that baffled all hand-holds— a square well of a thing with only a few feet of the arched roof left above the shifting sand and silt of ages. To climb out of it was impossible. Had it been deliberately built for a prison it could not have served that purpose better.

It took but a few moments for him to discover this. Holding his hurt wrist above his head so that it would not throb so keenly, he felt around the four walls. As high as he could reach in every spot there was no projection for him to cling to.

Once he shouted for help, then caught himself on the edge of the second cry. Of what use to call? If a European should hear him he would probably be taken back to Kairouan—to face the body of Dancherman. If an Arab should answer he would be unable to tell the man what he wanted; and he, too, might take him promptly back to Kairouan as the only solution of an un-Arabic dilemma.

In the meantime there was nothing to do but settle himself as comfortably as possible and wait for daylight. He lowered himself to the floor, leaning against a well and laying his wrist against the cold stone to soothe its hot aching.

At once, as his body relaxed into some degree of comfort, his mind raced back to the hotel, and painted pictures of the night's events: Dancherman cold in bed —the writhing thing beside him that crawled over the stiffened limbs—the smirk on the face of the snake-charmer as he sold him the gunny-sack with its deadly burden—the house-boy at the hotel with his stupid wonderment at sight of the foppishly dressed tourist carrying a filthy gunny-sack in his hand.

And through the shadowy memories wove the sinuous bodies of snakes; and back of them again laced tenuous figures with splayed necks, darting their forked tongues and striking out.

But this was delirium! His wrist—the pain of it—stealing his reason for a few minutes. He clamped his teeth shut and waved away the faces and figures that swam before his eyes. But the twining forms of the cobras persisted. No matter how tightly he closed his eyes he could still see the crawling, sluggish reptiles with their cold eyes and lightning tongues.

What would it feel like to be bitten by one? What had Dancherman felt when the needle points sank in his flesh? Probably as though his veins had been opened and molten iron poured in! Then —his face blackened by the poison, lying cold in bed beside the writhing cobra.

How dark in this ghastly pit! Black with the hopeless darkness that must belong to the blind. And quiet! The abysmal silence began to weigh on his nerves. It was so noiseless that he could hear the rasp of shirt fabric against coat as his chest rose and fell with his breathing. He moved his leg slightly, and could distinctly hear the rustle of cloth. A dry, scaly kind of rustling! Like the noise of——

His heart pounded in his ears as he strained to hear. It had seemed for an instant as though he could still hear the rustling after his leg had stopped moving! Like the rasping of a scaly body on the stone of the floor!

Logic instantly came to his relief. It could not be a cobra he had heard. Snakes hunt for sun-warmed rocks, not chill, lightless pits. And with the sheer walls, no serpent could den here. Impossible! He was imagining things.

Nevertheless he remained facing toward the spot where he thought he had heard the sound, bent forward as though he would force aside the curtain of blackness and see if a snake were really there.

A dry, leisurely rasping sounded out from another corner of the pit. He whirled to listen, leaning his weight full on his broken wrist in the heedless intensity of his effort to hear. The noise continued, stopped for an instant, came again as though nearer to him.

Like an answering whisper, the rustling was renewed in the corner where he had first thought he heard it. From each side sounded the rasping as of dry, cold scales on rough stone. And from each side the sound seemed to come ever closer.

Another murmurous rustle scraped his ears—and another. From all directions came the whisper of fat, thick coils looping over the rock of the floor—converging as they moved dully to see what strange thing had fallen into their home.

There must be dozens, scores of them. And all moving with that faint scratchy sound as they neared him. He drew up his knees, and huddled into his corner for fear at any moment he might feel one of the heavy coils wound around his leg.

His heart thudded in his throat until a little sheet of red spurted before his eyes at every throb. One man, defenseless and alone, in a pit that was literally carpeted with writhing cobras!

Nearer sounded the rustling. As though the darkness had suddenly been lifted, he could fairly see the slowly narrowing circle of snakes closing in on him. Nearer. . . .

The nerve ends in his skin jerked and fluttered as he felt in anticipation the contact of the reptiles. Soon, now, soon —and they would be touching him.

He put his hand to the floor to brace his trembling body—and cried aloud as his fingers came squarely down on a round, cold thing. Consciousness began to fade, till he was jerked back to alertness by the thought that he must not faint.

As the contact burned again and again in remembrance, it occurred to him that it might not have been a snake, but merely a ridge in the cold, smooth rock; he had not been bitten, and the thing, whatever it was, had not moved. But for no reward could he have forced his fingers to explore there again. The thought that a cobra might be coiled motionless within a foot of him was less horrible than the chance of deliberately touching one with his bare hand!

The dry rasping was louder now, and nearer. From all directions he could hear it. . . .

His leg jerked out spasmodically as there was the feeling of something brushing slowly against it. That would not do. He must not do that! His only hope—if any hope was left him—lay in remaining as motionless as the stone itself. He had read that somewhere. A motionless body is never bitten by a snake.

Something moved across his ankle, as though a section of rope were being pulled over it. Through his thin sock he could feel every flowing of chill, serpentine muscle. Sweat poured from his body, but he stayed quiet.

The snake curled up against the warmth of his leg. And as minute after minute ticked by, Weiss held himself motionless though the hair of his scalp prickled and each repressed breath caught in his throat.

From every part of the pit came the continued rasping of dry, cold bodies looping over the rock floor. Like the far-off rustling of leaves, it was. The rustling of leaves in pitchy blackness! And in the center of the deadly circle, he held himself as quiet as the rock against which he leaned.

THE strain was too much for any human will. With the cobras all about him, and the weight of one actually resting against his leg—he began to break! An instant more, and though he should be bitten a score of times for it—he would have to move. All over his body his muscles were twitching with agonized desire for blind, senseless action.

His hands, clenched in his lap, were touched by something cold and heavy that crawled over them and came to coiled rest on his waist. . . .

The thread of control was snapped. Screaming, he lashed out with his fists, battering the rock floor with his bare hands as far as he could reach. He could feel a dozen needle points sunk into his flesh. . . .

Without a sound he fell forward on his face and lay still.

It was so that Achmed and the vacationing cattle-man—sent out by Dancherman to bring him back quietly and avoid a scandal—found him in the red light of daybreak.

Noosing the tow-rope of the car around one of the stiffened arms, they raised the body of Weiss from the pit. As they laid it out on the ground, both drew back with a shudder from the staring, twisted face, and Achmed quickly covered it with his burnoose.

"It must be someone else!" marveled the cattle-man. "Weiss didn't have white hair."

"It is Weiss," said Achmed. "But—changed!"

"How could he have died—like that? Cobra bite?"

"No. As you see, his face—though not pretty—is unblackened by the poison. Besides, in the memory of man, there have been no cobras around here."

"But the one Dancherman threw out of his bed——"

"Brought up from far, far south by the charmer," said Achmed. "There are no cobras in this land, my friend. Unless"—he shrugged—"unless there are those most powerful ones of the imagination. . . ."

"Nonsense!" protested the rancher. "It takes more than imagination to kill a full-grown man!"

Incredulous, he searched minutely for signs of cobra bite. The body was absolutely unmarked!

"You see!" said Achmed. "It was too dark, and he was too much alone with the memory of what he had done. . . ."

Again he shrugged, and he raised his eyes from the huddled figure toward the throneroom of Allah.

Whether at Naishápúr or Babylon,
Whether the Cup with sweet or bitter run,
    The Wine of Life keeps oozing drop by drop,
    The Leaves of Life keep falling one by one.
                —Rubáiyát of Omar Khayyam.

The Black Camel

By G. G. PENDARVES

The Englishman attempted to wrest from their owners in the desert city of El Zoonda a string of gems that dated back to Tyre and Sidon

THE "L" train roared and rattled on downtown past Bleecker Street, bearing its load of weary passengers still farther on into the forbidding gloom ahead.

But it was not the inclement weather which caused one man to alight with such evident reluctance at Bleecker Street. Skulking in the shadows, he allowed his fellow-passengers to precede him through the clanking exit-barriers, and several times he glanced back apprehensively over his shoulder to make certain that no one followed him down the stairway to the street level.

The whites of his eyes gleamed as he found himself held up by a stream of traffic going south; and, rather than wait, he sped along under the "L," crossed over two blocks farther up and returned to Bleecker Street on the other side; then once more he turned his back on it and hurried downtown, dodging along Wooster Street for several blocks, turning east and finally returning uptown again by way of Greene Street.

He slipped and twisted through the crowd—commuters hurrying for homeward-bound trains, errand boys, shoppers, together with that indefinite drifting mass of humanity which form the neutral background of New York. Abel Gissing merged himself into this background without effort, for there was nothing in his slim body, his thin face and shadowed eyes to distinguish him from the hundreds of under-nourished men and women who washed to and fro, up and down

the streets, like refuse drifting on the bosom of a great tidal wave.

Only the glint of terror in his eyes, the nervous tension of his body, the quick hiss of an indrawn breath as a passer-by jostled him roughly, set him definitely apart from the mob. Here was a hunted thing seeking sanctuary!

Coming to Bleecker Street for the third time, Gissing looked furtively about him, hesitated, crossed the street, recrossed it; then, abruptly making up his mind at last, he pushed open the door of a dim little shop, entered and closed it quickly behind him, and stared speechlessly at the man who rose to face him.

Isaac Volk grasped the situation with the intelligence of one who has long lived by his wits, and was accustomed to turn all kinds of situations, no matter how complicated, to his own advantage.

Here was a man in the last extremity of terror! Evidently he had something to get rid of, or he would not have sought refuge in a pawn-shop; obviously he wished to be rid of it immediately and would not stay for long argument or bargaining.

The Jew's eyes narrowed, every instinct in him alert and keen; here was a bird to his hand for the plucking, and his fingers itched for the job.

Danger? A fig for the danger! Isaac Volk had been cradled and bred in the very lap of hazard; for one does not trade with the underworld, or hobnob with poisoners, thieves and cutthroats without risk. Danger . . . he had come to need

"His shot was followed by a fierce hiss of rage."

the taste of it as a sailor craves the tang of salt on his lips, or as a desert wanderer desires limitless horizons. He put his dirty claw-like hands on the counter in front of him, leaned over it, and watched his visitor in silence.

Yellow gleams of light, from a flickering oil lamp hung from the low-raftered ceiling, half revealed and half concealed the faces of the two men as they stood frozen into immobility, distrust warring with utter panic on Abel Gissing's pallid features; greed, craft, and infinite patience puckering the sallow, dirt-begrimed visage of the Jew.

Suddenly, with a light nervous tread, Gissing crossed swiftly to the counter, and drew a packet from under his coat.

"Take it!" he said in a low shaking voice. "Take it! I've heard of you . . . I know you fear nothing—no one! Take it, and may you never——"

He broke off as the door-latch rattled violently, and, leaping over the low counter, he crouched down between it and the wall, clutching Volk by the legs. A loud hoarse voice was audible from without, cursing the shop and everything in it, including the owner. Gissing rose with an audible sigh of relief.

"I thought it was . . . *him!*" he muttered.

Volk, meanwhile, was unwrapping the package, taking no notice at all of his client's behavior or of the noisy profanity which continued outside his locked door.

Removing the oilskin cover, Volk revealed a square box of sandalwood inset with ivory and carved about with Arabic lettering in relief. The "Hand of Fatima" was exquisitely cut where a keyhole might have been expected, and, turning this with eager exploring fingers, Volk found the box open in his hands, and even his hard eyes softened at sight of the treasure within.

He drew it forth deftly enough, holding the long shining string up to the light, and the blood coursed hot and quick in his veins as a man's might do after a draft of rare, long-mellowed wine.

"Rubies?"

"No," answered Gissing in a whisper, "Rose-emeralds! The Arabs call it the *Wrath of Allah* . . . the *Wrath of Allah!* It has a history, that string of stones . . . too long to tell you all now. It came from the East, the far East, in ancient times . . . long before the Arabs got hold of it."

"And you . . . where did you pick it up?" asked Volk, his black eyes boring into the shifting eyes of his companion.

"From . . . from . . . North Africa . . . the desert."

"So!" responded Volk. "And the clasp?"

"I never discovered," said Gissing. "It's not part of the original string, of course. I've never seen a black stone like it before, it's cut in the shape of a camel because the stones belong now to a secret society called the Black Camels. My God! . . . the Black Camels!" was Gissing's despairing whisper.

Volk retired to the back of his den, and remained there for a long time, examining the jewels and testing them, while the other man waited muttering and shivering by the counter.

"They seem to be genuine," was Volk's verdict at last.

"Genuine!" Gissing's voice cracked on a high note of hysteria. "Would I go through hell for a string of glass beads? They're worth more than you or any man in this city can pay. They're beyond all price! There's nothing like them in the whole world, I tell you! They date back to the days of Tyre and Sidon, and the period when the Phenicians built Tarshish, and owned silver mines in Spain. These stones were brought by them from Syria, and passed from their keeping to king after king. Now they belong to the Black Camels and their leader——"

"Who is he?"

"No names—not even here! I see his face everywhere . . . I hear his voice! He is a ruler in the desert . . . ruler of a terrible race in the desert. Their stronghold is a vast walled city, built of salt, and black with age. That string of stones was the glory of his people."

"But who are his people?" persisted the Jew.

"Touaregg Arabs . . . the scum of the desert . . . outlaws, murderers, robbers, bandits of every description, who have banded themselves together and call themselves the Black Camels because death walks ever at their side. The desert city is their headquarters, but their followers are everywhere. They are a very strong, very terrible secret society — followers of Zoroaster—fire-worshippers!"

Volk stared blankly and unbelievingly at this fantastic story. Silence fell in the little dusty shop. The owner of the voice outside had gone off with a last parting curse, and there was a lull in the roar of the traffic. Only the bubbling flicker of the lamp-flame overhead was audible.

"That clasp means danger . . . it is a symbol of death!" Gissing continued in a whisper. "Death to any one who violates the sanctuary of the jewels! Death to those who touch the *Wrath of Allah* with profane hands! Death to me . . . to you . . . to every one, I tell you!"

A wild laugh rose to Gissing's lips, but the Jew clapped a dirty hand over his mouth.

"Death for you, if you like! For me, I am not afraid of your Arabs and your secret societies. Besides—what has the desert to do with us here?"

"The Black Camel is death, I tell you! Does not death walk here as well as in the desert?"

"And how did you manage to get away with this?"

Gissing's eyes, which were fixed in unwilling, passionate admiration on the gleaming rose-red stones, darted fearfully toward his interlocutor.

"Don't ask me, man," he said heavily. "That's my business, not yours. I wish to God I'd never seen it, never heard of the Black Camels and their sacred jewels! Never seen an Arab—or been near the desert! If only I could——"

"Stow that!" interrupted the Jew roughly. "I'll give you my own price for these stones as you——"

"*Your* price!" a note of contempt strengthened the other's voice. "They're priceless . . . priceless! But yes—yes—take them," he added hurriedly, as a gust of wind rattled the crazy dwelling, hooting savagely through vents and holes in the roof and walls. "Hide them quickly before I change my mind. To think of the long years I spent in the desert to get hold of those cursed jewels . . . death almost every step of the way . . . and now——"

"Now you don't want them."

"I'm afraid . . . afraid!" The husky voice sank to its lowest note. "The Black Camels are on my track. *He* has followed me . . . he's here in this city . . . in this street perhaps. He is a devil—more awful than death itself. I dare not keep the stones. I dare not keep them . . . but . . . but——"

His hands went out to the wonderful shimmering length of jewels, each stone the glowing living heart of a rose—the very fire and essence of that perfect flower!

Isaac Volk dropped the jewels into the box, shut it, and wrapped the oilskin about it abruptly.

"Two thousand dollars," he said, his thin curved mouth closing over the words like a steel trap. "That'll take you a few miles from your Black Camels and all the rest of your fancy zoo, I reckon."

Gissing made no reply. As the shining rose jewels vanished from his sight, the last flicker of energy died out of him, and he collapsed amongst the greasy garments which hung against the wall behind the long counter.

The Jew brought a thimbleful of vile brandy and forced it down the other's throat; then he counted a roll of bills and gave it to Gissing.

"Better get out," Volk said. "I don't want any of your Camels in here—black or white! To say nothing of the cops. Come on now—out of this!"

Roughly assisting him, the Jew half carried, half pushed the unfortunate Gissing across the dusty room, drew back the bolt, and deftly deposited his visitor on the slimy uneven steps outside his door.

"Don't come near this place again," he warned. "What you've done, I don't know—or care. But don't bring your troubles here—that's all."

He re-entered his house, bolting the door on the inside again; and going straight to the box of sandalwood, he drew out the jewels, and sat down to examine them at leisure.

"Fellow was crazy, I guess!" he muttered at length. "I'd be hanged by my thumbs before I'd give them away like that. That yarn of his about the Black Camels! How the —— did he think that up? What *was* he running from, anyhow? Black Camels—huh! This beauty" —and he touched the clasp—"is the only camel I'll have round here, I guess."

IT WAS rather more than twenty-four hours later when Gissing returned to the pawn-shop.

Midnight had passed, and although in more fashionable quarters the glare of lights, the whirring of cars, the hooting of many horns still continued, down in Bleecker Street a heavy leaden silence enveloped the dingy neighborhood. The endless rows of gray roofs, the dreary windows, the towering factories, the flyblown stores, the vast warehouses, the gaudy picture-houses, and the lots of waste ground littered with bricks and paper and timber, all these were cloaked in merciful shadow by a setting moon, whose slanting silver beams lent romance even to the unbeautiful environs of Bleecker Street.

Lights shone dimly here and there as Gissing hurried along, but the small square window of Isaac Volk's house was in darkness, and the door was uncompromisingly shut.

Gissing put out a cautious hand and lifted the rusty latch of the battered door, and to his amazement found that the bolt had not been drawn within. The door opened slowly inward as he pushed it from him, and, as he stood hesitating, the murky fetid atmosphere of the room within rose like an evil cloud to his face.

Very cautiously he stole inside, very softly he closed the door behind him, and stood listening intently, his eyes wide and strained, trying to pierce the inky evil-smelling darkness of the den.

Gradually his heart slowed down, and he licked his dry lips and swallowed convulsively. He got out his torch and sent a slender pencil of light athwart the gloom, moving it across and across the dirty place as he grew bolder.

Suddenly the moving light was still, pointing at an obscure corner where Volk had stowed away an ancient four-post bed on which was piled some unspeakable bedding and a few mangy-looking fur coats.

Paralyzed by shock, Gissing held the light steady for an appreciable time, his eyes on the bold outline of a drawing sketched in black charcoal on the wall by the bed. It was the presentment of a camel—a black camel—which his torch revealed.

Not only that . . . there was something else . . . something at which Gissing stared and stared with dropped jaw and a cold sickness in his breast.

He began to back to the door at last, with a queer sobbing catch of his breath, afraid to turn his back on what he saw. When, with groping hand behind, his cold fingers touched the latch, he dashed down his torch, flung open the door, and, leaving it to swing to and fro in the night wind, he fled under the shadow of the iron roof of the "L" until he could run no farther.

He knew without shadow of a doubt who possessed the *Wrath of Allah* now!

It was Buzak, ruler of El Zoonda— that Arab city in the desert, the stronghold of the terrible brethren of the Black Camels.

Buzak the White-footed One, so called because of his burned foot, the skin of which was permanently bleached and wrinkled by its injury.

Buzak, who had pursued over desert and plain, across cities and the broad ocean, until he had found his jewels again.

Gissing's hands stole trembling to his throat as he recalled the bloated, distorted features of Isaac Volk, as he had dangled dreadfully from his own rafters. Volk had died slowly—inch by inch—the breath squeezed out of his body by infinitesimal degrees—with many pauses between the torture that the victim's lungs might fill again. Yes! Volk had died many deaths that night, Gissing knew well.

The latter had lived long enough in El Zoonda to be horribly familiar with Buzak's methods: for there, protected by his clever disguise, his intimate knowledge of the ways and speech of the Arabs, and above all by his painful initiation to the membership of the Black Camels, he had witnessed many unforgettable crimes of the White-footed One.

And yet . . . yet the shimmering rose-red radiance of the lost jewels began to beckon him again—to shine like a false marsh-light luring him to destruction.

That incomparable loveliness . . . the light and warmth of the whole world was imprisoned in those stones!

He forgot Isaac Volk . . . he forgot past perils . . . he forgot the almost super-human strength and cunning of Buzak his enemy.

He only remembered that Buzak had pursued him, had deprived him of a treas-ure he held dearer than life, and was bearing this treasure farther and farther away from him every passing minute.

Gissing's fear dropped from him like a cloak.

"I will track him as he tracked me," he resolved. "I will find him and kill him before he reaches his desert city, and the jewels shall be mine . . . *mine* once more."

2

IT WAS a transformed Gissing who dis-embarked at Algiers and took train for a little white-walled city on the edge of the desert.

Transformed outwardly by a beard and spectacles, a tweed suit of remarkable de-sign, gaiters, thick boots, and a greenish velour hat with a feather stuck in its band, he was the picture of an untravelled tourist from the land of Wagner and beer.

But inwardly the transformation was far more devastating. The whole char-acter of the man was altered astoundingly from that of the Gissing who had skulked, shivering with fear, into that pawn-shop in Bleecker Street only three short weeks ago.

An alienist would have realized that here was a man whose reason tottered to a fall; a man obsessed and driven by a fixed idea; a man who had ceased to re-flect or consider, and was rushing in blind hurrying circles toward the center of that whirlpool which would presently engulf him into its vortex of insanity and death.

His fear of Buzak was utterly swamped by the overmastering fury of desire which drove him like a demon. Blind, thwarted, sick desire which reached out to his lost treasure and burned up the obstacles in his way, as a devouring flame licks up wood and straw.

THE following evening Gissing made his way through the high-walled tor-tuous ways of the city until he stood before a nail-studded door which was very familiar to him. He lifted its heavy iron knocker, and, after a short interval, the door was opened to him. There was a swift question, an answer, and an ex-clamation in joyous guttural Arabic, as the door was held wide open for Gissing to enter.

It was fully an hour before he re-emerged, wrapped in a voluminous bur-nous with the hood drawn well down over his head and face, completely hiding the strange dress and mask he wore beneath. It was the Dress of Ceremony which every member of the Black Camels wore when assembling for any public function. At these meetings, brother disguised himself from brother as cautiously as from an enemy, and they were known to each other by numbers only. Even Buzak, the Arch-devil of them all, mingled with the lesser brethren as a number too, and no man could say what that number was.

Buzak alone held the key to each brother's identity, and that was why Gissing had skilfully altered the Arabic numerals sewn in silver thread on the veil he wore, and was now 901.

He had to risk the possibility of the genuine 901 being present at the gather-ing for which he was bound, but his whole life was now one gigantic risk—details did not worry him!

On and on he went through the evil-smelling labyrinthin native streets until he reached a dark tree-shaded avenue, and a massive iron gate set in a high white wall.

"The Black Camel walks swiftly," he said in Arabic, as a tall form approached, wrapped in a burnous like his own.

"Where does it walk?"

"Over the gray face of the desert," was Gissing's prompt reply.

The guardian of the gate waved him on, and in a few moments Gissing was unburdening himself of his heavy burnous, and stood in the rich black silk robes of his order.

Around him were dozens of similar figures, all in black, all wearing a head-dress in the likeness of a camel, all with a long black silk veil falling straight from beneath the eyes to the hem of their robes, and on each veil was blazoned a silver number. Even voices were disguised, and Gissing, with the rest, spoke through a little mouthpiece which rendered speech curiously shrill and sibilant.

Gissing knew that Buzak was in the city, getting together men and camels and provisions for the long journey across the desert to El Zoonda. This fact had been easy to ascertain. And, as leader of the Black Camels, his enemy would almost certainly be present at this, the most important function of the year.

Gissing mixed freely with the crowd, so eager to find Buzak that he lost sight of the danger of meeting his own number face to face. How to discover Buzak? How to distinguish him in this mass of black-robed brethren?

In pairs, in groups, sometimes singly, the brethren were beginning to settle like a flock of blackbirds about the great domed hall, reclining on piles of soft cushions, or squatting cross-legged on wonderful silken rugs which were strewn over the mosaic floor. Incongruous enough they looked—somber macabre figures in the spacious brilliant place, with its white carven pillars and Moorish arches, its Oriental lavishness of color, its perfume of incense and attar of roses, and its general air of ease and voluptuousness.

Then luck—blind luck—led Gissing to sink down in a certain alcove. Several other brethren already sat there, exchanging remarks in the peculiar speech their mouthpieces produced.

One of the occupants of the alcove moved slightly to give the latest comer room, and in so doing, he dragged the robe of a man by his side, exposing the sandalled foot of his neighbor for a moment. It was only a fleeting glimpse that Gissing had, but it was enough. He recognized that foot, with its bleached wrinkled skin, puckered and drawn up like the hand of a washerwoman.

This was the White-footed One himself—Buzak the White-footed One who sat within reach of his hand! Gissing trembled with the shock of his sudden discovery, and for a moment the silver number on his enemy's veil wavered and melted dizzily before his eyes.

He fought the blind swimming sensation desperately, afraid that his good luck would vanish before he could take advantage of it, and that Buzak and his number would disappear like a mirage in the desert. Clenching his hands under the long loose sleeves of his robe, he forced himself to calm. Slowly the blood stopped pounding and rushing in his ears, slowly his vision cleared, and he saw the glittering number sharp and distinct once more.

"27."

Gissing leaned back heavily against a yielding mass of cushions and closed his eyes.

"I've got him!" he told himself, tremendous exultation surging up within him. "I've got him! I'll claim my privilige tonight, while the luck's with me . . . it can't fail me now! What luck . . . what staggering colossal luck . . . in another hour the jewels . . . no, no . . . I mustn't think of them yet."

"BRETHREN of the Black Camel!" The strange sibilant twittering of many voices ceased abruptly, as brother 901 mounted a dozen steps to a dais at the east end of the great hall, and stood outlined against a heavy saffron-hued brocade curtain.

"Brethren of the Black Camel!" Gissing's voice was audible, even in its disguise, from end to end of the room. "I claim a boon and a privilege at your hands."

"Speak, brother!" voices answered from every direction.

"Tonight in this place hath my face been blackened, and the greatest insult that one man can offer to another have I suffered. Only death can wipe out the memory of my shame."

"Speak further," commanded shrill voices.

"I overheard talk between two of the brethren here tonight, as I sat in the deep shadow behind a pillar. One brother boasted to another that he is my wife's lover, and he cast mud and filth on my name for an old half-witted fool, not able to guard his own treasure."

One of the brethren, an exceptionally tall man, stood up and hissed:

"Great wrong has been done thee. What boon dost thou crave at our hands?"

"The privilege of the Hunt!"

A babel broke out at these words. Rarely indeed was this deadly privilege demanded, and the thought of the grim spectacle they were to witness roused the primitive emotions of the Arabs to fever-heat.

The tall brother spoke again:

"It is thy right, brother 901. Hast thou well considered the penalty of thy failure —should thy aim be untrue?"

Gissing's inflamed imagination was incapable of dealing with failure or penalty, and he answered:

"I can not fail."

"Speak then, brother 901. Who is he thou wilt hunt in the darkness . . . who shall flee before thy wrath in the shadows of the night?"

"He who hath brought shame and dishonor on my house is number—27!"

"Brother 27—27—27!"

The cry went hissing from mouth to mouth, all the grotesque camel-heads turning and bobbing furiously, as each brother sought to identify the owner of the fatal number.

Then a wide lane opened to disclose number 27 standing in a little space apart, very still and quiet and ominous. Eager hands seized him, jostled him, pushed him until he was standing on the platform opposite his accuser.

Brother 27 was indeed cornered! Only a genius or a madman could have conceived such a plan of checkmating him. As one of the brethren, even Buzak could not refuse the challenge of the Hunt, without breaking a most sacred and binding vow. To break his vows was to lose face irrevocably before the brethren, to lose prestige, and power, and ultimately leadership; and that also meant the end of him as ruler of El Zoonda, for the Black Camels were the power behind his throne and they alone kept the cruel inhuman chief safe in his own city.

The Hunt must proceed—and Buzak must creep like a jungle thing at the mercy of the Hunter, unless chance delivered him from his implacable foe.

Gissing laughed in his newly grown beard as he calmly stared at the black figure confronting him.

"What madness hath seized thee?" hissed a voice from beneath the veil of 27. "I spoke no word of thy wife—or of any woman."

"Wallahi! Thy memory is short as thy remaining life!"

" 'Tis thou shalt lie cold under the moon tonight," was the answer. "A hunted thing has teeth and claws!"

"Thou sayest well! Claws too long and sharp, therefore will I cut them for thee!" was Gissing's retort.

During this brief duologue all the silent-footed brethren had withdrawn, melting like flakes of soot from the spacious hall, but their rapid speech could be heard from all sides where the deep balconies ran round the four walls.

The lights went out with the swift suddenness of a blow, and only a red crescent moon, high in the central dome of the splendid roof, shed a portentous glow on the scene. The tall brother—spokesman for the evening, and chosen for that office by purely arbitrary method—now joined the two on the platform.

"I will recite the Rule, Brethren of the Black Camel!" He presented a revolver to Gissing. "Thou—the Hunter—receive this weapon. May thy aim be true if thy cause is just. Swear now to shoot only at the signal of the bell . . . swear by the Sacred Fires of thy oath, brother 901!"

"By the Red Fire of Eblis,
　By the White Fire of Sun, Moon, and
　　Stars,
　By the Fires of Love and Hate,
　By the sacred undying Fire on the
　　Altar of Zoroaster—I swear!"

The spokesman turned to brother 27:

"This for thee, O Hunted One! This to warn the Hunter that his prey walks abroad to kill or be killed. Ring it when they dost hear my word of command.

Swear now by thy oath to obey my voice!"

Brother 27 took the little brass bell from the tall Arab, and swore as Gissing had done.

"O Hunter!" went on the speaker, "only at the sound of the bell shalt thou shoot. Three times shall thy prey give warning of his nearness to thee . . . three times shall thy vengeance speak. But if thou dost fail to kill, then art thou proved a liar and accurst, and shalt die the death of the Seven Flames this night.

"O Hunted One!" continued the voice, "three times shalt thou sound thy bell at my word of command. May thy teeth and claws protect thee if thou art innocent!"

Taking Buzak by the arm, the spokesman led him to the west wall and withdrew, leaving the combatants facing each other across the length of the hall. In a brief time the voice sounded again from a balcony.

"The Moon sets! The Hunter and his prey are abroad in the darkness. Let the Hunt begin!"

The red crescent light blinked out, and the great hall was plunged into absolutely impenetrable darkness.

TIME seemed to stand still. Not a whisper, not a breath was audible. The brethren might have been changed into black marble, so profoundly still were they, while in the hall below them death stalked on noiseless foot.

As Gissing moved forward, the scented air seemed to be roaring past his ears with the booming fury of a New England blizzard; fiery comets flashed and whizzed before his straining eyes as he stared and stared into the hot thick blackness. His head felt like a balloon blown up to bursting-point and filled with scorching air, while his feet were heavy and cold and dragged at his ankles like bags of wet sand.

"Give warning, Hunted One!"

The command was like an electric shock. A bell tinkled, a spurt of light was followed by a sharp report; then there was the sound of falling glass, and Gissing realized his shot had found its billet in one of the great mirrors panelling the walls.

Again the darkness of the Pit, the awful silence, the terrifying sound of his own heartbeats, and the click of his dry tongue in his mouth. For years and endless years it continued, this walking in a hot black world, where hands stretched out to seize him by the throat! The hands of the Strangler feeling in the dark for him . . . feeling . . . feeling!

"Give warning, Hunted One!"

Again the bell—again the flash and the report! Again the soft thick silence fell, while Hunter and Hunted moved blindly to and fro in hell.

Gissing's instinct, tuned to abnormal sensitivity by his maddened brain, held him still, with his back against the wall one outstretched hand had touched. He stood there like a thing of stone, while the centuries slipped past him; he stood and suffered there alone—most awfully alone—while around him all the souls whizzed past and were released from hell, while he must stay alone . . . alone!

"Give warning, Hunted One!"

The bell rang almost at Gissing's elbow, and his shot was followed by a fierce hiss of rage and the thud of a fall.

Swift as light, he was at Buzak's side, feeling the inert helpless body, patting—probing—searching frantically! Ah! . . . here in the armpit was something! A jerk . . . another . . . and Gissing pulled a small chamois leather bag from under the broad bandage which had held it close to Buzak's body, and thrust it into his own girdle.

Then he ascertained with deft sure touch that his bullet had injured but not killed the Strangler, for the heart beat slow and strong. As the red moon glowed overhead once more, he dashed to meet the brethren, who were swarming back into the hall.

He ran like some swift fire in their midst, and with mad fury snatched off veil after veil from before the faces of the paralyzed brethren. His own, too, he tore off and trampled under foot, and as the unveiled began to shout and run and gesticulate as madly as Gissing himself, in a few seconds none could say who had begun the assault, for Gissing ran to and fro bewailing and crying out his unveiled state like the rest.

The confusion was appalling. Torn veils were picked up from the ground at random by the outraged brethren, each one seeking to cover his features, no matter how. Gissing, alone, chose his veil with an eye to the number he picked up, and that number was not 901!

He had fastened it securely, and stood quietly fingering that packet in his girdle, when suddenly the place was bathed in all the colors of a desert sunrise, as one tinted globe after another filled with light.

The spokesman came forward, and after ascertaining that brother 27 was wounded, but not killed, he accepted the situation with the true fatalism of the East, and took the most convenient way out of his predicament.

"This is the deed of some *Shaitan* [demon] who is amongst us tonight!" he said at last. "Who may strive against fate? It was written that we should be afflicted by this terrible devil . . . what is written, is written! Let us invoke the aid of the Mighty Ones, that this *Shaitan* shall be driven from our midst."

This idea diverted the braver of the brethren; but the majority were too shaken to linger under a roof which sheltered so evil a spirit, Gissing being among the latter, and with them he hastened to escape before worse ills befell.

3

AND now that the marvelous jewels were in his hands once more, Gissing knew again the cold shadow of a monstrous fear.

Buzak still lived—and where, under the broad arch of heaven, was there a place of safety and peace for the man who had twice stolen from him the sacred *Wrath of Allah?*

Gissing's thoughts turned hungrily toward America—to his own place and his own people; but the threat of Isaac Volk's dangling body lay like a hideous shadow over that vast continent, darkening and blotting out his pictured return to his native land as fast as his longing painted it.

Gradually, after sleepless hours of torturing indecision, he realized that only the thought of the great mysterious desert brought any peace to his mind. The haunting loveliness of the silent wilderness attracted him more and more strongly, as his mind threshed everlastingly in red-hot circles which seemed always to bring him nearer and nearer to Buzak.

In the reaction from his late ordeal, following the three weeks planning and striving to regain the jewels, he now magnified his enemy's omnipotence, and his own danger, as passionately as he had recently ignored both.

At last, in burnous and sandals, his skin stained to a desert swarthiness, the blue *littram* of the Touaregg fastened over nose and mouth, he went down to the *souk* [market] to hear the latest news and gossip of the city.

"*Maleish!* Wouldst thou have me grow oranges the size of watermelons? Lo, these of my orchard are beyond praise!

Like honey and dew they cool the parched throat, and——"

Gissing put a piece of money in the merchant's hand, and taking the oranges, dropped them into the hanging peak of his hood.

"A caravan?" he asked indifferently, jerking his head toward a busy group of men in a far corner of the market.

"Thou sayest," replied the merchant. "It is the Sheik Daouad el Wahab who returns to his tents in the Tueyk mountains."

"That is a far journey, by the prophets!" exclaimed Gissing.

"He hath bought him a new wife, for the first one is angry that she, having born him two sons, must yet do all the work of his household. She gives Daouad no peace, clamoring day and night!"

"So he will double his cause of unrest!"

"*Wah!* He becomes old and fat, and Kirfa, his first wife, doth not dip her tongue in honey."

"He starts now, this Sheik Daouad?"

"Even this night," replied the merchant. "But another and a greater caravan goes south ere the new moon rises."

Gissing's heart beat slow and heavy in his breast as he looked questioningly at his companion.

"This is not a good time for any caravan, small or great," he commented.

"By Allah, thou hast wisdom behind thy teeth. This caravan goes to El Zoonda."

"Buzak!" was Gissing's hoarse exclamation.

"Who else!" agreed the merchant.

"He goes in haste."

"Swift as the hot south wind when it blows across the desert. Moreover, he pursueth one who hath done him some evil turn."

Gissing wandered on through the *souk*, receiving confirmation and denial of the fruit-merchant's tale on every hand; the market buzzed with Buzak's name, but no two reports of him agreed.

At last he noticed a camel-driver watering his beasts, and from his unusual activity Gissing judged him to be one of Buzak's slaves; and, being far apart from the rest, the white man approached him with caution.

"Thou art in haste," he remarked.

"There is need," was the surly response; then, melting instantly as his willing fingers closed over a coin— "Buzak the Sheik will start at dawn."

"Whither, my brother?"

The slave hesitated, and another and larger coin was dropped into his hand.

"I will tell thee, because thou hast named me brother, who am but a slave beneath thy feet. Moreover, with thy gold, perchance I may yet win freedom."

"Speak, in Allah's name!" implored Gissing.

"The caravan will start at dawn, but Buzak the Sheik doth not ride forth with it! This is a thing I heard by chance, while I lay chained and forgotten in the courtyard—but it is the truth. Buzak, my master, will remain secretly in this city, that he may search for an enemy who hath done him great evil."

Gissing's red-rimmed bloodshot eyes looked long into the pock-marked wretched face of the slave.

"Thou dost swear, by Allah?"

"By Allah, and by Allah. May my bones rot in the wilderness, and jackals pick them if I lie! May my soul go down to Eblis, and *Shaitans* torment me forever if I hide the truth from thee. Moreover it is a white man who hath injured Buzak, one who speaks with the tongues of the desert, and is like us in all points. All this came to my ears as Buzak spoke with one—Hassan ibn Shesh. This Hassan is to lead the caravan to El Zoonda, and is to learn aught he can on the journey, if perchance Buzak's enemy hath already fled into the desert."

"Hassan ibn Shesh!" A new stab of fear went through Gissing, as he recalled the obscene mass of flesh and the very evil face of the owner of that name. This was Buzak's chief councillor, the court-jester extraordinary, whose business it was to administer fresh zest and amusement to life in El Zoonda by devising new and spectacular deaths for Buzak's victims.

Under the *littram* he wore, Gissing's face was distorted by his panic, and his impulse was to run . . . and run . . . and run! To get away from this city where Buzak was, to run blindly somewhere . . . anywhere . . . at all costs to run!

Violently he restrained himself, and, with shaking hands, dropped a third piece of money into the slave's eager hand.

"Allah's peace be with thee!" he murmured hoarsely, and, turning from the well, he began to make his way unostentatiously to the caravan of Daouad el Wahab. Mechanically he threaded his way among the booths, and pyramids of red-gold oranges, to where the venerable Sheik in snowy turban, blue and scarlet burnous and gold slippers, sat peacefully directing his servants.

"Thou dost journey south, O Sheik?" asked Gissing, after the customary greeting.

"Even so," was the dignified response. "Who art thou, and why dost thou ask?"

"I am a physician—Fahd el Raschid— and would return in haste to Aufiz, where my wife lies sick. I came to this city for certain drugs and must journey swiftly back to her. I would pay thee well for thy company and protection, and for aught else thou dost demand."

The old Sheik deliberated in his long snowy beard, while Gissing's hands worked nervously under his sheltering sleeves. Lengthy argument and haggling followed, in which Gissing forced himself to take part with the zest proper to a born Arab, and the bargain was struck at last.

All the long hot hours until noon, Gissing sat in one of Daouad's tents, watching the *souk,* and especially that part of it where Buzak's caravan was preparing for its journey.

It was during the siesta that the shadow of the colossal bulk of Hassan ibn Shesh, councillor of El Zoonda, fell across the opening of the tent where Gissing sat.

Gissing looked directly up into Hassan's little black eyes, buried in rolls of flesh, and the shock of it steadied the whirling thoughts that were driving him insane. The need for action was a vast relief, and his distraught mind grew suddenly cold and clear. Drawing the knife at his girdle he plunged it again and again into the quivering flabby body of the councillor.

No outcry had disturbed the profound quiet of the hot noontide hour, and Gissing dragged the mountainous body into his tent without observation, and looked at it dispassionately.

For long he sat gravely considering his problem, his brain finding relief in the concentration necessary. Presently he let down the flap of his tent, and kneeling, began to dig furiously in the soft sand. All through the grilling hours of the afternoon he toiled, and the sun was setting red and low in the west before he had accomplished his task.

Then he untied his tent flap, and sat once more in the opening—the sandy floor smooth under his feet—and of Hassan ibn Shesh there was no sign whatever. Gissing scarcely felt the terrible exhaustion of his body, for his brain burnt like a hot coal in his head, and his eyes stared glassily from under his twitching brows.

Darkness fell, and Daouad and his little retinue set out at last: the line of camels moving with protesting roars toward the south and the illimitable desert, and Gissing's hot fingers were clasped round a certain little chamois leather bag which hung suspended from a chain at his neck, as he watched the terraced lights of the white-walled city grow dim behind him.

IT WAS at dawn on the tenth day out that Daouad discovered the physician Fahd el Raschid was not in his tent, nor was his camel tethered with the rest. For as long as he dared delay on that weary waterless route, the old Sheik waited, while his slaves rode forth to discover some trace of the missing man. They searched in vain, however, and at last, very reluctantly, the old Sheik with his new wife and his slaves set out without the physician.

And far out over the wide-flung sea of sand, Gissing rode on and on, holding in his hands a rose-red shining string of beauty.

He was alone at last—alone with his treasure . . . that matchless splendor of ancient days. Here he could worship it . . . drink in its glowing life . . . feel the blood beat strongly within him once more as the terrible glorious thing he had won flashed in the sunlight.

His treasure . . . his life . . . his own!

He rode on and on across the blinding sands—on and on by sunlight and starlight—on and on until neither food nor water remained, and his camel sank down to her knees and never rose again.

It was all one to Gissing. He huddled down against the dying beast, and smiled at his rose-red jewels and whispered hoarsely to his treasure.

He never felt the bitter night wind that blew through his very bones, for the flame at the heart of each perfect stone he held warmed him to the soul.

At dawn his rapid whispering voice failed, and the cold hands which held his jewels before his darkening vision dropped heavily to his sides.

Very cold and still sat Gissing, as the last pale stars glimmered and vanished—unable any more to see the sun touch to life the dancing magic flames of the *Wrath of Allah* . . . for the shadow of the Black Camel was dark and heavy on his eyelids.

But the *Wrath of Allah* flashed and flashed again in the eye of the rising sun.

The Curse

By CAPTAIN ED SMITH

In India it is considered very dangerous to insult a Yogi, or holy man

JANKI was a very holy man indeed. Though his coarse matted hair was indescribably filthy and swarmed with vermin, though he smeared mud and ashes on his emaciated, almost naked body, wandering aimlessly through the length and breadth of teeming India, yet his begging-bowl was always full, there was always a bare-legged, ragged lad to make the rounds of the charitable who might wish to acquire merit. If the bowl came back heaped full of curried ghee with a great dab of melting rancid butter atop, who was Janki to begrudge the lad his just share of the spoils from the foray among the bazar habitués, or from the scrawny squalid mothers who dwelt beyond them? If that lad brought back even better provender and a timid request for a love philtre or a charm to assure the speedy birth of a son and heir, who was Janki to refuse so reasonable and modest a return? Impartially he gave such slight tokens, impassively he ate whatever was set before him; then, with the empty bowl hanging in its accustomed place at his girdle, he sat oblivious to sun and shade in the Silence. Truly Janki was a very holy man indeed!

He had come into the Aravalli Hills from the burning plains of Rajputana where the hot earth and its crops turned sere and yellow, even as the jungle itself; where the parched ground baked to a stone-like hardness and opened in huge gaping cracks, where the peasant brats died like flies of the cholera, and the burning-ghats were ever smoking.

The Feringhee, the Anglesi, had sought refuge in the cooler hills; Mount Abu was crowded with them—and with Rajputana princelings come to play polo, to gamble or to royster in such Oriental viciousness as they could find or else bring with them. All who could had left the parched plains for the Aravellis, the long hill road to Mount Abu was dotted with every conceivable conveyance as whites and natives alike fled the murderous heat of the lowlands.

Thither, too, came Janki, impervious alike to heat or cold, sun or rain, impervious also to feast or famine—though I will be frank to say that famines came but rarely to Janki's way.

Perhaps the multitudinous gods of Hind watched over him; perhaps they guided him into paths of peace and plenty — howbeit, when famine and drouth came, when disease spread its somber pinions over the land, Janki was always elsewhere. Truly Janki was a very holy man indeed!

There are Anglesi sahibs who will snort and declare that Janki was a charlatan—a fake and a fraud—instead of a very holy yogi. They will say that these very facts show that he was coldly calculating; that these very things prove their contentions conclusively instead of proving what every native believed about him regardless of his race or creed. I do not know. I refuse to be drawn into any controversy. Those same white sahibs will tell you that no man born of the fertile fruitful earth may peer into the future; they will discourse learnedly and long-windedly on coincidence when that subject happens to come up. Once more I refuse to be drawn into any argument.

But I shall tell you a tale of Janki and you may judge for yourself. The tale was told to me beside the leaping flames in the velvety darkness when the caravanserais and the bazars had been left far behind us, when the keen night winds of the high hills whistled sharply down the Pass and djinns and demons rode abroad on their wintry blasts. The shivering Plainsman who told it to me got it in the Serai that stands hard by the Motee Bazar, interposing its swarming colorful bulk between them and the great iron way that carries the sahibs on their foolish, furious, petty business trips across the great plains that have resounded to the footfalls of so many and so varied a horde of conquerors.

This Plainsman brought with him also a tale about another holy man—oh, such a salt, salt tale—but enough! The low-born one told me many tales, tales that he swore by the beard of his father were all true talk and he was bound to me by many ties other than that of marriage; but, having heard him bargaining in the horse bazars for the sorry nag that I bestrode, my faith in his probity and virtue was not then so strong as it once was. The tale came to him in the devious, round-about way that is the Orient, wherein a nautch, an Afridi and various and sundry others figured, so I myself can hardly vouch for it.

On that long steep hill that leads up to Mount Abu, lined with its sweetmeat stalls, horse-traders' camps, and those of vendors of this and that, Janki strode. The natives made a way for him through the press and accorded him far more respect than they did for the haughty hill rajah who had just preceded him.

As Janki stepped around a bend three horsemen spurred out of a narrow side road. White sahibs, all of them, they paid not a second glance at the natives who gave back on either hand. Not so, however, their horses; that of the youngest, a skittish sorrel, became unmanageable. Its rider sawed roughly on the bit as the animal wheeled and snorted, attempting vainly to control its sudden panic, yet unable to prevent it from bolting. In its sudden, furious rush the horse hurled Janki into the dust.

The yogi rose to his feet, his face a mask of diabolical anger. His eyes glared. He shook his fist after the swiftly receding form, mouthing curses after that devil and his demon steed.

Contemptuously the older of the two remaining sahibs tossed a few rupees at the holy man, who let them fall unheeded into the dusty way.

MOMENTS passed. The two sahibs sat their mounts impassively as they awaited the return of their comrade. The holy man raged and rained vituperations and nameless obscenities after the absent one. Flecks of foam dripped from his lips onto his heaving chest.

"Have done, beggar," the older sahib admonished Janki at last. "Pick up your rupees and begone!"

Janki swung about and glared at him; his curses stuck in his throat. He drew a deep breath.

"Beggar!" he snorted. "You dare to call me beggar — to think that a few miserable annas can right the wrong the accursed foreign devil——"

The sahib raised his riding-crop in a threatening manner.

"Peace, you!" he shouted.

His companion placed a restraining hand on his arm. The older man shook it impatiently aside as Janki darted between them, face contorted, a shaking accusing finger pointed at the choleric white.

"You, too!" he shouted. "You, too, I curse! Hear me, gods! Smite this impious one. Lay his proud form in agony before me. Teach him the folly of insulting your resistless might! As for that other, I call upon the wild beasts of the jungle to tear the life from his white throat. When he feels their claws rending his flesh, their hot breath in his face, may his dying thoughts be of the holy ones he has offended!"

About them the natives drew slowly back in superstitious awe as the shaking yogi seemed to swell and dwarf them into insignificance. Janki turned slowly away. Contemptuously leaving the silver coins lying in the road, he strode up the hill as the youngest sahib rejoined his fellows.

"Rubbish!" snorted the choleric sahib. "Damn him! What is India coming to? That dirty beggar dared to threaten me — and you, too, Sawyer!"

He turned to the youngster.

"The beggar had the impudence to threaten us because your mare bowled him

O. S.—8

over when she bolted. Damn his filthy hide!"

The youngster chuckled.

"That's rich! What was it, unk? The usual bunk? Hell-fire and brimstone, like the old rector at home?"

"It's no laughing-matter, Sawyer," Kensington interposed. "That was a yogi —a mahatma! When you've been here as long as I have——"

"You've been here too long, Kensington; that's the trouble!" The choleric major cut him short. "Listening every day to these superstitious beggars, living among them, has made you into an old woman afraid of the dark!"

Kensington subsided once more. Major Ellison turned to his nephew:

"That filthy beggar called on the wild animals of the jungle to claw you up, to tear open your throat——"

Sawyer Ellison chuckled.

"That's a ripping long shot, unk! How he knew of my passion for big game hunting beats me, unless he got it from some of Ken's native servants. Elephants in Africa — lions — bear in the Kodiak Island region, that tiger in Nepal—he almost got me—remember? Maybe one of them will get me yet, though I doubt it. Well, it's all in the game. It's a chance I take without thinking. What did he promise you, uncle?" Sawyer's eyes were merry.

The major turned to Kensington disgustedly.

"What was it, Ken?" he growled. "Something about stretching me out in agony, wasn't it?"

Kensington nodded soberly.

"Just the same, I wish you fellows would call that leopard hunt off for tonight, old chap." His eyes were gloomy.

"What! Call it off just because a balmy beggar goes musty when I upset his apple cart in the little old road? Nothing doing,

Ken!" Sawyer interposed quickly. "Why, the bait is set, the machin is built and the tonga will be around for us tonight after tiffin. Never! That's a bit too thick, old thing. No sir! the hunt goes on as per schedule—and may we bag the brace of them! Leopards! Big ones, too, from the size of their pugs—I measured them myself! I've got to have a leopard hide for the den; don't I, unk?" Sawyer turned to his uncle for support. The elder Ellison nodded dourly.

"Watch your step, then," Kensington said resignedly. "I'll go, of course," he added quickly.

"Good!" Major Ellison snapped. His grim face expanded with satisfaction. "That's all poppycock, Ken. I'll bet that old beggar has forgotten all about his momentary anger before this. . . . I hope we bag a big 'un. If we should shoot a pair of them—well, that *will* be a tale to tell at the club!"

He touched his horse lightly with his crop and the trio made their way swiftly to the Kensington bungalow.

DINNER was over. In the black night the tonga stopped abruptly. The three hunters dismounted with alacrity, saw to their guns, inspected the mutilated bodies of the goats that the two leopards had slain the night before and that had been left carefully untouched at Kensington's orders. Swiftly they climbed up to the machin, the hunter's platform, in the wild fig tree that overlooked the clearing, hurriedly built that very day by Kensington's numerous native servants.

Far up the hill above them the light of Mount Abu twinkled, vying with the fat tropical stars and the flitting, twinkling fireflies. Ghostly whisperings and furtive rustlings filled the air as the jungle awoke from its day-dreaming for the serious business of the night.

Sawyer Ellison slapped at the mosquitos that hovered about them in swarms, biting every exposed place. He stifled a groan as he rubbed cramped aching leg muscles. Fervently he wished that he dared to move, to stretch, to turn from that intolerable position, yet mindful that his companions suffered similarly, and stoically forbore to relieve themselves lest they scare away any lurking game.

The moon rose, flooding the opening with its silver. The minutes passed in maddening slowness. A twig snapped sharply. The three in the machin tensed to instant watchfulness.

From the dense, shadowy jungle stole a sleek spotted body. Sawyer's eyes widened. A leopard! He eyed its lithe, wicked grace, its huge bulk—a real trophy—one to be proud of—if he could manage to secure it. Slowly his rifle raised.

At that instant the leopard's mate crept into view on his right, another splendid cat, almost the equal of the other. The female leaped playfully at her mate; the two played like enormous cats, though their playful slaps at each other would have broken bones for any of the hunters had they been there on the ground with the two. Reluctantly the two Ellisons held their fire for a surer shot. The leopards ceased their playful antics and crept swiftly toward the mutilated carcasses of the goats.

At almost the same instant Ellison's guns roared. The female leopard leaped high, clawing and growling in her death agonies, tearing up the tough jungle grasses in flying shards. The other beast dropped like a stone.

Incredulously Kensington eyed his silent weapon. Sheepishly he slipped off the safety catch that had prevented an echoing, answering roar when his nervous finger had pressed the trigger.

"Buck fever!" Sawyer jeered softly as he watched in amusement. "After all

these years! Ken, old dear, I'm surprized!"

"Didn't need the other gun, anyway,"
the major muttered. "They're both
dead." He eased himself into a better
position.

Kensington misinterpreted the movement.

"Don't go down, my dear fellow," he
whispered. "I've known supposedly dead
leopards to charge and kill an over-hasty
hunter."

"Never thought of doing such a
thing," the major growled testily. "I'm
not such a greenhorn!"

An hour passed and still the clearing
lay as silently as before.

"I hear the tonga coming back!" Sawyer exclaimed. "Come on! Let's go!"

He slid swiftly down one side of the
rope ladder, sailor fashion, his gun slung
over his back. Kensington saw him carelessly kick the female with a hurried foot
as he passed the body. There was no response. The beast was dead. Sawyer Ellison ran over to the larger animal.

The major cautiously thrust his portly
bulk over the edge of the machin, feeling
with his legs for the rounds of the swaying, spidery rope ladder.

The supposedly dead leopard sprang
up with a roar. Before Kensington could
recover from his stupor Sawyer lay on the
ground with the snarling, raging beast
above him. Its murderous claws were
shredding his clothing, tearing his flesh
to ribbons, the snarling head was thrust
into his face as its white fangs sought his
throat.

With a hoarse shout Major Ellison

slipped from the edge of the machin and
fell heavily to the ground twenty feet below.

Twice Kensington sighted at that raging beast, each time pausing and staying
his eager finger lest he kill his friend. At
last, in desperation, he fired.

The beast rolled over and over, a snarling, spitting, clawing, squalling fury of
destruction. Gradually its struggles subsided, it lay sprawled in the white moonlight.

Kensington reloaded the empty barrel
and slid swiftly to the ground. The major
was groaning, his florid face ashen and
drawn. One glance was enough. Kensington felt sick. The fall had broken
both the major's legs; through the bloody
trousers protruded a splintered bone.
Before Kensington's eyes floated a wavering picture of a face screwed into a de-
moniac mask of rage under filthy matted
hair, of glowing, glaring eyes and foam-
flecked lips—in his ears sounded again
wild screaming curses. . . .

He hurried to the younger man. He
stared at the gaping, torn throat through
which life had already fled. He shuddered anew at the bloody mass of torn
flesh that had been his friend and school-
mate. . . .

From the dense jungle behind him
floated an elfin laugh, faint, clear, bell-
like—was it one of the memsahibs up
there at Mount Abu?

With excited gabblings, and swirling,
smoking torches held high above their
heads, that swayed in a wild grotesque
dance, his servants broke through the
jungle screen into the clearing.

Come, fill the Cup, and in the fire of Spring
Your Winter-garment of Repentance fling;
The Bird of Time has but a little way
To flutter—and the Bird is on the Wing.
—*Rubáiyát of Omar Khayyam.*

The Voice of El-Lil

By ROBERT E. HOWARD

*In the heart of African Somaliland was an Oriental city transplanted from
the Tigris-Euphrates valley—a modern tale of ancient Sumeria*

MASKAT, like many another port, is a haven for the drifters of many nations who bring their tribal customs and peculiarities with them. Turk rubs shoulders with Greek and Arab squabbles with Hindoo. The tongues of half the Orient resound in the loud smelly bazar. Therefore it did not seem particularly incongruous to hear, as I leaned on a bar tended by a smirking Eurasian, the musical notes of a Chinese gong sound clearly through the lazy hum of native traffic. There was certainly nothing so startling in those mellow tones that the big Englishman next me should start and swear and spill his whisky-and-soda on my sleeve.

He apologized and berated his clumsiness with honest profanity, but I saw he was shaken. He interested me as his type always does—a fine upstanding fellow he was, over six feet tall, broad-shouldered, narrow-hipped, heavy-limbed, the perfect fighting man, brown-faced, blue-eyed and tawny-haired. His breed is old as Europe, and the man himself brought to mind vague legendary characters — Hengist, Hereward, Cerdic—born rovers and fighters of the original Anglo-Saxon stock.

I saw, furthermore, that he was in a mood to talk. I introduced myself, ordered drinks and waited. My specimen thanked me, muttered to himself, quaffed his liquor hastily and spoke abruptly:

"You're wondering why a grown man should be so suddenly upset by such a small thing—well, I admit that damned gong gave me a start. It's that fool Yotai

Lao, bringing his nasty joss sticks and Buddhas into a decent town—for a half-penny I'd bribe some Moslem fanatic to cut his yellow throat and sink his confounded gong into the gulf. And I'll tell you why I hate the thing.

"My name," said my Saxon, "is Bill Kirby. It was in Jibuti on the Gulf of Aden that I met John Conrad. A slim, keen-eyed young New Englander he was —professor too, for all his youth. Victim of obsession also, like most of his kind. He was a student of bugs, and it was a particular bug that had brought him to the East Coast; or rather, the hope of the blooming beast, for he never found it. It was almost uncanny to see the chap work himself into a blaze of enthusiasm when speaking on his favorite subject. No doubt he could have taught me much I should know, but insects are not among my enthusiasms, and he talked, dreamed and thought of little else at first. . . .

"Well, we paired off well from the start. He had money and ambitions and I had a bit of experience and a roving foot. We got together a small, modest but efficient safari and wandered down into the back country of Somaliland. Now you'll hear it spoken today that this country has been exhaustively explored and I can prove that statement to be a lie. We found things that no white man has ever dreamed of.

"We had trekked for the best part of a month and had gotten into a part of the country I knew was unknown to the average explorer. The veldt and thorn forests gave way to what approached real

116

"Her dancing was a whirl of fire and passion."

jungle and what natives we saw were a thick-lipped, low-browed, dog-toothed breed—not like the Somali at all. We wandered on though, and our porters and askari began muttering among themselves. Some of the black fellows had been hobnobbing with them and telling them tales that frightened them from going on. Our men wouldn't talk to me or Conrad about it, but we had a camp servant, a half-caste named Selim, and I told him to see what he could learn. That night he came to my tent. We had pitched camp in a sort of big glade and had built a thorn boma; for the lions were raising merry Cain in the bush.

" 'Master,' said he in the mongrel English he was so proud of, 'them black fella he is scaring the porters and askari with bad ju-ju talk. They be tell about a mighty ju-ju curse on the country in which we go to, and——'

"He stopped short, turned ashy, and my head jerked up. Out of the dim, jungle-haunted mazes of the south whispered a haunting voice. Like the echo of an echo it was, yet strangely distinct, deep, vibrant, melodious. I stepped from my tent and saw Conrad standing before a fire, taut and tense as a hunting hound.

" 'Did you hear that?' he asked. 'What was it?'

" 'A native drum,' I answered—but we both knew I lied. The noise and chatter of our natives about their cooking-fires had ceased as if they had all died suddenly.

"We heard nothing more of it that night, but the next morning we found ourselves deserted. The black boys had decamped with all the luggage they could lay hand to. We held a council of war, Conrad, Selim and I. The half-caste was scared pink, but the pride of his white blood kept him carrying on.

" 'What now?' I asked Conrad. 'We've our guns and enough supplies to give us a sporting chance of reaching the coast.'

" 'Listen!' he raised his hand. Out across the bush-country throbbed again that haunting whisper. 'We'll go on. I'll never rest until I know what makes that sound. I never heard anything like it in the world before.'

" 'The jungle will pick our bally bones,' I said. He shook his head.

" 'Listen!' said he.

"It was like a call. It got into your blood. It drew you as a fakir's music draws a cobra. I knew it was madness. But I didn't argue. We cached most of our duffle and started on. Each night we built a thorn boma and sat inside it while the big cats yowled and grunted outside. And ever clearer as we worked deeper and deeper in the jungle mazes, we heard that voice. It was deep, mellow, musical. It made you dream strange things; it was pregnant with vast age. The lost glories of antiquity whispered in its booming. It centered in its resonance all the yearning and mystery of life; all the magic soul of the East. I awoke in the middle of night to listen to its whispering echoes, and slept to dream of sky-towering minarets, of long ranks of bowing, brown-skinned worshippers, of purple-canopied peacock thrones and thundering golden chariots.

"Conrad had found something at last that rivalled his infernal bugs in his interest. He didn't talk much; he hunted insects in an absent-minded way. All day he would seem to be in an attitude of listening, and when the deep golden notes would roll out across the jungle, he would tense like a hunting dog on the scent, while into his eyes would steal a look strange for a civilized professor. By Jove, it's curious to see some ancient primal influence steal through the veneer of a cold-blooded scientist's soul and touch the red flow of life beneath! It was new and strange to Conrad; here was something he couldn't explain away with his new-fangled, bloodless psychology.

"WELL, we wandered on in that mad search—for it's the white man's curse to go into Hell to satisfy his curiosity. Then in the gray light of an early dawn the camp was rushed. There was no fight. We were simply flooded and submerged by numbers. They must have stolen up and surrounded us on all sides; for the first thing I knew, the camp was full of fantastic figures and there were half a dozen spears at my throat. It rasped me terribly to give up without a shot fired, but there was no bettering it, and I cursed myself for not having kept a better lookout. We should have expected something of the kind, with that devilish chiming in the south.

"There were at least a hundred of them, and I got a chill when I looked at them closely. They weren't black boys and they weren't Arabs. They were lean men of middle height, light yellowish brown, with dark eyes and big noses. They wore no beards and their heads were close-shaven. They were clad in a sort of tunic, belted at the waist with a wide leather girdle, and sandals. They also wore a queer kind of iron helmet, peaked at the top, open in front and coming down nearly to their shoulders behind and at the sides. They carried big metal-braced shields, nearly square, and were armed with narrow-bladed spears, strangely made bows and arrows, and short straight swords such as I had never seen before—or since.

"They bound Conrad and me hand and foot and they butchered Selim then and there—cut his throat like a pig while he kicked and howled. A sickening sight —Conrad nearly fainted and I dare say I looked a bit pale myself. Then they set out in the direction we had been heading, making us walk between them, with our hands tied behind our backs and their spears threatening us. They brought along our scanty dunnage, but from the way they carried the guns I didn't believe they knew what those were for. Scarcely a word had been spoken between them and when I essayed various dialects I only got the prod of a spear-point. Their silence was a bit ghostly and altogether ghastly. I felt as if we'd been captured by a band of spooks.

"I didn't know what to make of them. They had the look of the Orient about them but not the Orient with which I was familiar, if you understand me. Africa is of the East but not one with it. They looked no more African than a Chinaman does. This is hard to explain. But I'll say this: Tokyo is Eastern, and Benares is equally so, but Benares symbolizes a different, older phase of the Orient, while Pekin represents still another, and older one. These men were of an Orient I had never known; they were part of an East older than Persia—older than Assyria—older than Babylon! I felt it about them like an aura and I shuddered from the gulfs of Time they symbolized. Yet it fascinated me, too. Beneath the Gothic arches of an age-old jungle, speared along by silent Orientals whose type has been forgotten for God knows how many eons, a man can have fantastic thoughts. I almost wondered if these fellows were real, or but the ghosts of warriors dead four thousand years!

"The trees began to thin and the ground sloped upward. At last we came out upon a sort of cliff and saw a sight that made us gasp. We were looking into a big valley surrounded entirely by high, steep cliffs, through which various streams had cut narrow canyons to feed a good-sized lake in the center of the valley. In the center of that lake was an island and on that island was a temple and at the farther end of the lake was a city! No native village of mud and bamboo, either. This seemed to be of stone, yellowish-brown in color.

"The city was walled and consisted of square-built, flat-topped houses, some apparently three or four stories high. All the shores of the lake were in cultivation and the fields were green and flourishing, fed by artificial ditches. They had a system of irrigation that amazed me. But the most astonishing thing was the temple on the island.

"I gasped, gaped and blinked. It was the tower of Babel true to life! Not as tall or as big as I'd imagined it, but some ten tiers high and sullen and massive just like the pictures, with that same intangible impression of evil hovering over it.

"Then as we stood there, from that vast pile of masonry there floated out across the lake that deep resonant booming—close and clear now—and the very cliffs seemed to quiver with the vibrations of that music-laden air. I stole a glance at Conrad; he looked all at sea. He was of that class of scientists who have the universe classified and pigeonholed and everything in its proper little nook. By Jove! It knocks them in a heap to be confronted with the paradoxical-unexplainable-shouldn't-be more than it does common chaps like you and me, who haven't much preconceived ideas of things in general.

"The soldiers took us down a stairway cut into the solid rock of the cliffs and we went through irrigated fields where shaven-headed men and dark-eyed women paused in their work to stare curiously at us. They took us to a big, iron-braced gate where a small body of soldiers equipped like our captors challenged them, and after a short parley we were escorted into the city. It was much like any other Eastern city—men, women and children going to and fro, arguing, buying and selling. But all in all, it had that same effect of apartness — of vast antiquity. I couldn't classify the architecture any more than I could understand the language. The only thing I could think of as I stared at those squat, square buildings was the huts certain low-caste, mongrel peoples still build in the valley of the Euphrates in Mesopotamia. Those huts might be a degraded evolution from the architecture in that strange African city.

"OUR captors took us straight to the largest building in the city, and while we marched along the streets, we discovered that the houses and walls were not of stone after all, but a sort of brick. We were taken into a huge-columned hall before which stood ranks of silent soldiery, and taken before a dais up which led broad steps. Armed warriors stood behind and on either side of a throne, a scribe stood beside it, girls glad in ostrich-plumes lounged on the broad steps, and on the throne sat a grim-eyed devil who alone of all the men of that fantastic city wore his hair long. He was black-bearded, wore a sort of crown and had the haughtiest, cruelest face I ever saw on any man. An Arab sheikh or Turkish shah was a lamb beside him. He reminded me of some artist's conception of Belshazzar or the Pharaohs—a king who was more than a king in his own mind and the eyes of his people—a king who was at once king and high priest and god.

"Our escort promptly prostrated themselves before him and knocked their heads on the matting until he spoke a languid word to the scribe and this personage signed for them to rise. They rose, and the leader began a long rigmarole to the king, while the scribe scratched away like mad on a clay tablet and Conrad and I stood there like a pair of blooming gaping jackasses, wondering what it was all about. Then I heard a word repeated continually, and each time he spoke it, he indicated us. The word sounded like 'Akkaddian,' and suddenly my brain reeled with the possibilities it betokened. It couldn't be — yet it had to be!

"Not wanting to break in on the conversation and maybe lose my bally head, I said nothing, and at last the king gestured and spoke, the soldiers bowed again and seizing us, hustled us roughly from the royal presence into a columned corridor, across a huge chamber and into a small cell where they thrust us and locked the door. There was only a heavy bench and one window, closely barred.

" 'My heavens, Bill,' exclaimed Conrad, 'who could have imagined anything equal to this? It's like a nightmare—or a tale from *The Arabian Nights!* Where are we? Who are these people?'

" 'You won't believe me,' I said, 'but —you've read of the ancient empire of Sumeria?'

" 'Certainly; it flourished in Mesopotamia some four thousand years ago. But what—by Jove!' he broke off, staring at me wide-eyed as the connection struck him.

" 'I leave it to you what the descendants of an Asia-Minor kingdom are doing in East Africa,' I said, feeling for my pipe, 'but it must be—the Sumerians built their cities of sun-dried brick. I saw men making bricks and stacking them up to dry along the lake shore. The mud is remarkably like that you find in the Tigris and Euphrates valley. Likely that's why these chaps settled here. The Sumerians wrote on clay tablets by scratching the surface with a sharp point just as the chap was doing in the throne room.

" 'Then look at their arms, dress and physiognomy. I've seen their art carved on stone and pottery and wondered if those big noses were part of their faces or part of their helmets. And look at that temple in the lake! A small counterpart of the temple reared to the god El-lil in Nippur—which probably started the myth of the tower of Babel.

" 'But the thing that clinches it is the fact that they referred to us as Akkaddians. Their empire was conquered and subjugated by Sargon of Akkad in 2750 B. C. If these are descendants of a band who fled their conqueror, it's natural that, pent in these hinterlands and separated from the rest of the world, they'd come to call all outlanders Akkaddians, much as secluded Oriental nations call all Europeans Franks in memory of Martel's warriors who scuttled them at Tours.'

" 'Why do you suppose they haven't been discovered before now?'

" 'Well, if any white man's been here before, they took good care he didn't get out to tell his tale. I doubt if they wander much; probably think the outside world's overrun with bloodthirsty Akkaddians.'

"At this moment the door of our cell opened to admit a slim young girl, clad only in a girdle of silk and golden breastplates. She brought us food and wine, and I noted how lingeringly she gazed at Conrad. And to my surprise she spoke to us in fair Somali.

" 'Where are we?' I asked her. 'What are they going to do with us? Who are you?'

" 'I am Naluna, the dancer of El-lil,' she answered—and she looked it—lithe as a she-panther she was. 'I am sorry to see you in this place; no Akkaddian goes forth from here alive.'

" 'Nice friendly sort of chaps,' I grunted, but glad to find some one I could talk to and understand. 'And what's the name of this city?'

" 'This is Eridu,' said she. 'Our ancestors came here many ages ago from ancient Sumer, many moons to the East. They were driven by a great and cruel king, Sargon of the Akkaddians—desert people. But our ancestors would not be slaves like their kin, so they fled, thousands of them in one great band, and traversed many strange, savage countries before they came to this land.'

"Beyond that her knowledge was very vague and mixed up with myths and improbable legends. Conrad and I discussed it afterward, wondering if the old Sumerians came down the west coast of Arabia and crossed the Red Sea about where Mocha is now, or if they went over the Isthmus of Suez and came down on the African side. I'm inclined to the last opinion. Likely the Egyptians met them as they came out of Asia Minor and chased them south. Conrad thought they might have made most of the trip by water, because, as he said, the Persian Gulf ran up something like a hundred and thirty miles farther than it does now, and Old Eridu was a seaport town. But just at the moment something else was on my mind.

" 'Where did you learn to speak Somali?' I asked Naluna.

" 'When I was little,' she answered, 'I wandered out of the valley and into the jungle where a band of raiding black men caught me. They sold me to a tribe who lived near the coast and I spent my childhood among them. But when I had grown into girlhoood I remembered Eridu and one day I stole a camel and rode across many leagues of veldt and jungle and so came again to the city of my birth. In all Eridu I alone can speak a tongue not mine own, except for the black slaves—and they speak not all, for we cut out their tongues when we capture them. The people of Eridu go not forth beyond the jungles and they traffic not with the black peoples who sometimes come against us, except as they take a few slaves.'

"I asked her why they killed our camp servant and she said that it was forbidden for blacks and whites to mate in Eridu and the offspring of such union was not allowed to live. They didn't like the poor beggar's color.

"Naluna could tell us little of the history of the city since its founding, outside the events that had happened in her own memory—which dealt mainly with scattered raids by a cannibalistic tribe living in the jungles to the south, petty intrigues of court and temple, crop failures and the like—the scope of a woman's life in the East is much the same, whether in the palace of Akbar, Cyrus or Asshurbanipal. But I learned that the ruler's name was Sostoras and that he was both high priest and king—just as the rulers were in old Sumer, four thousand years ago. El-lil was their god, who abode in the temple in the lake, and the deep booming we had heard was, Naluna said, the voice of the god.

"At last she rose to go, casting a wistful look at Conrad, who sat like a man in a trance—for once his confounded bugs were clean out of his mind.

" 'Well,' said I, 'what d'you think of it, young fella-me-lad?'

" 'It's incredible,' said he, shaking his head. 'It's absurd—an intelligent tribe living here four thousand years and never advancing beyond their ancestors.'

" 'You're stung with the bug of progress,' I told him cynically, cramming my pipe bowl full of weed. 'You're thinking of the mushroom growth of your own country. You can't generalize on an Oriental from a Western viewpoint. What about China's famous long sleep? As for these chaps, you forget they're no tribe but the tag-end of a civilization that lasted longer than any has lasted since. They passed the peak of their progress thousands of years ago. With no intercourse with the outside world and no new blood to stir them up, these people are slowly sinking in the scale. I'd wager their culture and art are far inferior to that of their ancestors.'

" 'Then why haven't they lapsed into complete barbarism?'

" 'Maybe they have, to all practical purposes,' I answered, beginning to draw on my old pipe. 'They don't strike me as being quite the proper thing for offsprings of an ancient and honorable civilization. But remember they grew slowly and their retrogression is bound to be equally slow. Sumerian culture was unusually virile. Its influence is felt in Asia Minor today. The Sumerians had their civilization when our bloomin' ancestors were scrapping with cave bears and sabertooth tigers, so to speak. At least the Aryans hadn't passed the first milestones on the road to progress, whoever their animal neighbors were. Old Eridu was a seaport of consequence as early as 6500 B. C. From then to 2750 B. C. is a bit of time for any empire. What other empire stood as long as the Sumerian? The Akkaddian dynasty established by Sargon stood two hundred years before it was overthrown by another Semitic people, the Babylonians, who borrowed their culture from Akkaddian Sumer just as Rome later stole hers from Greece; the Elamitish Kassite dynasty supplanted the original Babylonian, the Assyrian and the Chaldean followed—well, you know the rapid succession of dynasty on dynasty in Asia Minor, one Semitic people overthrowing another, until the real conquerors hove in view on the Eastern horizon—the Aryan Medes and Persians—who were destined to last scarcely longer than their victims.

" 'Compare each fleeting kingdom with the long dreamy reign of the ancient pre-Semitic Sumerians! We think the Minoan Age of Crete is a long time back, but the Sumerian empire of Erech was already beginning to decay before the rising power of Sumerian Nippur, before the ancestors of the Cretans had emerged from the Neolithic Age. The Sumerians had something the succeeding Hamites, Semites and Aryans lacked. They were stable. They grew slowly and if left alone would have decayed as slowly as these fellows are decaying. Still and all, I note these chaps have made one advancement—notice their weapons?

" 'Old Sumer was in the Bronze Age. The Assyrians were the first to use iron for anything besides ornaments. But these lads have learned to work iron—probably a matter of necessity. No copper hereabouts but plenty of iron ore, I daresay.'

" 'But the mystery of Sumer still remains,' Conrad broke in. 'Who are they? Whence did they come? Some authorities maintain they were of Dravidian origin, akin to the Basques——'

" 'It won't stick, me lad,' said I. 'Even allowing for possible admixture of Aryan or Turanian blood in the Dravidian descendants, you can see at a glance these people are not of the same race.'

" 'But their language——' Conrad began arguing, which is a fair way to pass the time while you're waiting to be put in the cooking-pot, but doesn't prove much

except to strengthen your own original ideas.

"NALUNA came again about sunset with food, and this time she sat down by Conrad and watched him eat. Seeing her sitting thus, elbows on knees and chin on hands, devouring him with her large, lustrous dark eyes, I said to the professor in English, so she wouldn't understand: 'The girl's badly smitten with you; play up to her. She's our only chance.'

"He blushed like a blooming school girl. 'I've a fiancée back in the States.'

" 'Blow your fiancée,' I said. 'Is it she that's going to keep the bally heads on our blightin' shoulders? I tell you this girl's silly over you. Ask her what they're going to do with us.'

"He did so and Naluna said: 'Your fate lies in the lap of El-lil.'

" 'And the brain of Sostoras,' I muttered. 'Naluna, what was done with the guns that were taken from us?'

"She replied that they were hung in the temple of El-lil as trophies of victory. None of the Sumerians was aware of their purpose. I asked her if the natives they sometimes fought had never used guns and she said no. I could easily believe that, seeing that there are many wild tribes in those hinterlands who've scarcely seen a single white man. But it seemed incredible that some of the Arabs who've raided back and forth across Somaliland for a thousand years hadn't stumbled onto Eridu and shot it up. But it turned out to be true—just one of those peculiar quirks and back-eddies in events like the wolves and wildcats you still find in New York state, or those queer pre-Aryan peoples you come onto in small communities in the hills of Connaught and Galway. I'm certain that big slave raids had passed within a few miles of Eridu, yet the Arabs had never found it and impressed on them the meaning of firearms.

"So I told Conrad: 'Play up to her, you chump! If you can persuade her to slip us a gun, we've a sporting chance.'

"So Conrad took heart and began talking to Naluna in a nervous sort of manner. Just how he'd have come out, I can't say, for he was little of the Don Juan, but Naluna snuggled up to him, much to his embarrassment, listening to his stumbling Somali with her soul in her eyes. Love blossoms suddenly and unexpectedly in the East.

"However, a peremptory voice outside our cell made Naluna jump half out of her skin and sent her scurrying, but as she went she pressed Conrad's hand and whispered something in his ear that we couldn't understand, but it sounded highly passionate.

"Shortly after she had left, the cell opened again and there stood a file of silent dark-skinned warriors. A sort of chief, whom the rest addressed as Gorat, motioned us to come out. Then down a long, dim, colonnaded corridor we went, in perfect silence except for the soft scruff of their sandals and the tramp of our boots on the tiling. An occasional torch flaring on the walls or in a niche of the columns lighted the way vaguely. At last we came out into the empty streets of the silent city. No sentry paced the streets or the walls, no lights showed from inside the flat-topped houses. It was like walking a street in a ghost city. Whether every night in Eridu was like that or whether the people kept indoors because it was a special and awesome occasion, I haven't an idea.

"We went on down the streets toward the lake side of the town. There we passed through a small gate in the wall—over which, I noted with a slight shudder, a grinning skull was carved—and found ourselves outside the city. A broad flight of steps led down to the water's edge and the spears at our backs guided us down them. There a boat waited, a strange high-prowed affair whose prototype must have plied the Persian Gulf in the days or Old Eridu.

"Four black men rested on their oars, and when they opened their mouths I saw their tongues had been cut out. We were taken into the boat, our guards got in and we started a strange journey. Out on the silent lake we moved like a dream, whose silence was broken only by the low rippling of the long, slim, golden-worked oars through the water. The stars flecked the deep blue gulf of the lake with silver points. I looked back and saw the silent city of Eridu sleeping beneath the stars. I looked ahead and saw the great dark bulk of the temple loom against the stars. The naked black mutes pulled the shining oars and the silent warriors sat before and behind us with their spears, helms and shields. It was like the dream of some fabulous city of Haroun-al-Raschid's time, or of Sulieman-ben-Daoud's, and I thought how blooming incongruous Conrad and I looked in that setting, with our boots and dingy, tattered khakis.

"WE LANDED on the island and I saw it was girdled with masonry—built up from the water's edge in broad flights of steps which circled the entire island. The whole seemed older, even, than the city—the Sumerians must have built it when they first found the valley, before they began on the city itself.

"We went up the steps, that were worn deep by countless feet, to a huge set of iron doors in the temple, and here Gorat laid down his spear and shield, dropped on his belly and knocked his helmed head on the great sill. Some one must have been watching from a loophole, for from the top of the tower sounded one deep golden note and the doors swung silently open to disclose a dim, torch-lighted entrance. Gorat rose and led the way, we following with those confounded spears pricking our backs.

"We mounted a flight of stairs and came onto a series of galleries built on the inside of each tier and winding around and up. Looking up, it seemed much higher and bigger than it had seemed from without, and the vague, half-lighted gloom, the silence and the mystery gave me the shudders. Conrad's face gleamed white in the semi-darkness. The shadows of past ages crowded in upon us, chaotic and horrific, and I felt as though the ghosts of all the priests and victims who had walked those galleries for four thousand years were keeping pace with us. The vast wings of dark, forgotten gods hovered over that hideous pile of antiquity.

"We came out on the highest tier. There were three circles of tall columns, one inside the other—and I want to say that for columns built of sun-dried brick, these were curiously symmetrical. But there was none of the grace and open beauty of, say, Greek architecture. This was grim, sullen, monstrous—something like the Egyptian, not quite so massive but even more formidable in starkness— an architecture symbolizing an age when men were still in the dawn-shadows of Creation and dreamed of monstrous gods.

"Over the inner circle of columns was a curving roof—almost a dome. How they built it, or how they came to anticipate the Roman builders by so many ages, I can't say, for it was a startling departure from the rest of their architectural style, but there it was. And from this dome-like roof hung a great round shining thing that caught the starlight in a silver net. I knew then what we had been following for so many mad miles! It was a great gong—the voice of El-lil. It looked like jade but I'm not sure to this

day. But whatever it was, it was the symbol on which the faith and cult of the Sumerians hung—the symbol of the godhead itself. And I know Naluna was right when she told us that her ancestors brought it with them on that long, gruelling trek, ages ago, when they fled before Sargon's wild riders: And how many eons before that dim time must it have hung in El-lil's temple in Nippur, Erech or Old Eridu, booming out its mellow threat or promise over the dreamy valley of the Euphrates, or across the green foam of the Persian Gulf!

"They stood us just within the first ring of columns, and out of the shadows somewhere, looking like a shadow from the past himself, came old Sostoras, the priest-king of Eridu. He was clad in a long robe of green, covered with scales like a snake's hide, and it rippled and shimmered with every step he took. On his head he wore a head-piece of waving plumes and in his hand he held a long-shafted golden mallet.

"He tapped the gong lightly and golden waves of sound flowed over us like a wave, suffocating us in its exotic sweetness. And then Naluna came. I never knew if she came from behind the columns or up through some trap floor. One instant the space before the gong was bare, the next she was dancing like a moonbeam on a pool. She was clad in some light, shimmery stuff that barely veiled her sinuous body and lithe limbs. And she danced before Sostoras and the Voice of El-lil as women of her breed had danced in old Sumer four thousand years ago.

"I can't begin to describe that dance. It made me freeze and tremble and burn inside. I heard Conrad's breath come in gasps and he shivered like a reed in the wind. From somewhere sounded music, that was old when Babylon was young, music as elemental as the fire in a tigress's eyes, and as soulless as an African midnight. And Naluna danced. Her dancing was a whirl of fire and wind and passion and all elemental forces. From all basic, primal fundamentals she drew underlying principles and combined them in one spin-wheel of motion. She narrowed the universe to a dagger-point of meaning and her flying feet and shimmering body wove out the mazes of that one central Thought. Her dancing stunned, exalted, maddened and hypnotized.

"As she whirled and spun, she was the elemental Essence, one and a part of all powerful impulses and moving or sleeping powers—the sun, the moon, the stars, the blind groping of hidden roots to light, the fire from the furnace, the sparks from the anvil, the breath of the fawn, the talons of the eagle. Naluna danced, and her dancing was Time and Eternity, the urge of Creation and the urge of Death; birth and dissolution in one, age and infancy combined.

"My dazed mind refused to retain more impressions; the girl merged into a whirling flicker of white fire before my dizzy eyes; then Sostoras struck one light note on the Voice and she fell at his feet, a quivering white shadow. The moon was just beginning to glow over the cliffs to the East.

"The warriors seized Conrad and me, and bound me to one of the outer columns. Him they dragged to the inner circle and bound to a column directly in front of the great gong. And I saw Naluna, white in the growing glow, gaze drawnly at him, then shoot a glance full of meaning at me, as she faded from sight among the dark sullen columns.

"Old Sostoras made a motion and from the shadows came a wizened black slave who looked incredibly old. He had the withered features and vacant stare of a deaf-mute, and the priest-king handed the golden mallet to him. Then Sostoras

fell back and stood beside me, while Gorat bowed and stepped back a pace and the warriors likewise bowed and backed still farther away. In fact they seemed most blooming anxious to get as far away from that sinister ring of columns as they could.

"There was a tense moment of waiting. I looked out across the lake at the high, sullen cliffs that girt the valley, at the silent city lying beneath the rising moon. It was like a dead city. The whole scene was most unreal, as if Conrad and I had been transported to another planet or back into a dead and forgotten age. Then the black mute struck the gong.

"At first it was a low, mellow whisper that flowed out from under the black man's steady mallet. But it swiftly grew in intensity. The sustained, increasing sound became nerve-racking—it grew unbearable. It was more than mere sound. The mute evoked a quality of vibration that entered into every nerve and racked it apart. It grew louder and louder until I felt that the most desirable thing in the world was complete deafness, to be like that blank-eyed mute who neither heard nor felt the perdition of sound he was creating. And yet I saw sweat beading his ape-like brow. Surely some thunder of that brain-shattering cataclysm re-echoed in his own soul. El-lil spoke to us and death was in his voice. Surely, if one of the terrible, black gods of past ages could speak, he would speak in just such tongue! There was neither mercy, pity nor weakness in its roar. It was the assurance of a cannibal god to whom mankind was but a plaything and a puppet to dance on his string.

"Sound can grow too deep, too shrill or too loud for the human ear to record. Not so with the Voice of El-lil, which had its creation in some inhuman age when dark wizards knew how to rack brain, body and soul apart. Its depth was unbearable, its volume was unbearable, yet ear and soul were keenly alive to its resonance and did not grow mercifully numb and dulled. And its terrible sweetness was beyond human endurance; it suffocated us in a smothering wave of sound that yet was barbed with golden fangs. I gasped and struggled in physical agony. Behind me I was aware that even old Sostoras had his hands over his ears, and Gorat groveled on the floor, grinding his face into the bricks.

"And if it so affected me, who was just within the magic circle of columns, and those Sumerians who were outside the circle, what was it doing to Conrad, who was inside the inner ring and beneath that domed roof that intensified every note?

"Till the day he dies Conrad will never be closer to madness and death than he was then. He writhed in his bonds like a snake with a broken back; his face was horribly contorted, his eyes distended, and foam flecked his livid lips. But in that hell of golden, agonizing sound I could hear nothing—I could only see his gaping mouth and his frothy, flaccid lips, loose and writhing like an imbecile's. But I sensed he was howling like a dying dog.

"Oh, the sacrificial dagger of the Semites was merciful. Even Moloch's lurid furnace was easier than the death promised by this rending and ripping vibration that armed sound-waves with venomed talons. I felt my own brain was brittle as frozen glass. I knew that a few seconds' more of that torture and Conrad's brain would shatter like a crystal goblet and he would die in the black raving of utter madness. And then something snapped me back from the mazes I'd gotten into. It was the fierce grasp of a small hand on mine, behind the column to which I was bound. I felt a tug at my cords as if a knife edge was being passed along

them, and my hands were free. I felt something pressed into my hand and a fierce exultation surged through me. I'd recognize the familiar checkered grip of my Webley .44 in a thousand!

"I acted in a flash that took the whole gang off guard. I lunged away from the column and dropped the black mute with a bullet through his brain, wheeled and shot old Sostoras through the belly. He went down, spewing blood, and I crashed a volley square into the stunned ranks of the soldiers. At that range I couldn't miss. Three of them dropped and the rest woke up and scattered like a flock of birds. In a second the place was empty except for Conrad, Naluna and me, and the men on the floor. It was like a dream, the echoes from the shots still crashing, and the acrid scent of powder and blood knifing the air.

"THE girl cut Conrad loose and he fell on the floor and yammered like a dying imbecile. I shook him but he had a wild glare in his eyes and was frothing like a mad dog, so I dragged him up, shoved an arm under him and started for the stair. We weren't out of the mess yet, by a long shot. Down those wide, winding, dark galleries we went, expecting any minute to be ambushed, but the chaps must have still been in a bad funk, because we got out of that hellish temple without any interference. Outside the iron portals Conrad collapsed and I tried to talk to him, but he could neither hear nor speak. I turned to Naluna.

" 'Can you do anything for him?'

"Her eyes flashed in the moonlight. 'I have not defied my people and my god and betrayed my cult and my race for naught! I stole the weapon of smoke and flame, and freed you, did I not? I love him and I will not lose him now!'

"She darted into the temple and was

out almost instantly with a jug of wine. She claimed it had magical powers. I don't believe it. I think Conrad simply was suffering from a sort of shell-shock from close proximity to that fearful noise and that lake water would have done as well as the wine. But Naluna poured some wine between his lips and emptied some over his head, and soon he groaned and cursed.

" 'See!' she cried triumphantly, 'the magic wine has lifted the spell El-lil put on him!' And she flung her arms around his neck and kissed him vigorously.

" 'My God, Bill,' he groaned, sitting up and holding his head, 'what kind of a nightmare is this?'

" 'Can you walk, old chap?' I asked. 'I think we've stirred up a bloomin' hornet's nest and we'd best leg it out of here.'

" 'I'll try.' He staggered up, Naluna helping him. I heard a sinister rustle and whispering in the black mouth of the temple and I judged the warriors and priests inside were working up their nerve to rush us. We made it down the steps in a great hurry to where lay the boat that had brought us to the island. Not even the black rowers were there. An ax and shield lay in it and I seized the ax and knocked holes in the bottoms of the other boats which were tied near it.

"Meanwhile the big gong had begun to boom out again and Conrad groaned and writhed as every intonation rasped his raw nerves. It was a warning note this time and I saw lights flare up in the city and heard a sudden hum of shouts float out across the lake. Something hissed softly by my head and slashed into the water. A quick look showed me Gorat standing in the door of the temple bending his heavy bow. I leaped in, Naluna helped Conrad in, and we shoved off in a hurry to the accompaniment of

several more shafts from the charming Gorat, one of which took a lock of hair from Naluna's pretty head.

"I laid to the oars while Naluna steered and Conrad lay on the bottom of the boat and was violently sick. We saw a fleet of boats put out from the city, and as they saw us by the gleam of the moon, a yell of concentrated rage went up that froze the blood in my veins. We were heading for the opposite end of the lake and had a long start on them, but in this way we were forced to round the island and we'd scarcely left it astern when out of some nook leaped a long boat with six warriors—I saw Gorat in the bows with that confounded bow of his.

"I had no spare cartridges so I laid to it with all my might, and Conrad, somewhat green in the face, took the shield and rigged it up in the stern, which was the saving of us, because Gorat hung within bowshot of us all the way across the lake and he filled that shield so full of arrows it resembled a blooming porcupine. You'd have thought they'd had plenty after the slaughter I made among them on the roof, but they were after us like hounds after a hare.

"We'd a fair start on them but Gorat's five rowers shot his boat through the water like a race-horse, and when we grounded on the shore, they weren't half a dozen jumps behind us. As we scrambled out I saw it was either make a fight of it there and be cut down from the front, or else be shot like rabbits as we ran. I called to Naluna to run but she laughed and drew a dagger—she was a man's woman, that girl!

"GORAT and his merry men came surging up to the landing with a clamor of yells and a swirl of oars—they swarmed over the side like a gang of bloody pirates and the battle was on! Luck was with Gorat at the first pass, for

I missed him and killed the man behind him. The hammer snapped on an empty shell and I dropped the Webley and snatched up the ax just as they closed with us. By Jove! It stirs my blood now to think of the touch-and-go fury of that fight! Knee-deep in water we met them, hand to hand, chest to chest!

"Conrad brained one with a stone he picked from the water, and out of the tail of my eye, as I swung for Gorat's head, I saw Naluna spring like a she-panther on another, and they went down together in a swirl of limbs and a flash of steel. Gorat's sword was thrusting for my life, but I knocked it aside with the ax and he lost his footing and went down—for the lake bottom was solid stone there, and treacherous as sin.

"One of the warriors lunged in with a spear, but he tripped over the fellow Conrad had killed, his helmet fell off and I crushed his skull before he could recover his balance. Gorat was up and coming for me, and the other was swinging his sword in both hands for a death blow, but he never struck, for Conrad caught up the spear that had been dropped, and spitted him from behind, neat as a whistle.

"Gorat's point raked my ribs as he thrust for my heart and I twisted to one side, and his up-flung arm broke like a rotten stick beneath my stroke but saved his life. He was game—they were all game or they'd never have rushed my gun. He sprang in like a blood-mad tiger, hacking for my head. I ducked and avoided the full force of the blow but couldn't get away from it altogether and it laid my scalp open in a three-inch gash, clear to the bone—here's the scar to prove it. Blood blinded me and I struck back like a wounded lion, blind and terrible, and by sheer chance I landed squarely. I felt the ax crunch through metal and bone, the haft splintered in my

O. S.—**9**

hand, and there was Gorat dead at my feet in a horrid welter of blood and brains.

"I shook the blood out of my eyes and looked about for my companions. Conrad was helping Naluna up and it seemed to me she swayed a little. There was blood on her bosom but it might have come from the red dagger she gripped in a hand stained to the wrist. God! it *was* a bit sickening, to think of it now. The water we stood in was choked with corpses and ghastly red. Naluna pointed out across the lake and we saw Eridu's boats sweeping down on us— a good way off as yet, but coming swiftly. She led us at a run away from the lake's edge. My wound was bleeding as only a scalp wound can bleed, but I wasn't weakened as yet. I shook the blood out of my eyes, saw Naluna stagger as she ran and tried to put my arm about her to steady her, but she shook me off.

"She was making for the cliffs and we reached them out of breath. Naluna leaned against Conrad and pointed upward with a shaky hand, breathing in great, sobbing gasps. I caught her meaning. A rope ladder led upward. I made her go first with Conrad following. I came after him, drawing the ladder up behind me. We'd gotten some half-way up when the boats landed and the warriors raced up the shore, loosing their arrows as they ran. But we were in the shadow of the cliffs, which made aim uncertain, and most of the shafts fell short or broke on the face of the cliff. One stuck in my left arm, but I shook it out and didn't stop to congratulate the marksman on his eye.

"Once over the cliff's edge, I jerked the ladder up and tore it loose, and then turned to see Naluna sway and collapse in Conrad's arms. We laid her gently on the grass, but a man with half an eye could tell she was going fast. I wiped the blood from her bosom and stared aghast. Only a woman with a great love could have made that run and that climb with such a wound as that girl had under her heart.

"Conrad cradled her head in his lap and tried to falter a few words, but she weakly put her arms around his neck and drew his face down to hers.

" 'Weep not for me, my lover,' she said, as her voice weakened to a whisper. 'Thou hast been mine aforetime, as thou shalt be again. In the mud huts of the Old River, before Sumer was, when we tended the flocks, we were as one. In the palaces of Old Eridu, before the barbarians came out of the East, we loved each other. Aye, on this very lake have we floated in past ages, living and loving, thou and I. So weep not, my lover, for what is one little life when we have known so many and shall know so many more? And in each of them, thou art mine and I am thine.

" 'But thou must not linger. Hark! they clamor for thy blood below. But since the ladder is destroyed there is but one other way by which they may come upon the cliffs—the place by which they brought thee into the valley. Haste! They will return across the lake, scale the cliffs there and pursue thee, but thou may'st escape them if thou be'st swift. And when thou hearest the Voice of El-lil, remember, living or dead, Naluna loves thee with a love greater than any god.

" 'But one boon I beg of thee,' she whispered, her heavy lids drooping like a sleepy child's. 'Press, I beg thee, thy lips on mine, my master, before the shadows utterly enfold me; then leave me here and go, and weep not, oh my lover, for what is—one—little—life—to—us—who—have—loved—in—so—many——'

"Conrad wept like a blithering baby, and so did I, by Judas, and I'll stamp the lousy brains out of the jackass who twits me for it! We left her with her arms folded on her bosom and a smile on her lovely face, and if there's a heaven for Christian folk, she's there with the best of them, on my oath.

"Well, we reeled away in the moonlight and my wounds were still bleeding and I was about done in. All that kept me going was a sort of wild beast instinct to live, I fancy, for if I was ever near to lying down and dying, it was then. We'd gone perhaps a mile when the Sumerians played their last ace. I think they'd realized we'd slipped out of their grasp and had too much start to be caught.

"At any rate, all at once that damnable gong began booming. I felt like howling like a dog with rabies. This time it was a different sound. I never saw or heard of a gong before or since whose notes could convey so many different meanings. This was an insidious call— a luring urge, yet a peremptory command for us to return. It threatened and promised; if its attraction had been great before we stood on the tower of El-lil and felt its full power, now it was almost irresistible. It was hypnotic. I know now how a bird feels when charmed by a snake and how the snake himself feels when the fakirs play on their pipes. I can't begin to make you understand the overpowering magnetism of that call. It made you want to writhe and tear at the air and run back, blind and screaming, as a hare runs into a python's jaws. I had to fight it as a man fights for his soul.

"As for Conrad, it had him in its grip. He halted and rocked like a drunken man.

" 'It's no use,' he mumbled thickly. 'It drags at my heart-strings; it's fettered my brain and my soul; it embraces all the evil lure of all the universes. I must go back.'

"And he started staggering back the way we had come—toward that golden lie floating to us over the jungle. But I thought of the girl Naluna that had given up her life to save us from that abomination, and a strange fury gripped me..

" 'See here!' I shouted. 'This won't do, you bloody fool! You're off your bally bean! I won't have it, d'you hear?'

"But he paid no heed, shoving by me with eyes like a man in a trance, so I let him have it—an honest right hook to the jaw that stretched him out dead to the world. I slung him over my shoulder and reeled on my way, and it was nearly an hour before he came to, quite sane and grateful to me.

"Well, we saw no more of the people of Eridu. Whether they trailed us at all or not, I haven't an idea. We could have fled no faster than we did, for we were fleeing the haunting, horrible mellow whisper that dogged us from the south. We finally made it back to the spot where we'd cached our dunnage, and then, armed and scantily equipped, we started the long trek for the coast. Maybe you read or heard something about two emaciated wanderers being picked up by an elephant-hunting expedition in the Somaliland back country, dazed and incoherent from suffering. Well, we were about done for, I'll admit, but we were perfectly sane. The incoherent part was when we tried to tell our tale and the blasted idiots wouldn't believe it. They patted our backs and talked in a soothing tone and poured whisky-and-sodas down us. We soon shut up, seeing we'd only be branded as liars or lunatics. They got us back to Jibuti, and both of us had had enough of Africa for a spell. I took ship for India and Conrad went the other way—couldn't get back to New England quick enough, where I hope he married that little American girl and is living happily. A wonderful chap, for all his damnable bugs.

"As for me, I can't hear any sort of a gong today without starting. On that long, gruelling trek I never breathed easily until we were beyond the sound of that ghastly Voice. You can't tell what a thing like that may do to your mind. It plays the very deuce with all rational ideas.

"I still hear that hellish gong in my dreams, sometimes, and see that silent, hideously ancient city in that nightmare valley. Sometimes I wonder if it's still calling to me across the years. But that's nonsense. Anyway, there's the yarn as it stands and if you don't believe me, I won't blame you at all."

But I prefer to believe Bill Kirby, for I know his breed from Hengist down, and know him to be like all the rest—truthful, aggressive, profane, restless, sentimental and straightforward, a true brother of the roving, fighting, adventuring Sons of Aryan.

Strange, is it not? that of the myriads who
Before us pass'd the door of Darkness through,
    Not one returns to tell us of the road,
Which to discover we must travel too.

                —Rubáiyát of Omar Khayyam.

The Circle of Illusion

By LOTTIE LESH

A peculiar story was that told by the Collector of Antiques—a tale of the Unfinished Buddha and the love of a Japanese priest for the daughter of the emperor

AS HAMMERSMITH opened the low door of shop number seven, the clear-throated tinkle of a bell above the lintel announced his arrival. Presently a thin, stoop-shouldered man wearing an ill-fitting coat appeared through a curtain at the far end of the dimly lighted room, hesitated a moment, peering through the gloom at his visitor, then laying down the book he was holding, came timidly forward.

He had nothing of the suavity of the efficient salesman. Even Hammersmith noted the contrast between his dignified, scholarly bearing and the obsequious eagerness of the hook-nosed hagglers who sold antiques in the same street. Bowing gravely, he regarded Hammersmith with a searching expression which seemed to indicate that he wished this visitor to announce his business at once and be gone. His pallid skin, his dark, melancholy eyes and the thin graying mustache which accentuated the lines of his drooping, sorrowful mouth gave his face a venerable, world-weary expression. He had the drawn, soul-starved features of a man who has spent all his days within the confines of a gloomy house, poring over musty manuscripts of long-forgotten dead men.

"I have bought a house in Madison Row," said his visitor portentously, looking down to see how the collector took this significant announcement. "My wife wishes to fill it with antiques—antiques of the best kind. She don't want to be outdone by anybody when it comes to class. Something real ancient is what she wants."

The collector cast a doubtful glance at the dusty shelves of his shop, littered with plate and pottery of uncertain age.

"Nothing I have would suit you, I fear," he murmured, more to himself than to his visitor. "Yonder on the third shelf are some Egyptian vases but they are rather common. I had a rare Ming vase, a beauty," he added, "but yesterday an Englishman who had sought it for years offered me a price which I dared not refuse. I sold it. You see," he explained in a gentle tone in which humor and humility mingled, "I have been a victim of the slings and arrows of outrageous fortune. When young, I collected as did my ancestors, for the love of possessing beautiful things. My family disdained those who commerced in art. We did not seek treasures at the ends of the earth in order to sell them for gold."

"But see here," urged Hammersmith aggressively, "if you had such a rare treasure yesterday, surely you have others equally rare. Something ancient is what we want. My wife would like to own something that a dead queen had possessed if she could get it. You see how particular she is; she won't be outdone by none, now she can afford fine things."

The collector shuddered slightly.

"I have nothing that would suit you, I fear—short of the family treasure." He hesitated, waiting for the stranger to go, then bowed gravely. "I bid you good-day."

132

The persistent seeker after antiquities took a step toward the door, but suddenly struck with an ingenious idea, turned back and called to the collector persuasively.

"Even though you do not wish to sell this family treasure you mentioned, surely you would not object to telling one who appreciates such things about it. Art is what I am interested in too. Come, tell me about your treasure."

The earnestness in Hammersmith's voice appeared to arrest the collector; moreover he was a courteous man, and to refuse such a request was hardly possible.

"When I mentioned my family treasure," he explained quietly, "I supposed that you knew to what I referred—the Unfinished Buddha. Have you never heard of it? Its name is a classic in the art world. You have never heard of it?"

Hammersmith admitted that he had not. The collector regarded him keenly, with an expression of complete incredulity.

"How strange!"

Hammersmith's face grew red. He was about to offer some excuse for his ignorance, when he perceived that the collector was no longer conscious of his presence. The little man had sunk languidly into a chair and with hands clasped in his lap seemed absorbed with some inner image of beauty. After a moment of deep meditation, he arose, and going to the back of the shop, drew forth a heavy chest which had been concealed under a cot behind the counter. Here, under lock and key, reposed the treasure. The little man lifted it gently from its resting-place and brought it forward. Carefully removing the bit of old yellow silk in which it was wrapped, he revealed within the palms of his hands a tiny green Buddha. The hand of the carver had never smoothed it; it was incomplete, but no suggestion of crudeness marred it.

"Death stayed the hand of the sculp-tor," murmured the collector softly, "but the hand of the brooding centuries has effaced the scars."

He sank into his chair, sighing gently.

"EVERY excursion into the wise old East is a glorious adventure, if one's heart is open to romance," he said. "For such an one, mystery lurks behind every gray wall. Once again, like wine in the blood, comes the thrill that I knew on first visiting Japan's ancient imperial city, that subtle charm which still lingers like ghostly melodies echoing down the dusty centuries. I remember the golden summer morning when I visited the shrines at Nikko and stopped breathless before the Yomei-mon, the most beautiful gate in Japan, called the sunrise to sunset gate, where three hundred years ago a pair of immortal lovers met and tarried the whole long day.

"In Japan three hundred years ago it was not customary for a woman to be from under authority; but O-Miyuku-san was an orphan; moreover she was an emperor's daughter and a descendant of the gods over whom no mortal had any authority. At sunrise she had come unattended to the shrine at Nikko to do honor to the spirit of her father, the emperor, lately dead. Long after her prayers were said, she lingered in the holy place, drinking in the beauty of the shrine, richly embellished with carvings from the enchanted hand of Jingoro, filled with child-like wonder at the sight of the marvelous painted dragons which looked so life-like that they were said to uncoil from their pillars at night to drink from the lotus pool. In a dream, she paused before the Yomei-mon, wondering if it could, indeed, be the gate of Paradise through which her father would presently beckon her.

"Time does not exist in the presence of beauty. O-Miyuku-san did not know how long she stood gazing at the Yomei-mon before she became aware that a tall priest was standing beside her. Then she drew her robes swiftly about her and would have fled, but the beauty of his face held her. It was a noble face, strangely diffident and other-worldly. O-Miyuku-san, returning his gaze, clasped her little hands tightly to conceal their trembling. Was it for the daughter of an emperor and a lineal descendant of the gods to fear a mortal? She did not know that it was love which had met her at the Yomei-mon.

"Strange that Hasaki with a lifetime's study of the Sutras and all his esoteric philosophy concerning the illusion of earthly things would have tarried to gaze at a maiden. But Hasaki was only a youth, and like many another ascetic, he made the discovery of an unsuspected wisdom in the saying: 'He was created a man before he became a priest.'

"At dusk, the maiden fled. But for her there was no escape, nor for Hasaki; neither the walls of the imperial palace nor the sacred presence of the Buddha could shut out the remembrance of that which had passed before the Yomei-mon. Both knew in their hearts that 'even the knot of rope tying our boats together was knotted long ago by some love in a former birth.'

"But to love with desire O-Miyuku-san, the daughter of Heaven, was a calamity. Hasaki spent the still hours of the night in breathless repetition of the Sutras, prostrating his body before the Buddha. It was to no avail. In the gray dawn of morning he stood before the high priest, his distraught young face, white in the glow of the andon, lifted to the gentle, unmoved countenance of his wiser brother.

" 'Return to the Sutras, my son,' droned the older man. 'It is not for an emperor's daughter to marry a priest.

Take this image of the Buddha; keep it in the folds of your girdle, and in the hour of your temptation recite the Treasure Sutra to the Compassionate One.'

"But not even a high priest of Buddha has authority over the daughter of Heaven. When night fell O-Miyuku-san returned to the shrine. Crossing the slumberous courtyard on winged feet, she found Hasaki kneeling before the Buddha with open prayer roll, devoutly repeating the Sutras. When the priest beheld the princess before him, fairer even than he had remembered her, he covered his face with his hands.

"Leaning toward him, she whispered faintly, 'If you send me away, I shall die.'

"Hasaki arose, and abandoning his priest's robes, went with her out of the city.

"The palace in which the daughter of the emperor and her lover dwelt was an idyllic earthly paradise where royal peacocks feathered in emerald and dazzling gold guarded the gates as effectively as flashing swords. Here these two dreamed that they had created a paradise whose walls no power could shatter.

"Not entirely forgetful of his past life, Hasaki spent many hours fashioning tiny images of the Buddha, even as the ancient priests had done to embellish their temples. The art of carving became a passion with him, second only to his love for the princess; and presently he became known throughout the kingdom as the most exquisite artist of his day. Only one pure in heart could have conceived the works from his hand which were filled with a lofty charm and an other-worldly beauty. But one work, the most perfect of them all, a jade image of the Buddha, Hasaki never completed.

"A cholera swept the land, destroying the people by thousands. It struck down the coolies by the wayside and on the wharves, where they died miserably like rats. It entered the palaces of the rich; and the gods remained as ineffably unmoved by the implorations of the powerful as they had been by the wailings of the weak.

"The little daughter of Heaven commanded her palace gates to be barred against Death, and she ordered one thousand guardsmen outside the gates to forbid his entrance. But not even the thousand guardsmen had power against that day when Hasaki lay heedless of his princess, when the agonized prayers of the daughter of Heaven fell back against her lips unanswered.

"Just before death, Hasaki spoke to O-Miyuku-san, bidding her cherish the beautiful Unfinished Buddha. 'Nirvana is profitless without you,' he whispered. 'I shall dwell beside you in the image of the god until death sets you free; thus we shall never be parted either in life or in death or in Paradise which we shall enter together.'

"In this promise the princess found comfort after her lord's body was taken from her; and the story of the incarnation of the artist, Hasaki, in the form of the Unfinished Buddha became the wonder of the Eastern world.

"Now there was a famous collector of antiques in those days, a European with a palace on the river Rhine. This man had traveled even into Asia and the islands farthest east and south in search of ancient and precious beauty. While journeying in the Orient, it happened that the tale of this marvelous incarnation reached his ears, and he was filled with an insatiable desire to possess the Unfinished Buddha. He did possess it. After incurring the sentence of death for insolently offering money in exchange for the sacred treasure, he escaped from prison, and stole the god from the royal treasury at night, after slaying the guard. He succeeded in fleeing the kingdom unscathed; although a terrible price was set on his head. But the daughter of Heaven, learning that the robber had his palace on the other side of the world, followed him secretly, taking with her two faithful servants.

"The palace of Brasswell, the collector, was a mediæval castle, filled with ancient storied riches of the past. It stood on a high hill overlooking a city, with the river Rhine flowing so near the base of its walls that the collector, from the turret of his castle, could see the waves of the river creaming on the beach beneath him. Here, remote from the garish life of the world, he dwelt in Oriental splendor, dreaming that he was the imperial emperor of an ancient, exotic world.

"Everything surrounding him was foreign; the tapestries on the walls, the treasures in the treasury room at the top of the castle — even the servants were foreign. A score had been imported from the ends of the earth for the sake of his pleasure. Among them were Egyptians, Nubians, Arabs and Malays; and there were also two Chinese who had lately come into his service.

"These Chinese pleased him inordinately. Their ceremonial deference to him and their noble pedigree, their ancestors having been servants of emperors for centuries, made him prize them above all his servants. He even came to honor these two with his confidence, made them his trusted counselors, and in time, showed them his priceless treasures—took them into his holy of holies at the top of the castle, into the dim religious light of that vast room whose entrance was guarded on either side by the colossal statue of a ferocious Deva king. Within that chamber gilded statues gleamed solemnly in the spacious obscurity. Colors, like tongues of flame, flared out from the shadowy places; colors of the mysterious East; lapis lazuli and emerald, the vermilion of lacquer and pomegranates, purple of Syria and crimson of Tyre.

"There, for the first time, Brasswell displayed his treasures: the work of skilled craftsmen of past centuries, art long since supposed to have perished; yellowed scrolls bearing ancient inscriptions, exquisite stone Amidas fashioned by slender delicate Japanese hands, and wood carvings showing the unmistakable trace of Unkei's handicraft. Before the barred and recessed casement golden peacocks trailed plumages of sapphires and emeralds across richly brocaded palanquin cloths. Against the purple velvet banners on the walls hung the ancient weapons of the shoguns; and from a lacquered chest, breathing the spirit of plum blossoms, caught ages ago from some queen's garden, Brasswell drew forth a ceremonial coat heavily crusted with jewels and bearing the family crest of a Chinese emperor.

"Then, a little flown with the softly murmured adulation of his servants, he brought forth a heavy iron key which had been concealed in the folds of his garment. With this key he unlocked the dragon-guarded lid of a huge stone coffin. Calling his trusted servants close, he lifted the lid of the coffin. Within lay the beautiful Unfinished Buddha.

"A murmur of horror escaped the lips of his servants. Falling on their knees, they begged their master to return the god at once to the Japanese princess, reminding him with awe-stricken faces of the terrible curse which inevitably befalls those who do injury to a priest. Brasswell laughed at their fears, relocked the coffin, hung the key once more around his neck, and informed his servants that his superior wisdom lifted him above the ignorant superstitions of the East.

" 'Yours is the wisdom of the fool,'

replied Li King, the elder, gently. 'For this, I foresee that in one night the curse of madness will destroy you. It is already upon you, August One; otherwise you would have read the expression of vengeance which now conceals the features of that Buddha you have stolen. There was only lofty sweetness there before.'

"Greatly surprized and displeased with this unexpected attitude on the part of his servants, Brasswell ordered them from his presence and forbade them to speak of what they had seen. Thereafter, he conferred with them less often, finding that their quiet scrutiny made him strangely ill at ease. Becoming increasingly annoyed by the curious manner with which they came to observe him, he began to watch them covertly. Once, after passing his former confidants in a corridor, Brasswell turned suddenly to discover the two in whispered conference, the elder pointing to his master with one hand and with the other significantly touching his head.

"Brasswell began to conceal himself when he heard the two approaching. He was watching them one day from behind an arras, when Li King accidentally surprized his master by carelessly sweeping aside the concealing curtain. Brasswell, crouched on the floor, looked up to see the sorrowful eyes of his servant resting upon him. Li King exchanged significant glances with his companion and shook his head sadly.

" 'It has come to pass,' he murmured.

"After this incident, Brasswell tried desperately to win back the respect of his servants and re-establish his claim to sanity. But fate seemed to have conspired against him; for when he willed to act most normally, he found himself doing strange, unnatural things.

"Once, in a studied attempt to appear

entirely at ease in his servants' presence, he pretended to be vastly delighted with the contents of a manuscript which he held before him. Not until he saw the observant Li King make a silent gesture to his companion did he realize that the manuscript was upside down in his hands.

"Then, softly, almost imperceptibly, the entire household was corrupted. All the servants came to regard their master as a madman. Protesting at first with mighty threats against this treatment, Brasswell gradually subsided into silence; for his angry ravings only strengthened their conviction that he was mad.

"The eyes of all his house were upon him; they followed him from the tower room to the dungeon; they were everywhere. He could not escape them. At length a terror of his own kind seemed to possess him, and he ran when he heard his servants approaching. He ceased to sleep in his usual bedchamber; and his servants, searching through the gloomy castle for their demented master, often found him hiding with the spiders in some sunless hole.

"At length, a night of terrible storm descended upon them. The thunder blasts rocked in the battlements, and the lightning, darting into the enormous shadows like phantom rapiers, revealed Brasswell huddled in a heap of decaying tapestry in an uninhabited quarter of the castle. Awakened by the tumultuous storm, he became sharply conscious of a presence near him. Too terrified to move, he lay shivering miserably, when a blinding flash of lightning, illuminating the place for an instant, revealed a figure towering over him, a tall figure with ashen face, wearing the garb of a Buddhist priest.

"Like a thing pursued, Brasswell fled shrieking through the echoing corridors and up the circling stairways, until he reached the top of the castle. Flinging himself into the tower room, he unlocked the massive stone coffin and seizing the beautiful Unfinished Buddha, he rushed to the casement and threw it into the storm. The fitful lightning revealed it lying on the beach below, the waves of the river creaming around it. Brasswell's Chinese servants braved the storm to recover the god. Returning to the tower room, they found their master dead. Seeing that the huge stone coffin in which the Buddha had been entombed was now empty, they placed their master's body within it, and locking the lid, they threw the key in the Rhine.

"At dawn, they carried the Buddha to the private dwelling of a Japanese lady in the city below; but the lady had departed life in the storm of that night, gone out as if in answer to a moonbeam sent from the deep deep water world as a signal that he was waiting for her."

THE strange recitative had come to a close. The collector sighed deeply:

" 'And they are gone: ay, ages long ago
Those lovers fled away into the storm.' "

In the silence that fell, Hammersmith sat staring at the gentle, musing countenance of the Buddha. As if in answer to his unspoken question the collector answered softly, "It is quiescent now; the spirit has fled. It is as it was in the beginning; but the beauty of the past clings to it with the same charm that invests a room in which a long-dead queen has slept."

Hammersmith cleared his throat.

"I am a rich man. Name your price; I will pay it."

The collector shook his head.

"It is beyond price. See," he murmured, caressing the Buddha, "see with what ineffable calm it reposes, wise in the understanding that human desires are but as tiny ripples on the Infinite Ocean of Illusion. Age can not wither nor custom stale that august restfulness. Only the favored few can fathom the wisdom of its quiet. If I believed you were such," he added reluctantly, "I might entrust it to you. I am growing old—and have none to whom I can leave it."

The wistful envy that the aged feel toward those in the prime of life betrayed his earlier firmness. Then Hammersmith saw that the animation in his face had burned out and that he was indeed old. Smiling confidently, he towered over the shriveled little man.

"Name your price," he said.

A shadow of horror crossed the face of the collector.

"To take money in exchange for it would be a sacrilege. Do not speak of that again." He sighed heavily. "Take it as a gift, and in the name of friendship give me a mere fraction of what a king would pay to possess such a treasure—in the name of friendship, never as payment, remember! Five thousand dollars, perhaps. Truly that is a trifle; but I am an old man. I can not guard my treasure after death."

With Hammersmith's check folded carefully in the parchment-like hands, the collector followed his visitor to the entrance of the shop.

"Farewell," he murmured, "you take with you that which is precious. Guard it well, for the wisdom it teaches is priceless. That wisdom you will realize sooner or later—that all is illusion."

Wrapped in revery the collector watched Hammersmith disappear into the writhing crowd that surged perpetually before his dimly lighted shop. Gazing with quiet eye upon the passing pageant, he saw, as in a vision, humanity hopelessly caught in the whirling Circle of Illusion, irresistibly swept into the vortex by its own tumultuous desires.

The silken rustle of a woman's garment aroused him from his meditation. The curtains at the rear of the shop parted noiselessly, and the face of the collector's wife appeared in the aperture. It was a dark, luminous face with heavy-lidded eyes and tiny heart-shaped mouth.

"Abel," exclaimed the woman softly, "thou'rt a marvelous teller of tales; thy lyric tongue hath made us. Soon all this tawdry stock will be sold, and then, praise Allah, we shall set up a shop in Regent Street and buy some real antiques."

The Man Who Limped

(Continued from page 31)

as the law will allow—who pluck their eyebrows, kohl their eyes, dye their cheeks, make scarlet their lips with red grease, and flirt with men. But I am also informed that you have a few females whose becoming modesty forbids these things, and who are, therefore, bright and shining examples of virtue in an otherwise vicious and depraved world.

If I were of your people, *effendi*, I should never cease extolling the excellence of these modest and reticent maidens who *seem* too good to be true—but I would select a wife from among the others.

Ho, Silat! Bring the sweet and take the full!

THE SOUK

"THE East never sleeps, never rests. Its maze of confusion and mystery flows onward endlessly."

With these words Frank Owen, in *Singapore Nights,* hits off the appeal of the Orient. It will be the purpose of ORIENTAL STORIES to present in fiction the glamor and mystery of the East. There seems a genuine need for such a magazine, to fill a want that has long been felt. The Orient makes a romantic appeal to the imagination that no other part of the world can equal. The inscrutable mystery of Tibet, the veiled allure of Oriental harems, the charge of fierce Arab tribesmen, the singing of almond-eyed maidens under a Japanese moon, the whirling of dervishes, the barbaric splendor of mediæval sultans, the ageless life of Egypt—from all these the story-writers weave charms to shut out the humdrum world of everyday life, and transport the reader into a fairyland of the imagination, but a fairyland that exists in its full reality in Asia.

ORIENTAL STORIES will publish not only tales of Asia and Asia Minor, but will include also fascinating tales of the East Indies, of Egypt, and of the littoral of North and East Africa, which is Oriental in language and character though not in geography. We shall present for your delectation not only vivid tales of romance, intrigue and red war in present-day Asia, but will offer you also vivid historical tales—of Genghis Khan the Red Scourge, of Tamerlane the Magnificent, of Saladin the Intrepid, of the wars between the Cross and the Crescent, of the spread of the Mogul conquerors into India, of the British conquest, of the awakening of China and Japan, and of Russian intrigue to set Islam against the British Empire. Samarcand, Singapore, Delhi, Bagdad, Damascus, Cairo, Herat and its Hundred Gardens, Ispahan, and a host of other cities whose very names weave a spell, will be the locales for these stories; Karakorum the desert capital of Genghis Khan; Xanadu the wonder-city of Kubla Khan; the Vale of Cashmere, long famed in song; Angkor, the fabled city in the forests of Cambodia; the Taj Mahal, tomb of Shah Jehan's favorite wife—where except in the Orient can such marvelous settings be found for fascinating stories?

We have been fortunate in obtaining a number of original poems by the contemporary Chinese poet, Hung Long Tom. These are not translations from the Chinese, but are written in English. However, as the style is entirely different from that of English poetry, a word or two about them might not be out of place. "Chinese poetry," writes Hung Long Tom, "is different from the poetry of other countries in so far as it attempts to be a picture rather than a poem. In China at times tiny bits of verse are written on squares of silk and hung on the walls. They are known as written pictures." So that is what these poems by Hung Long Tom are: written pictures. We will use two or three of these in each issue.

ORIENTAL STORIES will follow no hard and fast rule as to the spelling of Oriental proper names. The Punjaub or the Punjab, dakaits or dacoits, Sheykh or Sheik —the authors will be allowed full license to follow whatever Oriental spellings they wish. Several of the Oriental languages, notably Arabic, contain sounds that can not be represented in English pronunciation; and to attempt to insist upon any set scheme of transliteration of these sounds would be foolish.

When T. E. Lawrence, who led the Arabs in their successful revolt against Turkey during the Great War, wrote his book, *Revolt in the Desert*, he spelt the same Arabic words in different ways even in the same paragraph, and his publisher's proofreader objected strongly to the apparent inconsistencies of spelling. A long and entertaining correspondence ensued between author and publisher, and as this colloquy bears directly upon the diversity of spelling of Oriental words which will be found in this magazine, we think a few extracts from that correspondence will be interesting to our readers. The publisher wrote: "I attach a list of queries raised by F, who is reading the proofs. He finds these very clean, but full of inconsistencies in the spelling of proper names, a point which reviewers often take up. Will you annotate it in the margin, so that I can get the proofs straightened?" To this Lawrence replied: "Annotated: not very helpfully perhaps. Arabic names won't go into English, exactly, for their consonants are not the same as ours, and their vowels, like ours, vary from district to district. There are some 'scientific systems' of transliterations, helpful to people who know enough Arabic not to need helping. I spell my names anyhow, to show what rot the systems are." The proofreader queried: "Jeddah and Jidda used impartially throughout. Intentional?" To which Lawrence replied: "Rather!" The proofreader noted: "Bir Waheida was Bir Waheidi." Lawrence replied: "Why not? All one place." Again the proofreader noted: "Nuri, Emir of the Ruwalla, belongs to the 'chief family of the Rualla.' On Slip 33 'Rualla horse,' and Slip 38, 'killed one Rueili.' In all later slips 'Rualla'." Lawrence replied: "Should have also used Ruwala and Ruala." Another query was: "Jedha, the she camel, was Jedhah on Slip 40." Lawrence answered: "She was a splendid beast." Again the proofreader queried: "Sherif Abd el Mayin of Slip 68 becomes el Main, el Mayein, el Muein, el Mayin, and el Muyein." Lawrence commented: "Good egg. I call this really ingenious."

E. Hoffmann Price, one of the authors whose work will be published in this magazine for your delectation, comments in a letter to the editor: "Lawrence is right; Arabic can't be transliterated. Of course, a great deal can be passably approximated with Latin letters, but when you come to words involving certain sounds peculiar to the Arabic language, you are stuck. One sound can not be expressed by any letter or combination of letters in our alphabet; although some of the lesser terrors can be closely approximated by comparison with German, as in 'acht.' Worse than that, the pronunciation is difficult to approximate, to say nothing of transliteration. Lawrence was entitled to his little jest. Any Occidental who becomes proficient in that language is entitled to any flights of fancy he may find amusing."

Readers, it will help us to keep the stories in this magazine in line with your wishes if you will tell us which stories you prefer in this issue. Either write a letter, or fill out the coupon on page 31, and mail it to The Souk, ORIENTAL STORIES, 840 North Michigan Ave., Chicago.

Singapore Nights

(*Continued from page 19*)

It was good to have a friend so close at hand. The mystery of the house was nerve-racking.

As Dick leaned from the window, Wing Lo whispered softly, "Master can sleep. Through the night I will watch the approach to your window. I can easily lie hidden in the garden. The shadow tapestries will conceal me."

The next moment Wing Lo was gone. In the distance a dog howled dismally as though it were crying for the moon. It had been a wild, exciting day and Dick was exhausted. He had not been in bed many minutes before he was asleep. How long he slept he did not know, but the next thing he knew he was sitting bolt upright in bed. He scarcely realized what had awakened him, although he was vaguely conscious that he had heard a scream. Even as he endeavored to get his scattered wits together, the scream was repeated. He sprang from his bed and rushed to the window. By the light of the moon which flooded the garden he beheld Wing Lo gripped in the powerful arms of Yeh Ming Hsin. In the eerie light the latter looked like a misshapen baboon.

In a moment Dick had sprung through the window and was climbing down the vines. When he was about ten feet from the ground he jumped, landing full force on the shoulders of Yeh Ming Hsin. So terrific was the impact that Wing Lo was released. Yeh Ming Hsin was somewhat dazed by the unexpected interference and Dick Varney made the most of his bewilderment. He struck him flush on the chin with all his might and followed up with a frightful left jab in the stomach which sent the Chinaman sprawling. All the fight was taken out of him. He lay on the ground scarcely breathing. Wing Lo sprang forward. He drew a rope from his clothing and bound Yeh Ming Hsin hand and foot. Then together they carried the subdued Chinaman to a small building at the foot of the garden, a small pump-house that had been discarded. Wing Lo examined his bonds to see that there was no chance of his escaping. Then together they returned to the house and climbed up the vines to Dick Varney's room.

"I DID not scream," explained Wing Lo, "until I knew that I was overpowered. I feared for your life." He paused for a moment, then he continued speaking rather hurriedly. "The time for action has come. When Mortimer Davga discovers that Yeh Ming Hsin is missing, his wrath will be uncheckable. Up till now he has at least shown exceeding courtesy toward you. I know, for I watched by the window while you were eating. But now all restraint will be cast aside. It will be a finish fight. The prize is enormous. John Cravat, my old master, was one of the wealthiest tea-merchants in the East. To gain control of his fortune, Davga will stop at nothing. I know that in the wilder quarters of Singapore he is known as Mr. Isaacs. But I have not worried my little mistress with my suspicions. She does not know. In her interest I have followed him many times. Some unsavory tales have been whispered about the strange Mr. Isaacs. He seems to be a power here in the underworld. But Davga enjoys a reputation without a blemish. In meeting him, you have a sly and clever foe. It is much like fighting the wind. But you must succeed. The little mistress must be found at any cost."

A great clock in the hall sounded two. The gong boomed out so ominously it seemed at drum-pitch.

"What do you suggest doing?" asked Dick rather helplessly.

"We must find Dolores Cravat," replied Wing Lo emphatically. "And we must begin our search at once. I believe she is hidden somewhere in the house. It would be the logical place to seclude her. No labyrinth in Singapore is less known than the long winding halls of this house. What it was built for, I do not know. It is like a gigantic ugly blot on the color of the city. And Singapore is a town that does not stop at anything. I believe we should begin our search in the library, the room in which Mortimer Davga spends most of his time. It is his custom to keep the door of the room locked when he is away. If there were not many secrets buried there he would not be so careful of it. Other rooms there are in the house filled with treasures equally as rare, yet he guards them not."

So together Wing Lo and Dick crept down the immense winding halls, halls of dazzling blackness that bore down upon them like bales of black wool. They were afraid to strike a light, for such carelessness might spell death. It was slow work, for there were numerous chests and cabinets in the halls, statues and vases which they had to use care not to overturn. Once they paused breathless. They imagined they had heard a door close stealthily in the floor above. They waited, expecting each moment the brewing storm to break. But the silence continued, a silence that tore at their nerves by its intensity.

As they continued onward, Dick held the arm of Wing Lo so that they would not be separated. Wing knew the halls well. He was on familiar ground. But without him Dick would have been utterly lost. The corridors had been lighted dimly when he passed through them to the bedroom. If there had been light, despite the vastness of the house, he might have found his way back, but in that impenetrable jet he was helpless.

And now they reached the library. There was only a slim chance that the door would be unlocked. If Davga carried the key always with him, it was scarcely creditable it would be unlocked now. Yet luck was with them. It was not only unbarred but it was standing wide open. It was a bit of neglect on Davga's part and it served their purpose. Cautiously they crept into the room. The blackness even there was intense. Slowly step by step they edged their way toward the farthest wall. And now it seemed as though they could hear some one calling, calling faintly for help. Was it purely imagination? Was it the wind in the willows outside the window? Or was it Yeh Ming Hsin? Had he succeeded in freeing himself from his bonds?

They listened breathlessly. Presently the sound came again, more distinctly. Dick's heart commenced to pound wildly, for it was the voice of Dolores and she was calling to him. He worked his way to the wall and placed his ear against it. Once more he heard her voice, a voice which he could never forget. He decided to risk everything. "Dolores," he murmured softly, "Dolores." At that there came a tapping on the wall. It was true! It was not imagination. She was imprisoned in the wall. Perhaps there was a hidden room with a secret panel leading to it. This was the reason Mortimer Davga kept the chamber locked.

Dick Varney uttered an oath. "The lights!" he cried. "Turn on the lights!" Wing Lo obeyed at once. Death might stalk in that room, but what did it matter? His beloved mistress had been found again. As the lights flared up, they beheld Mortimer Davga standing near the chimney corner. There was an ugly smile on his face. He had been sleeping on a couch in the room. But now he was wide awake.

"Gentlemen, gentlemen," he purred, "may I inquire the cause of this intrusion?" As he spoke in a calm gentle voice he whipped out a revolver. But his action was not quick enough. Even as he beheld him, Dick had leaped. The revolver flew from Davga's hand as he lurched backward. The next moment Dick had him by the throat. Unmercifully his fingers closed until Davga's eyes grew wild with horror.

"Where is Dolores?" cried Dick. "Unless you show me how to get to her, this hour will be your last!"

He released his relentless grip somewhat. Davga moaned. Then he smiled, a smile that was a leer. Once more the fingers closed. This time Dick held him breathless for a few seconds longer. Then once more his fingers relaxed.

"This is your final chance," he said tensely. "If I tighten them again they will not loosen until their work is done."

He dragged Davga to his feet and pushed him headlong toward the wall, at the same time drawing a revolver. In the interim Wing Lo had walked across the room and bolted the door. For a while at least they would be free from interference.

Mortimer Davga whined like a whipped animal. A fortune was slipping through his fingers. Better to lose a fortune than his life. He fumbled along the baseboard of the wall and presently a panel swung open. Dick handed the revolver to Wing Lo. Then he stepped

into the blackness of the hidden room. The next moment Dolores was in his arms. He was kissing her lips.

"We must never be separated again," he whispered fervently.

Gently he led her to the next room. She was unharmed. The hidden room had been cozily furnished. She had been well fed. What Davga's intention had been they did not know, nor did they care. All that mattered was that she was free again.

WHEN they re-entered the library, Dick took the revolver from Wing Lo.

"Allow me to present my wife," he said to Mortimer Davga. "We were married yesterday morning. I believe under the terms of her father's will the estate passes to her control after her marriage."

Mortimer Davga laughed gratingly. "You perhaps are not aware that there is a proviso," said he, "that I must sanction the wedding. Control passes to her only at my option. You are a mighty clever fellow, but it looks as though in me you have met your master."

Dick smiled cruelly. "Looks are often deceiving," said he. "I think they are in this case. I had not meant to mention it unless I had to, but you may as well know I am a detective. I pride myself on never being beaten. I hate to spoil your day, but you are under arrest. This procedure, I admit, is rather out of the ordinary. May I point out that necessity knows no law? Usually a crime is discovered and then a criminal is sought. In this case, however, we reverse the procedure. A criminal has been discovered. Now we will seek a crime. Until our mission is accomplished I'm afraid you'll have to be a prisoner. I know that you are sometimes known as Mr. Isaacs. Mr.

Isaacs has an unsavory reputation in some sections of Singapore. He is unscrupulous, lawless. I do not think it will take long to connect him with a capital crime. I myself have good reason to doubt him. I was his guest and he threatened my life. When proof of a crime has been established I will turn you over to the authorities whose pleasure it is to deal with criminals."

Dick had taken a wild chance that Davga was really a criminal. He went on the theory that the house which he had kept under the name of Mr. Isaacs was a hotbed of crime. It seemed to reek of it.

Mortimer Davga collapsed into a chair. His face was ashen. By his expression, Dick knew that his words had struck home.

"I will see my lawyer at once," said he huskily, "and have the necessary papers drawn. After all, there is no reason why Dolores should not marry whom she likes."

"That is good," replied Dick. "Nevertheless we'll hold you prisoner until the proper papers have been prepared." As he spoke he seized Mortimer Davga by the arm and thrust him into the hidden chamber. Then he closed the panel and returned to Dolores.

He took her into his arms. "I've decided not to give you up," he whispered softly.

"I guess," she drawled, "I don't want to be given up."

He did not bother telling her that although she believed she was marrying a poor man, he was really as rich as she. He had inherited a fortune and had left New York to escape the countless people who wanted him for his money, not for himself. He had sailed for Singapore in quest of adventure and romance. He had found both. Having found Dolores, he had found all.

O. S.—9

www.ingramcontent.com/pod-product-compliance
Lightning Source LLC
Chambersburg PA
CBHW080816250626
47159CB00010B/3399